PRAISE FOR
THE ELEMENTAL DETECTIVES

"A beautifully written book, bristling with magic, set in an ancient London filled with dragons, ghosts, water spirits, and a mysterious, creeping sleeping-sickness that must be fought by the brave young heroes. I loved it"
Cressida Cowell, author of *How to Train Your Dragon*

"*The Elemental Detectives* is a rip-roaring magical adventure… Patrice Lawrence has done a marvellous job of building an imaginative and creative mythology which lurks just under the city streets"
Catherine Johnson, author of *Freedom*

"*The Elemental Detectives* is a richly imagined, inventive and immersive fantasy adventure"
E. L. Norry, author of *Fablehouse*

"I loved reading about a re-imagining of London with so much invention and energy. The world-building is, well … out of this world. Patrice Lawrence is among the greatest voices for young people writing today. I'm honoured to be a peer of hers"
Alex Wheatle, author of *Cane Warriors*

"BRILLIANT … history and fantasy woven magnificently into a thrilling, magical adventure"
Sophie Anderson, author of *The House with Chicken Legs*

"A fantastic adventure, packed with rich world building and stunning elemental magic"
Peter Bunzl, author of *Cogheart*

PATRICE LAWRENCE was born in Brighton and brought up in an Italian-Trinidadian household in Sussex. Her first novel *Orangeboy* was one of the most talked-about YA books of 2016. It was shortlisted for the Costa Children's Award and won the Waterstones Children's Book Prize for Older Fiction and the Bookseller YA Book Prize. She has written books for children of all ages from picture books to young adults. Patrice has been shortlisted for the Carnegie Award and won a number of awards including the Crime Fest Award for Best Crime Novel for Young Adults (twice), the Jhalak Children's and Young Adult Prize for Book of the Year by a Writer of Colour and the Little Rebels Award for Radical Children's Fiction. Patrice has been awarded the MBE for services to literature and is a Fellow of the Royal Society of Literature.

OTHER BOOKS BY PATRICE LAWRENCE

The Elemental Detectives

The Case of the Chaos Monster:
An Elemental Detectives Mystery

People Like Stars

The Case of the Dreaming Dragon

PATRICE LAWRENCE

Illustrated by Paul Kellam, Amanda Quartey and Luke Ashforth

■SCHOLASTIC

Published in the UK by Scholastic, 2025
Scholastic, Bosworth Avenue, Warwick, CV34 6UQ
Scholastic Ireland, 89E Lagan Road, Dublin Industrial Estate, Glasnevin, Dublin, D11 HP5F

SCHOLASTIC and associated logos are trademarks and/or
registered trademarks of Scholastic Inc.

Text © Patrice Lawrence, 2025
Cover illustration by Paul Kellam © Scholastic, 2025
Map illustration by Luke Ashforth © Scholastic, 2025
Chapter-head illustrations by Amanda Quartey © Scholastic, 2025

The moral rights of the author have been asserted by them.

ISBN 978 0702 31565 7

A CIP catalogue record for this book is available from the British Library.

All rights reserved.
This book is sold subject to the condition that it shall not, by way of trade or
otherwise, be lent, hired out or otherwise circulated in any form of binding
or cover other than that in which it is published. No part of this publication
may be reproduced, stored in a retrieval system, or transmitted in any form
or by any other means (electronic, mechanical, photocopying, recording or
otherwise), or used to train any artificial intelligence technologies without prior
written permission of Scholastic Limited. Subject to EU law, Scholastic Limited
expressly reserves this work from the text and data-mining exception.

Printed in the UK
Paper made from wood grown in sustainable forests and other controlled sources.

10 9 8 7 6 5 4 3 2 1

This is a work of fiction. Any resemblance to actual people,
events or locales is entirely coincidental.

The publisher does not have any control over and does not assume any
responsibility for any third-party websites or other platforms, or their content.

www.scholastic.co.uk

For safety or quality concerns:
UK: www.scholastic.co.uk/productinformation
EU: www.scholastic.ie/productinformation

This book is dedicated to everyone who's been taught a certain history and asked, 'What if…?'

ELEMENTALS OF LONDON!

The Air Elementals (aka the Fumis)

The **Fumis** are made from air and absorb everything around them, including the stinking smoke billowing from London's chimneys. They have a face shaped like a spade and a body like a pole. They hold a grudge against the Solids (humans) for polluting the air in the first place.

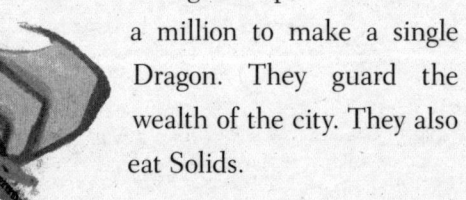

The Fire Elementals (aka the Dragons)

The **Dragons** are made up of tiny indestructible creatures that come together to form a dragon shape. It takes over a million to make a single Dragon. They guard the wealth of the city. They also eat Solids.

The Water Elementals (aka the Chads)

The **Chads** are shape-shifting guardians of the overground and underground springs and rivers in London. Their leader – the riverhead – is the terrifying Lady Walbrook. They dislike the Solids for the nastiness they throw into the rivers that makes Chads sicken and die.

The Earth Elementals (aka the Magogs)

The **Magogs** are the ancient giants, Gog and Magog, thought to be slumbering in the riverbed of the Thames. They have a network of spies across London, including some of the city's statues, who keep an eye on things.

A GUIDE TO LONDON'S GUILDS

The City of London, the tiny central borough within wider Elemental London, has been home to **guilds** for more than four hundred years. They were set up to help people who followed the same trade – for instance, the Guild of Bakers or the Guild of Ironmongers – and the person in charge is known as the Master. In Elemental London, there is a **Guild of Goldsmiths**, and the person in charge of that Guild is also known as **the Goldsmith**. Ever since the Guild was created, the Goldsmith has always wanted to be the richest and most powerful person in London.

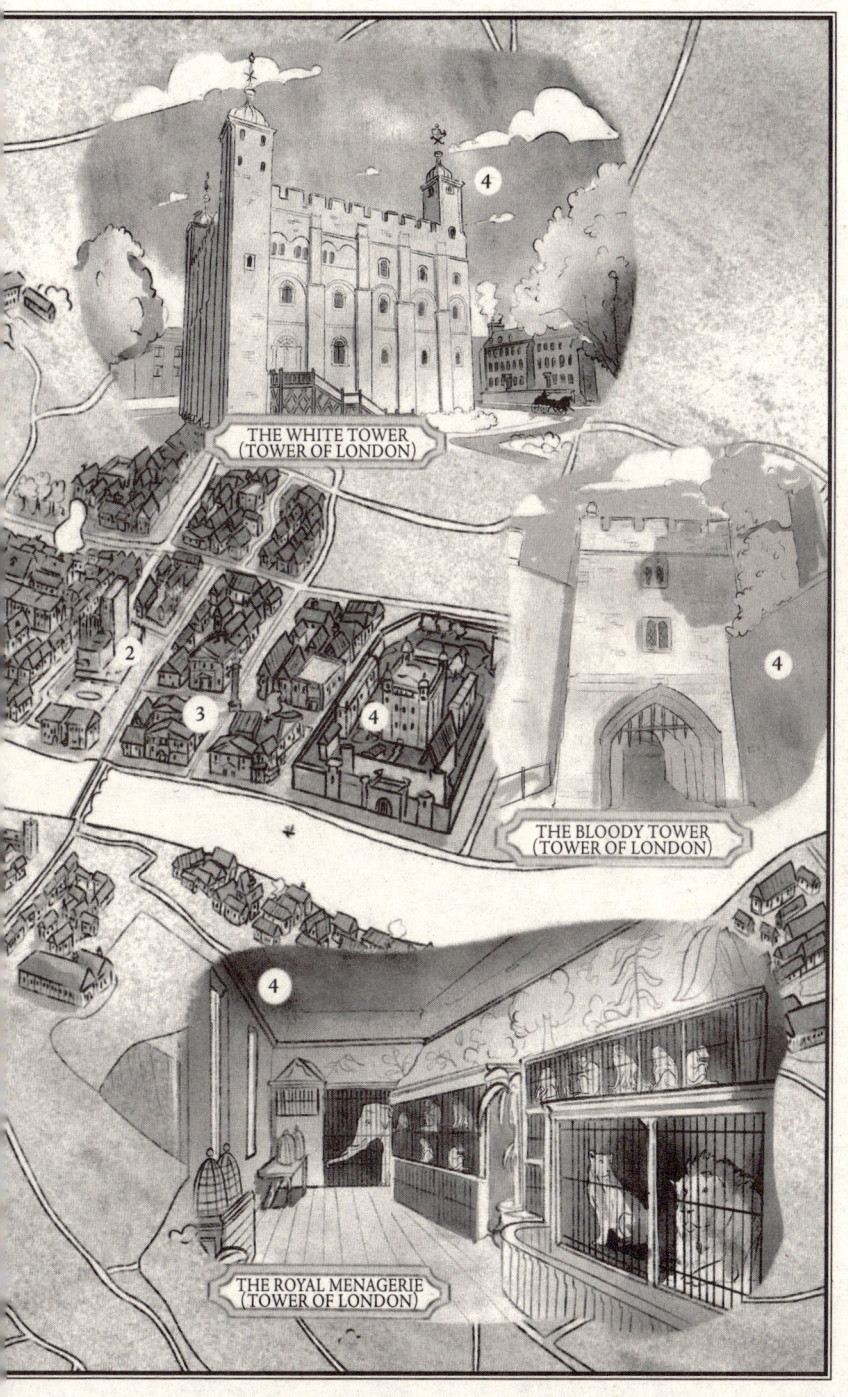

THE WHITE TOWER
(TOWER OF LONDON)

THE BLOODY TOWER
(TOWER OF LONDON)

THE ROYAL MENAGERIE
(TOWER OF LONDON)

THE DRAGON OF MARY-LE-BOW

The Dragon swung in a full circle against the wind. She'd been moored to the great golden weathervane for nearly a hundred years. It was such a short time, but how the city had changed. Before she was here, the Great Fire had surged through the streets of London, turning everything to embers and ash. Then, slowly, she had watched the city being rebuilt along the traces of the old roads: new houses, new shops, new churches.

She could leave if she wanted to, separating into

the thousands and thousands of black fiery creatures that formed her. She could swarm away and hide in the cracks between the cobblestones and reform into a Dragon elsewhere. But she stayed here, watching the streets below.

The great Bow bells in the belfry beneath her had rung nine o'clock a while ago. At night-time, the streets of London were dark but rarely empty. Her Dragon eyes shone into the shadowy nooks, seeing everything. A rag seller was tucked against the wall in the churchyard, wrapped in scraps of linen and silk as a shroud against the cold night. He smiled. His dreams must have been taking him somewhere warm and kind. Candles flickered in the windows of the grand Mercers' Hall on Ironmongers Lane and, behind that, faint ghosts moved around St Olave's churchyard.

And here were the children, hungry and barefoot, searching for treasure – dropped coins, lost handkerchiefs, an apple rolled to the side of the road and forgotten. There were six of them, keeping close together for safety, with one guttering candle between them. The Dragon heard them laughing and calling each other's names as they darted about. They stopped by the slumbering rag seller. One stooped down and tugged at the shroud, but they moved on, leaving him to his dreams.

The Dragon spun round again, surveying east to west – the Lord Mayor's Mansion House where her Dragon cousin was locked, starving, in the cellar by the devious Goldsmith. Then past the Royal Exchange and the Bank of England and the crowded, stinking Poultry Compter, crammed with despairing prisoners. A nightman's cart headed north along King Street, the barrels, scrapers and brooms rattling in the back. While Londoners slept, the nightmen cleaned the stinking cesspits.

She swung back round and—

Where were the children? Oh, there they were, picking their way through George Yard, gathering splinters of wood and twigs. But something was wrong.

Two bright sparks like eyes. She looked more closely. They *were* eyes. Burning rat-red eyes in a child's face.

The Dragon wasn't good at understanding human age – she'd lived far too long and human years were like seconds to her. The rat-eyed child was small, but old enough to walk and talk. Perhaps eight or nine human years? It moved quickly, its nose twitching, hunched forward as if smelling the air around it. Then it squeezed its body into a nook beneath a crumbling wall.

There was a second rat-child, though this one was upright, like a human. It was only the sudden red shine from its eyes that gave it away. The gang of street children stopped still, the candle raised higher. The rat-child stretched out its hand. Perhaps it held food or coin. The Dragon wanted to roar at the street children, warn them, but the Whittington Articles forbade Elementals from revealing themselves to humans unless there were very special circumstances. The Goldsmith harshly punished those who broke rules.

The first rat-child leaped from the darkness by the wall. The children jumped back. The candle fell and was extinguished. A child shouted for help, but the humans that came seized the street children, binding their wrists and ankles. Hoods were thrown over their heads. They were thrown into the back of a cart that clattered away to the east.

The Dragon twisted full circle, again and again, thinking about what she had seen. She should have warned those children of the danger! She should have ignored the Goldsmith and accepted any punishment dealt to her! Those weren't the first eyes she'd seen burning through the darkness. These weren't the first street children that had disappeared. It had happened before – a century ago, when the deadly Plague had raged through London. Was it happening again?

No! It must never happen again! That time, she'd only looked on and done nothing. This time she would act. Who could she trust? Certainly not her own kind: fire spirit Dragons who obeyed the Goldsmith's every word. The Fumi air spirits had no interest in helping the Solids – the humans, who pumped stinking smoke into the skies. The earth spirits, the Magogs, were only interested in waiting for their leaders to awaken – the giants Gog and Magog, who slept on the Thames riverbed. The Chad water spirits also had no sympathy for the humans, who made London's rivers dirty and sluggish. And as for the humans, they had no interest in anything but themselves.

No! That wasn't completely true. She spun round until she faced north. There *were* two humans that she could trust – children that had saved London from destruction twice before.

Marisee Blackwell and Robert Strong, where are you?

A SECRET MEETING

Robert Strong still couldn't believe he was free. He'd always been free in his heart, although for most of his life he'd been treated like an object that could be bought or sold, like a rug or a milk churn.

Robert had been born on the hateful Hibberts' cocoa plantation in Barbados. When he was ten, he'd been separated from his mother and sisters and brought to London as an unpaid servant for Lady Hibbert. He'd first met his best friend Marisee Blackwell when they'd solved the mystery of the Shepherdess and the enchanted sleep that had trapped poor people in their dreams until they withered away. He'd run away from the Hibberts last year after he and Marisee had saved London from another disaster. London's music had been stolen by a rogue air spirit. When the city lullaby was silenced, a Chaos Monster had awoken, crushing everything in its fury.

Robert should have been happy that he'd been awarded his freedom for his bravery. The Lord Mayor had even signed a letter confirming that Robert was under the mayor's protection, and Robert always carried the letter with him everywhere. But why did he have to be brave to be free? Why couldn't *everyone* just be free? Even with the letter, he worried that he'd be scooped off the street by some unscrupulous slave merchant and sent back to the West Indies.

That letter wouldn't keep him safe from other things either, because Robert's enemies weren't always human. There were magical beasts in the hidden places in London that wanted to hurt him. He shivered when he thought of them. He'd been attacked by a plague monster at the bottom of the Serpentine lake. Last year, a giant oyster in the Thames had pulled him into its shell and almost clamped shut around him.

The two worst creatures he'd faced had been almost human, like the strange tithe-master, who lived in the tunnel beneath the Foundling Hospital. He wore a coat made of live swans and had stolen all Robert's memories of his older brother, Zeke, who had died when Robert was younger. Robert and Zeke would never make new memories together.

And there was Haakon, a Variegate – part human, part polar bear. He was known as "the capture-creature" because he was a ruthless hunter who'd almost seized Robert twice. Sometimes Robert was sure he'd caught Haakon's wild animal smell in the alleyways of London, but when he looked around, he saw nothing.

But no – Robert had to try to really believe that he was free. Wasn't this everything he'd wanted? He breathed in. The only smell was the mustard seeds he was pounding for a poultice. He emptied the smashed seeds into a bowl and wiped the mortar and pestle clean. He enjoyed being an apothecary's assistant, watching Mr Boussay, the apothecary, mix the pastes and potions to cure London's ailments. Robert even brought him water from Madam Blackwell's magical well in Clerkenwell – it cured sicknesses of the eye. Robert sometimes wondered if it was the only medicine in the shop that was guaranteed to work!

The shop door burst open. Robert's breath stopped.

"Are you ready? We can't be late!"

Robert let himself breathe again. It was Marisee.

"Grandma says the meeting starts at six o'clock," she said. "And we want to be right in the front."

Robert nodded. He'd been holding down his excitement all day. Mr Boussay was kind but strict. The medicines had to be measured precisely. If Robert didn't get everything correct, he might lose his chance of being taken on as Mr Boussay's apprentice. As a proper apprentice, he could eventually trade as an apothecary and perhaps raise enough money to go and find his family in Barbados. Though, by that time, who knew where they could be, or even – and he hated to think this – whether they were alive.

That was why tonight was so important. He was going to meet someone who could have news about his mother and sisters.

"Turnmill says we can take the tunnels," Marisee said. "That way we'll be sure no one's following us. But hurry up!"

Marisee was never the most patient person, but this evening Robert felt the same impatience. He wanted to be out of the door and on his way.

"Just a moment," he said to Marisee.

He went into the back room where Mr Boussay was examining a glass jar of leeches, the slick, dark creatures curled together in the water. The apothecary didn't use them himself, but always kept extra in case the surgeons ran short.

"Do I have your permission to leave now, Mr Boussay?" Robert asked.

"Of course! Of course!" Mr Boussay said, without looking away from the jar. "But I expect you soon after sunrise tomorrow. Lord Frant's footman is coming early to collect a jar of alkermes for the lord's tender stomach."

"Yes, Mr Boussay," Robert said, even though last week the footman had told him that his master's bellyache came from eating too many pickled onions, and no amount of crushed beetles would make a difference.

Marisee checked the street outside and beckoned Robert to follow. They crept through the alleyway at the side of the shop, then slipped through the side gate into Mr Boussay's back yard, weaving between pots of herbs. Robert savoured the smell of thyme and lavender as they brushed past. Crouching low, they hurried towards the well.

Robert peered into the well's dark mouth.

"Are you sure someone will catch us?" he asked.

"Yes," Marisee reassured him. "Turnmill's already waiting."

He couldn't see anyone down there, but he trusted Marisee. They couldn't have survived their two London adventures together if they hadn't trusted each other.

Marisee went first, scurrying over the well wall and dropping inside. Robert waited. There was no splash – just silence. Then Marisee's echoey voice called up to him.

"Your turn!"

Robert glanced back towards the shop. Mr Boussay's lamp glimmered in the window. The apothecary was intently dusting the alligator skin and certainly wouldn't notice his assistant jump into a well. Robert clambered on to the well wall, sitting with his legs dangling over the side. He didn't dare look down – if he did, he would never jump. He closed his eyes and pushed himself into the darkness – and dropped.

Then stopped dropping, as if a soft cupped hand had caught him.

He opened his eyes. The well's water was flowing up the walls, corkscrewing around the bricks. He was entwined in a silky, silver mesh and the air was filled with the scent of cress and lilies, violet and sedge. Tiny silvery leaves and petals spun in the water. He was spinning too, slowly descending. Inches from the bottom, the mesh dissolved and he landed with a thud. He crawled through a small hole in the well wall and into a tunnel. Behind him, the water whooshed back into place.

Marisee was standing a way down the tunnel next

to a tall woman in breeches and a waistcoat. Her thick plaited hair was fixed in place by shards of pottery. She was Turnmill, the water spirit that cared for the Turnmill brook, part of the River Fleet. Hooves thundered in the tunnel behind her. Marisee and Turnmill jumped aside as an enormous wild boar charged past them, its great grizzled tusks sparking with magic. Robert's stomach lurched, and his body yelled at him to hurl itself out of the way.

He didn't. Robert stayed perfectly still, staring into the boar's tiny dark eyes. The boar halted, the curve of its tusks touching Robert's arms, the earth rutted around its hooves. The strange silvery-green gleam inside the well made the scars across its flank glisten.

The boar opened its mouth. "Well stood, Robert!"

"Thank you."

Robert hoped that his voice didn't give away how hard his heart was beating. Although he knew this was the Fleet Ditch Boar, a water spirit who guarded one of the entrances into the underground Fleet, Robert still baulked when this enormous beast hurtled towards him – despite the fact that Ditch usually greeted him this way. It was Ditch's idea of a joke.

"Enough of the theatrics," Turnmill called. "Let's get you to Fleet Street."

Robert felt safe in the tunnels, even though the Chaos

Monster had crushed a few wells when it had smashed its way through London. Some of the tunnels were old Roman waterways, lined with rotting wood. Others were channels left by ancient streams that had long ago dried up or been diverted. Sometimes there were old things pressed into the walls – thin medieval coins, pewter dagger handles, a sprinkling of nails from Roman sandals.

"Tell me again who this man is," Turnmill said.

"His name is Elijah," Robert said. "Elijah Hibbert. Or it used to be."

"Ah," Turnmill said. "Hibbert. So he was imprisoned on the same plantation as you, Robert."

Robert nodded. "He was sent from Barbados – it must be the same plantation."

And that's why Robert was excited. Elijah would have news about Robert's family. Ever since the tithe-master had taken all Robert's memories of his older brother, Robert thought about his mother and sisters even more. Yes, Marisee and her grandmother were like family to him, but sometimes he still felt so alone.

"Grandma said that Elijah was supposed to replace Robert in the Hibberts' Bloomsbury mansion," Marisee said. "Elijah escaped when the boat docked in Liverpool. The ship's captain was drunk and had fallen asleep. Elijah walked all the way to London!"

"That must have taken some strength," Turnmill said.

"Plantation people have to be strong," Robert said quietly. "Or we won't survive."

They trudged on in silence for a while.

"What happened when Elijah reached London?" Turnmill asked.

"One of the brook Chads on Hampstead Heath saw him sleeping under a tree and got the message to Grandma," Marisee said. Robert heard the pride in her voice. "Grandma asked Mr Williams to send a coach for him."

"Mr Williams?"

"He's a Quaker from Kensington," Marisee said. "When he can, he helps the escaped."

"Doesn't Elijah fear being caught again?" Turnmill asked.

"I'm sure he must do," Robert said. "Every moment of every day. But if he always hides away, no one will ever hear what he has to say about the cruelty of the plantations. Tonight's meeting is in the cellar of St Bride's. There's a secret way out at the back, just in case."

Turnmill stopped suddenly and touched the tunnel wall. "I'm sure it's here," she said, brushing away dirt. "Oh, yes."

A small brass plaque like a coffin plate was fixed on an upright wooden plank.

"Stand back," Turnmill ordered.

Robert and Marisee stepped aside as Turnmill prodded the plaque hard. The plank pivoted – Robert would have been clouted under his chin and sent flying upwards if he hadn't moved. The space that was revealed was just big enough for Robert and Marisee to fit through.

"There's a staircase ahead of you," Turnmill said. "Feel for the banister on the left and let it guide you. You'll come up into an old pelt cellar. The door sticks, so push it hard. It stinks to high heaven. That's why no one ever goes down there. Once you're outside, turn left in the alley on to Fleet Street."

Robert didn't mean to shove in front of Marisee, but all the hope he'd pushed away for such a long time was rushing back through him. Tonight, he'd find out about the people he loved. He knew he had to brace himself in case the news was bad, but he *had* to know if his mother and sisters were still alive.

By the light of the tunnel, he saw the stairs ahead.

"Good luck!" Turnmill called after them.

The plank swung shut and they were in total darkness. Robert shuffled his way forward until his toes bumped the bottom stair. He reached out and grabbed the banister, stumbling as he hurried.

"Careful!" Marisee said from behind him. "I don't think any of Mr Boussay's salves or poultices can fix a broken leg!"

Robert tried to slow down but his heart was beating so hard – he *had* to move fast. He stumbled again as the steps ran out and his hand slid off the end of the banister. He caught himself from falling right over. The stink from the room ahead was seeping under the door and down the stairs. Robert wondered how many animal skins had been stored in that room. Had the pelts just been left there to rot? It brought back horrible memories of the time he and Marisee had been locked in the Lord Mayor's cellar with a hungry Dragon. That place had stunk too.

Robert moved slower, arms stretched out. His fingertips touched something ahead of him.

"I've found the door," he said.

"Is there a handle?" Marisee called. "Does it open?"

Robert ran his hand across the surface. "No," he said. "But remember Turnmill's instructions?"

He set his shoulder against the rough wood. Marisee took her place beside him. They braced themselves, and together shoved as hard as they could. It flew open quickly, and they almost fell into the cellar. The stink seemed to slap him back. But, thankfully, there was no sign of a Dragon! The top half of the window was above the ground, but there was no light outside to be let in. Robert buried his nose in his sleeve and ran through the cellar to the door opposite. There should be one more flight of steps before he was on the street, and then only a few more minutes before he met Elijah.

"Be careful outside!" Marisee reminded him.

He didn't need to be reminded. In spite of the letter that confirmed his freedom, he was always careful. He eased this last door open – it wasn't even locked. Slowly, he climbed the shadowy steps. He took a deep breath. No one could call the grimy London air "fresh", but it was better than the cellar's fug. He peered into the alley. There was no one about.

"It's safe," he said.

Turn left, Turnmill had told them. He hurried on, but Marisee grabbed his shirt before he ran straight on to Fleet Street.

"There may be spies watching the church," she said. "Let me go first."

Robert nodded, even though he longed to race down the street towards St Bride's. If he got there early, maybe he could speak to Elijah before the meeting started.

Marisee stepped on to Fleet Street and walked slowly, like she was taking a stroll. She stopped, looking into a draper's window. Robert glanced up and down the street, then joined her. St Bride's Church was ahead of them – its strange tiered steeple was unmistakable, though it was hard not to imagine a spy keeping watch in every one of those high arches.

Marisee sniffed. "Can you smell burning, Robert?"

He sniffed the air too. "I think so," he said. Yes, he definitely could. Perhaps someone had started a small fire in an alleyway to stay warm. Or an uncleaned chimney might have caught fire. It would be hard to see the billowing smoke in the winter darkness.

"Robert?" Marisee said, pointing at the sky.

Like embers from a bonfire, tiny orange sparks streamed towards them, dotted with gold.

Marisee squinted up. "Is it … a Dragon?"

Why … why would a Dragon be seeking them out? He peered harder at the ribbon of sparks. Suddenly, Robert knew exactly which Dragon it was. Only the Mary-le-Bow Dragon was threaded with gold. Why would she leave her post to come here? He wished that Marisee hadn't seen it. He was desperate to continue on towards the church.

The sparks clustered together, then clicked into place as if they were scales. First came a long head, then a heavy, strong jaw and small eyes set beneath a ridged brow. A shimmering band of gold spilled eastwards across the sky towards Mary-le-Bow, tethering the Dragon to her church's steeple.

The Dragon's mouth opened. Robert and Marisee felt a flash of heat, but only words followed. No flames.

"Children are being stolen!" the Dragon said. "You must help them!"

"Stolen?" Robert echoed. "You've come for my help now?"

He hadn't meant to sound impatient, but he of all people knew that children were being stolen. *He* was here in London because *his* family had been stolen. But St Bride's was so close! Couldn't he meet Elijah first and find out about his mother and sisters?

Marisee touched his shoulder. "Robert, it must be important for the Dragon to come and find us."

"But … but … if we go to the meeting first…" His voice trailed away.

In his heart, Robert knew that Marisee was right. The Elemental spirits trusted Marisee and Robert to fight the enemies that threatened the city. He mustn't let them down. But… He glanced at the church one last time. Elijah must already be there.

"Can't we come afterwards?" he pleaded.

"What if that's too late, Robert?" Marisee said. "Imagine how many more poor people would have withered away in their sleep if we'd taken longer to find the Shepherdess. Most of London would have been in rubble if we hadn't stopped the Chaos Monster when we did. We have to help *now*."

Robert's head almost felt too heavy to nod, but he just managed it.

"I'll come," he said, so quietly that perhaps only the Dragon heard him.

BRING OUT YOUR DEAD!

The Dragon dissolved into sparks, coiling back towards Mary-le-Bow. Marisee felt a guilty rush of excitement. Was this going to be another adventure? But Robert's shoulders were slumped. His disappointment felt so strong that it could have been her own. She moved closer to him.

"I know how much you miss your family," she said, "because I miss my mother too. We've saved London twice and I'd give anything to tell her about it. I think she'd be so proud of me." Marisee shrugged. "But I'll never really know if she's proud. I don't know where she is, or whether she's even alive or dead. I'd do anything to find her. But if children are disappearing… I thought the Dragon never left the church. She must have come because we're the only people who can help her" – she met Robert's eyes – "and who can help the children."

Marisee turned away from St Bride's. She knew that Robert would follow her, but for a moment he needed to be by himself.

The church of St Mary-le-Bow stood on Cheapside, a wide road that ran from east to west through the City of London. Marisee went ahead of Robert through the church door. The last time they'd been here, they were chased up the bell tower by Haakon. They'd assumed that Haakon was kidnapping Robert to send him back to a plantation in the West Indies, but they'd learned that someone else wanted Robert, right here in London. They still didn't know who that was or why.

There'd been no sign of Haakon since the Chaos Monster adventure, over a year ago. Maybe he'd been ordered to leave Robert alone. After all, the Lord Mayor *had* signed a letter confirming that Robert was safe. And Marisee was sure that the Dragon wouldn't lead them into a trap. Nevertheless, Robert paused before entering the church, looking about just in case Haakon was lurking in the shadows. He glanced up at the cherub statues above the door to the bell tower, then finally closed the church door firmly and followed Marisee up the stairs to the bellringers' room below the belfry.

"We're here," Marisee whispered, looking at the trapdoor to the belfry above them.

The Dragon's sparks teemed through the gaps in the wooden planks above them. Her head was smaller this time. Marisee was pleased about that. As much as she trusted this Dragon, standing in a small wooden room alongside a giant Dragon's head was not a comfortable thought. The Dragon's voice was quieter too but still filled the air. Marisee's skin prickled with the heat of the fire magic.

"The humans came with rope for the children's hands and feet," the Dragon said, "and blankets to hide them. They brought children who were not human to lure the little ones into the trap."

"I don't understand," Marisee said. "How can a child not be human?" *Actually*, she thought, *there could be a few reasons for that.* "Was the child a ghost? Or a Chad like Sally Fleet?"

"No," the Dragon replied. "The child was a Solid and also an animal."

Marisee and Robert looked at each other.

"Like Haakon?" Robert asked, shocked. "A Variegate?"

Marisee shivered. Were children being turned into Variegates? Part human and part predator animal? That was one of the worst cruelties that she could imagine.

"Tell us what you saw," Marisee said.

"I keep a watch on the children," said the Dragon. "Especially the ones with no families to care for them. They were searching for food or some token to sell."

"The children with no families to care for them," Robert repeated. "Like the Red Guard Gang."

Marisee knew he was thinking about his friends – Emma, Spindrift, the brothers Duval and Turpin, and little Garnet. They had all been left alone to fend for themselves and survived by stealing. They were like a family to each other and had hidden Robert when he had nowhere to go.

"Did you recognize any of the children that were taken?" he asked.

"No," the Dragon answered. "It isn't easy for me to tell one human from the other. But there was a child… I'm sure that I sometimes heard her singing as she followed the others through the street."

"Singing?" Robert said sharply. "Garnet's always singing. Did you hear the child's name?"

Robert visited Garnet whenever he could. Marisee

knew that it made him feel like a big brother again, now that his sisters were so far away. Grandma always packed a basket of food, including Garnet's favourite – muffins.

"I do not recall that name," the Dragon said. "And I remember none from the time before."

"Tell us what happened before," Robert urged. "Tell us everything."

"I will show you," the Dragon said.

The air filled with tiny black and gold flecks, gusting around like windblown fog until Marisee could barely see Robert. They coated her face. She tried to brush them off, but they pasted themselves to her, pressing into her skin like tiny stones.

"Ouch!" she cried. "Stop it!"

"Be still," the Dragon ordered. "Or you will not see."

How could Marisee be still when those stony flecks were sticking to her eyelids, thickening until her lids were heavy, heavier, closing, closed…? Her lips were thick with them too. If she opened her mouth, she'd swallow them. She clamped her mouth shut.

Through the haze of sparks, she had seen Robert weakly flailing them away before a band of gold and black pressed his arms to his side and held them there.

Above Marisee, the mighty Bow bells were tolling: seven, eight, nine and then silence.

It was daylight. Marisee could see again, even though her eyelids remained heavy. How? Was the Dragon sleeping? Had she been trapped in its dreams?

"We hold the City's memories," the Dragon whispered, "deep in every part of us. Watch. Witness."

Marisee looked around. She was staring at an empty road. There was a row of shops opposite, but all were closed and shuttered. Many of the doors were marked with a big red cross. *Red cross?* Marisee knew that was important but couldn't remember why. She seemed to be in London, but where was the noise? All she could hear was... Was that the rush of the River Thames? How come she couldn't see it but could hear it so clearly? Where were the street vendors yelling about their wares? And the fiddle players sawing out popular tunes with their caps ready to receive coins? Where were the ballad singers and the mackerel sellers? There should be crowds of people drifting in and out of the shops, maids carrying packages, footmen calling to each other from passing coaches. Where were the porters striding between them, hauling barrels from the dock? Where was everybody?

And where was Robert? She tried to lift her hand. She couldn't. She couldn't even see her hand. So, where was she – the real her? Was she still in the St Mary-le-Bow tower? She wasn't dreaming because she couldn't dream – no one in her family could.

This feels so real, she thought.

The silence was broken by the clattering of hooves. At last! A cart! As the driver led the horse past Marisee, he rang a bell.

"Bring out your dead!" he called. "Bring out your dead!"

The cart was high-sided. She couldn't see inside. It stopped as the door of a draper's shop opened. A red cross was painted across the door. The red cross… The silence…

Grandma had told Marisee the stories passed down from grandmother to grandchild for a hundred years, about the time when an incurable plague had swept through London. Homes that were infected with the plague would scrawl a red cross on the door. The sick remained in their houses, and carts would call for people to bring out their dead.

Then suddenly the world darkened and, like a blink, there was light again – a shadowy, fiery light. Marisee was swooping through the air, low over the rooftops. Nearly every door was painted with a red cross and the scrawled words "Lord Have Mercie On Us". Bonfires blazed at the corner of the streets. Marisee's eyes watered and her chest heaved as she flew through the dense smoke. Men were hacking away at the hard ground, digging pits to bury the bodies. The despair was thicker than the smoke. Her eyes prickled and she knew that, back in 1766, tears were running down her cheeks.

"No more," she called out. "Please, Dragon, no more!"

But she was lifted higher and the streets below her became narrower. She was being swept eastwards, following the loop of the river. She could just about see the windmills on the Isle of Dogs. She thought for a moment of her friends: Henry, the lion-man Variegate and ex-assassin, who lived on the Isle of Dogs with his friend the Squall, a badly behaved air spirit. But she'd met them a hundred years in the future, in her real life.

Soon, she was descending towards a castle. She definitely knew this building – it was the Tower of London. Robert said that whenever he passed the Tower, he felt the anger pulsing out from it, though Marisee couldn't. But it was a place where many people had been executed and both humans and animals had been caged. Grandma had refused to take her to visit the famous Royal Menagerie – she was adamant that the poor animals were not treated well. Haakon had been partly created from a polar bear brought to the Tower from Norway hundreds of years ago. The necro-alchemists had placed the bear's beating heart into the body of a human murderer. The bear's rage and power had only strengthened as it was transformed into Haakon, the ruthless assassin.

Marisee's stomach lurched as she dropped from the sky. The Tower's stone battlements rushed towards her. She was going to smash into them... She tensed herself, a scream rising in her throat.

Darkness again. The stink, the stink! It was worse than the rotting pelts in the cellar near Fleet Street. Light filtered into the room through narrow windows high in the wall. A shriek made Marisee flinch. It was followed by another, even louder shriek, then scream after harsh scream. A creature – it must be a creature because no human could make that sound – roared so loud that Marisee was sure that the walls shook. She tried to clamp her hands over her ears, make her legs run away, but she couldn't move.

She could see more now, as if it had taken a moment for the Dragon's eyes to adjust to the darkness in its memory. The chamber was filled with cages, some on the floor, others set against the walls on ledges. Each cage contained an animal. This had to be the Royal Menagerie. The monkeys in the higher cages gripped the bars, screaming. A tiger stretched, its head and feet clipping the corners of its tiny prison. The roar came again. This time the Dragon must have turned because Marisee was suddenly staring at a lion. He grasped the bars of his cage in his teeth, tugging at them. They didn't move. He lifted his head away and his fury spread to the other animals. The noise was unbearable. Was this what Robert felt whenever he passed close by?

Sudden darkness again, but then, as Marisee blinked, she was in a cluttered chamber. It was cut through the middle by a long narrow table. A heavy ledger lay open on the table, its yellowing pages filled with diagrams and tiny writing. There was a stone shelf of spluttering candles. An apothecary's cabinet filled with bottles, jugs and jars. The empty eye sockets from the skull of a small animal stared at her from a bench crowded with dishes and strange equipment. Another case was crammed with books, both inside and on top of it. More books were piled in columns against the wall. Drawings were nailed to the bricks – the parts of a microscope, a rat's skeleton with the bones labelled, an engraving of plants marked "Poisons" with the writing beneath too small for Marisee to read.

A splashing sound came from a pot-like vessel on a desk by the far wall. A tentacle slapped over the side.

Is that an octopus? The vessel seemed too small to fit an octopus.

Marisee wanted a closer look, but she was bound inside the Dragon's memories and could only witness what the Dragon had chosen to remember. The door of the room creaked open and a man entered. Even in the gloom, Marisee could see that he was dressed richly. His clothes were very different from the ones in her time, full of ruffles and ribbons. His hair was thick and curly, so long that it reached past his fussy lace collar. Surely that had to be a wig! How did he keep it clean? Though this wasn't the time to think about that… She knew she should be watching and listening.

He was followed into the room by another man, dressed all in black with a cloak that hung in a dark wave from his neck. His hat was tipped forward, shadowing his brow.

The man dressed in ruffles suddenly spun round and grabbed the other man's arm.

"Where is my army, Mr Pipes?" he demanded.

Mr Pipes tried to pull his hand free, but the man in ruffles grasped it too tight.

"I need more time," Mr Pipes said. "These are delicate experiments, Lord Gullinn."

Lord Gullinn yanked Mr Pipes closer towards him. "You have had time, Pipes," he said. "You have had money. You have been given every piece of equipment demanded of me. You promised me soldiers with gills like fish who swim silently up rivers. You promised me soldiers that see through darkness like cats, and stalk their enemies for miles without sleep or food. Where are they?"

He released Mr Pipes' arms.

"I didn't promise…" Mr Pipes stuttered, stepping back. "There is never a guarantee. I'm sure there are others with better skills than me."

Lord Gullinn smirked. "You have earth magic inside you, Pipes," he said. "My spies have seen you talking to the statues."

Mr Pipes' mouth fell open. "You … know…?"

"I make it my business to know everything," Lord Gullinn said. "They have told me how you creep through the deep, dark passages below the castle at night." He clasped the hilt of his sword, stepping towards Mr Pipes. "Shall I show you what they found?"

Mr Pipes' face froze in fear. "Lord?"

"Bring the prisoners!" Lord Gullinn called out.

A guard shoved two children into the chamber. A boy and a girl, both thin and hunched over. Marisee gasped. She tried to clap her hand over her mouth even though no one could hear her. Her arms still wouldn't move. A tail curled out from above the waistband of the boy's breeches. A pair of ears stuck out from the top of the girl's head – round, pink and alert like a rat's. For a moment, the children's eyes flashed red.

"I've found your little *friends*," Lord Gullinn said. "Or perhaps they are pets."

The children whimpered. Mr Pipes reached out to them, but the guard yanked them away.

"You lied to me, Pipes!" Lord Gullinn hissed. "Your experiments did not fail. These are rat-children!"

"Tommy," Mr Pipes said. "Helen. I'm so sorry. I thought you were hidden away and safe."

The children reached out for him.

"Please, Mr Pipes," the rat-girl – Helen – said. "Change us back to how we were before."

Lord Gullinn crouched down next to the children.

"Oh," he said. "Mr Pipes will do no such thing. I want Mr Pipes to make more exactly like you!"

"No," Mr Pipes gasped. "I can't! I won't! Look how the poor creatures suffer! Wouldn't our learning be better spent on finding a cure for this plague?"

Lord Gullinn laughed. "Cure? Why should I search for a cure? London is weak, Pipes." He stood up. "This is the perfect time to strike. This city bursts with riches because of us, the goldsmiths. Our Guild has paid for ships and sailors to explore the world and return with gold, jewels and spices. The goldsmiths built London. But do we profit? No! The king takes taxes. He rewards his favourites. He has turned his back on me." Lord Gullinn swept the sword from its scabbard. Candlelight glinted across its blade. "It's unwise to turn your back on me."

"The rat-children were a mistake—" Mr Pipes started. "They're too young to be soldiers."

Lord Gullinn loomed over Mr Pipes. "Do you know what's more valuable than soldiers, Pipes? Spies! No one will keep secrets from me. And we know all about rats, don't we? They climb walls. They lurk unseen in cellars and attics. They squeeze themselves into the smallest of spaces. I want more ratlings, Pipes – a battalion of ratlings. The guards are already gathering children to bring to you. In this time of sickness, who will notice a few missing brats?"

Mr Pipes backed away. "No! This must never happen! It's cruelty."

"You will give me more ratlings," Lord Gullinn said calmly. "These..." He cast a disgusted glance at the children. "These abominations are in my care now. I decide who lives and who dies. If you want them to live, do as I say. And you know, Pipes, I am not a patient man."

The guard pulled the children out of the room. Lord Gullinn followed.

"The people will stop you, if I can't!" Mr Pipes shouted

after him. "They will never allow such inhumanity. Your ill work will be discovered. You cannot hide an army of rat-children in London."

Lord Gullinn's laugh echoed back into the chamber. Mr Pipes stared at the empty doorway, brushing away tears. He turned towards the pot, though the octopus had disappeared.

"I will never give him what he desires," he said.

Marisee wanted to lean forward, see and hear more, but the room crumbled into darkness and the Dragon's memories were squeezing her through the stone walls and out into daylight. She was on the street again. She was sure that she recognized this place... Surely it was Fish Street Hill? But there was a church where the Monument should be, the tall white column with its golden flame that she could see from nearly anywhere in London. But of course – the Monument was built to remember the Great Fire of 1666. These were the Dragon's memories from *before* the fire.

It was a sunny day and the market was busy despite the plague. Perhaps the people here thought they would be spared the sickness, or had already survived it.

A woman prodded a flat, spotted fish on a stall. "It's all scale and bone," she grumbled.

The fishmonger ignored her and served someone else.

Small figures darted through the crowds – children looking for dropped coins and begging for food. Taller figures moved through the crowd too, dressed in the uniform of the guards from the Tower of London. They spread out until they surrounded the children, closed in on them and grabbed. The struggling children were led away. No one did anything to help them. Some of the stallholders laughed and praised the guards for protecting them from thieves.

The day quickened like a waterwheel on a fast-flowing river. One moment it was afternoon, then twilight and then night. The fishmongers packed away their stalls, but the smell of their wares lingered. Small children appeared, crouching over the slimy cobbles, still searching for dropped pennies. Two pairs of red eyes flashed by the church gates. Two shadows scurried out. Marisee's heart pulled. She tried to reach out to the street children, warn them that something bad was about to happen, but, of course, she couldn't. She watched helplessly as the hungry children cautiously approached the rat-children. What did the rat-children show them? Money? Food? Marisee couldn't see. But she *could* see the high-sided cart waiting behind the church to steal the street children away.

Marisee was scooped from Fish Street Hill and squeezed between a rotting window frame and a wall.

The smell! A much better smell! Fresh bread and pies. She breathed it in. The room was dark apart from a spluttering candle and a dying fire in the hearth. The door opened and Marisee shrank back into the shadows – even though she wasn't actually there. What memories did the Dragon have of this place?

A maid came in, carrying a bowl of water. She raked the fading embers of the fire and threw the water over them. A man stood in the doorway watching her. As she turned round, he said, "Is this the last one, Anne?"

"Yes, Mr Farryner."

Mr Farryner? Wasn't that the name of the baker who started the Great Fire of London? Right where the Monument now stood. Was this *the* Mr Farryner?

"Please return to all of the rooms and ensure that the fires are dead," he ordered the maid. "I will follow afterwards."

The maid scurried past him. Mr Farryner sat down on a stool, stirring the cooling embers with a poker. Nothing glowed – it was all ashes. Finally content, Mr Farryner left the room, closing the door quietly behind himself.

Marisee felt herself moving through the darkness, but could see nothing until she was standing in front of a counter stacked with cake rings. Another lone candle flickered in its holder. The walls were hung with graters and tongs and all sizes of spoons, the floor coated with flour. She was in the bakehouse.

The Dragon's memories pushed her towards the chimney, until she was in front of a wide beehive-shaped oven. The baker had laid out bundles of wood ready for the following morning. The oven door was open – it was cold and empty.

Marisee frowned. She could smell smoke and hear voices shouting.

Suddenly, she was back in the alleyway, but it was no longer dark and quiet. Thick smoke pressed around her. People burst through it clutching buckets of water, then disappeared again. Marisee couldn't breathe – no, she could! She wasn't really here – but her body didn't believe it. She could taste scorched wood, feel the soot coat her skin.

A ball of fire landed on the thatched roof in front of her. The dry straw sparked like tinder, then burst into flame, crackling and roaring, shooting sparks out to the houses on either side. Timber beams smouldered, then burned. Windows cracked – and the heat, the heat! Marisee wiped her stinging eyes. She imagined smearing the dark ash across her face.

The heat wasn't real. It wasn't real! But it hurt.

She couldn't breathe! She couldn't see!

"Enough, Dragon! Enough!" she shrieked. "Take me away from here!"

Marisee was back in the bell tower, slumped against the wall. She looked down at her hands – there was no soot. They were clean. But she could still taste the fire, still smell it.

She would never ever enter a Dragon's memories again.

THE RED GUARD GANG

Robert and Marisee sat across from each other in the bell tower, shivering. Robert couldn't talk. His throat felt scorched, as if he'd been breathing in fiery smoke. The Dragon's memories whirled around his brain.

"Did *you* see Mr Pipes and Lord Gullinn?" Marisee asked.

Robert nodded. "And the rat-children." How could he find the words to describe his feelings? Fury and sadness and a gnawing fear. "You saw the children being taken away?"

"Yes," Marisee said. "And the fire. I'd always thought that the Great Fire had been started by…"

Robert let her voice fade in his head. He didn't care about how the Great Fire started – it wasn't his history to care about. What he did care about was what the Dragon had told them earlier. She'd witnessed men seizing a child who was always singing. Could the child be Garnet? She'd lived with the Red Guard Gang since they'd found her alone, crying on the street. They always protected her. Even though Robert lived with Marisee and her grandmother now, he still worried about his Red Guard Gang friends all the time. Even children could be hung from the gallows if they were caught stealing.

And now they were being stolen from the streets.

Robert raced down the stairs. His skin stung as if he'd been too close to flames. He paused at the bell-tower door. The cold night air soothed his face, but the darkness pulsed with threat. And that threat may have already taken Garnet.

"Hear anything useful?" came a voice from overhead.

It was one of the stone cherubs carved above the entrance. He'd heard their quiet chuckles as he'd raced into the tower.

"Know anything useful?" Robert replied.

The cherub giggled. "Everything you need to know's in the Tower."

"What? Did the statue talk?" Marisee asked as she rushed out of the door. "Did it say anything?"

Robert glanced at the cherub. It blinked quickly, then was still.

"Only that everything we need to know is in the Tower," he said.

Marisee glanced up at the dark bell tower. "I'm sure there's much, much more that we need to know," she said.

Robert started walking away from the church. "I need to be certain that Garnet's safe," he said. "I saw Turpin and Duval on Henrietta Street last Tuesday. They took me to their new den. It's on Cattle Court, off Milk Street."

Marisee touched Robert's shoulder. "Garnet isn't the only child who likes to sing," she said gently. "It most likely isn't her."

Robert knew that. He also knew that Garnet wasn't allowed out after sunset, but what if, for once, she had been? Or she'd crept out without telling anyone? Robert's legs moved quicker.

What if it is Garnet?
It must be Garnet!
Please don't be Garnet!

He slowed down as he slipped along the narrow

passageway to Cattle Court, glancing back and forth, searching for moving shadows and rat-red eyes. He could see none. He pulled aside a loose panel in an old fence and slipped through, followed by Marisee. They stood in a shabby yard that fronted a dilapidated house. He could just see an old post for tethering the cows, and two stalls, both with their doors hanging off. Turpin had told him that the owner had died and the place had yet to find new tenants.

Robert pushed the front door open. The room beyond it was dark and empty. It felt like the house was holding its breath, waiting to see what he would do.

"Emma!" he hissed. "Spindrift! It's Robert!"

There was a moment of silence, then a loud tap like a stone landing on wood. It came from the middle of the room. A candle appeared in a gap in the ceiling. Robert recognized the meaty smell of tallow. A ladder followed. It was made of ship's rope and was swinging like a noose.

"Hurry up!"

Robert recognized Spindrift's voice. Marisee had already moved towards it and was climbing up. She was always so brave! He went next, bracing himself as the ladder twisted and turned. At last, his head poked through the gap and he heaved himself through.

He was in a room under the roof that stretched across the whole building, eaves sloping down either side. It reminded Robert of the scullery maids' room in the garret of Lord Hibbert's Bloomsbury mansion. Spindrift was sat on a bale of cloth, leaning against the brick wall. The tallow candle had been jammed into the candle holder by his feet. He gave Robert a nod, but his eyes beneath his wide hat were, as always, wary.

"Robert!"

Two voices at the same time – the brothers Duval and Turpin. Duval was slicing a sorry-looking apple into chunks.

"Did you bring food, Robert?" Duval asked.

"Lots and lots of tasty food?" Turpin added.

"Did you dare to come empty-handed?" A girl's voice, with a laugh in it. Emma.

She was dressed in breeches with a Scots bonnet over her shorn hair. Robert was sure that it was the same hat she'd been wearing when he'd first met her. He peered into the shadows, heart hammering.

"Where's ... Garnet?" His voice was tight with panic. "Is she here? I can't see her!"

Emma held her finger to her lips. "Shhh. She's sleeping. She hasn't been well."

Spindrift raised the candle so Robert could see into the far corner. A small dark shape was curled up on a blanket.

"It's their fault." Emma pointed at Turpin and Duval. "They helped themselves to biscuits from a baker's shop on Poland Street. I think he used bad flour. They've got stomachs like wild dogs – I don't think anything makes *them* ill. Garnet ate more biscuits than anyone. Luckily, she finished all her puking before you arrived."

Robert had to look for himself. He crept over to the corner and sank down on to the bare boards by the sleeping child. It *was* definitely a child – their little fingers grasped the edge of the blanket. But was it Garnet? He eased away the blanket. The child was lying on their side, facing away from him. He could see the shape of their head, but … there was so little light. He couldn't tell!

"Robert?" Emma sounded annoyed. "What are you doing? She's only just fallen asleep."

"I have to be sure that it's really Garnet."

Marisee was saying something to Emma. Robert couldn't quite hear because he was leaning closer to the child. He should believe Emma. Why would she lie? But he needed to know for himself. The sleeping form wriggled, flopped on to its back, then sat up so quickly that its head almost collided with Robert's.

"My stomach hurts," Garnet wailed. And it was definitely Garnet! "I want the hurt to go away!"

"It will go away soon," Robert whispered in her ear.

"Those horrible biscuits know how brave you are! They'll run away from your stomach and never come back."

"There's already been too much running," Emma muttered.

Garnet turned to Robert. Even in the deep shadows he knew her face, in the same way that he would have recognized his young sisters in the darkest gloom of the plantation cabins.

Garnet sniffed. "I want them to run away now!"

Robert wrapped his arm around her shoulders. "They're too frightened of you, Garnet. They're waiting for you to go back to sleep so they can escape."

Garnet sniffed again. Robert gently wiped her face with the edge of the rough blanket.

"When I wake up again, will all the hurt be gone?" Garnet asked.

"It should be," Robert said. "But in case it hasn't, I'll bring some medicine for you tomorrow."

Garnet nodded. "I'll go back to sleep again."

She eased herself back down and Robert pulled up the blanket. Soon, her breathing was heavy and even. He touched her forehead. Thankfully, there was no fever. He crept back to the others. He was confident that Mr Boussay wouldn't mind him giving a tiny dose of alkermes to Garnet.

The guttering light flickered across Emma's worried face. "You know about the missing children?"

Robert nodded. "And you?"

There was a silence. Duval and Turpin stopped munching apple and looked at him.

"We've heard rumours," Spindrift said. "Of children being stolen by men with ropes and nets, and..." He faltered. Spindrift never faltered. He only spoke when he was sure of what he wanted to say.

"And rat-children with red eyes?" Robert asked.

"Yes," Spindrift said quietly. "Rat-children with red eyes."

Marisee and Robert swapped a look. "Have you seen the rat-children?"

"*I* have."

The voice came from above Garnet's bed. A child emerged from between the eaves. If Robert had only looked up, he would have seen them earlier. They came and sat on the floor between Spindrift and Emma, chin resting on their knees. They were thin, small and pale, their face streaked with dirt. Their toes poked out of battered old slippers and a pair of oversized breeches was held up by a band of dirty linen. The child's sleeve cuffs were solid with dirt.

"When did you see the rat-children?" Marisee asked gently.

"When they took me." The child's voice was muffled as their head sank further into their knees. "But I was a lucky one. I escaped."

"Tell them what you told me, Joe," Emma said softly.

Joe nodded.

"It was low tide," Joe said. "So me and the others were out in the mud. My friend Maud told me she'd found a load of buttons last Friday. She'd sold them to a draper and got a good few pennies. She was going to show me where they'd washed up. Sometimes you have a feeling in your heart that it's going to be a good day."

So Joe was one of the mudlarking children, Robert realized. They searched the Thames foreshore for treasure to sell. It was dangerous work. Sometimes the tide came in suddenly. Robert had heard about more than one mudlark who'd only just been rescued in time.

"It was sunset," Joe continued. "We should have left the shore, but the tide was late. We wanted to make sure we had a good look before the river swept everything away. And when you're looking, you have to get right down on your knees and dig around in the sand, especially when it's getting dark. I thought I'd found a coin. And I was…"

His fingers moved as if they were digging sand. He gave a little sob. Emma patted his shoulder.

"I heard a whisper," Joe said. "I thought it was a lark,

like me. I couldn't see properly because they were standing with the sun behind them. When I looked up, they said they'd found a coin. Asked if I wanted to have a look." Joe wiped his face with his dirty sleeve. "I was pulling my feet out of the mud, when I heard a scream. It could have been a gull, but it sounded more like a scream. All the other larks I knew had gone. It was only me and this other boy. Except, he wasn't a boy. He was like ... he was like a rat. Sniffing and twitching and moving like a rat. And he smelled like a rat too – as if he'd just been dug out of some stinking hole."

Joe sobbed again. Robert wished he could comfort him, but he knew that despair – when it was so deep inside you that nothing could touch it.

"His eyes." Joe's voice had sunk low. Robert held his own breath to be able to hear the boy. "They were as red as the devil's. I was so scared I couldn't move when the men came."

"They had boats," Emma said. "They take the children up towards the Tower of London."

Tower, Robert thought. *Was that the Tower that the cherubs meant?*

"How did *you* escape?" Marisee asked. She sounded suspicious.

"They tied our hands and feet with rope," Joe said.

"But the men were in a hurry. They didn't tie my hands too tight. They were laughing about how much money they were going to get for us and joking about what was going to happen next."

"What did they mean?" Marisee interrupted before Robert could.

"They said that there's a cauldron," Joe replied. "They throw children and rats in it together like they're making a soup, and they come out all mixed together."

"A cauldron?" Robert asked. "Like a magic cauldron?"

Joe shrugged. "Sounds like a witches' tale, doesn't it? But that boy got turned ratty somehow. I knew I'd rather be dead than like him. One of the other larks started screaming. When the net-men went to her, I threw myself over the side of the boat. I didn't care what happened. I closed my eyes and let God decide."

"Joe was lucky," Emma said. "The tide was coming in. The river carried him to London Bridge."

"God gave me enough strength to hold on to a mooring post. A lighterman saw me and rescued me from the water. Mr Spindrift found me by a barrel of nutmeg, wet to the core and stinking of the river. I was shaking so hard I'm surprised I have any teeth left in my head."

"Are they making rat Variegates again?" Marisee was talking to herself. "Why now?"

"What's *vairy-gates*?" Joe asked.

"It's happened before," Marisee said. "Long ago, there were experiments in the Tower of London. Necro-alchemists created Variegates, who were part human criminal and part animal. They were turned into a Guild of Assassins to hunt and catch other criminals."

"I met Emma when she rescued me from the capture-creature," Robert said. "He's a Variegate that's part polar bear." Robert shuddered. "He enjoys hunting his prey."

Joe looked like he was going to ask what a polar bear was, but Marisee cut in.

"Henry's also a Variegate." She smiled fondly. "He's partly lion. But he's our friend."

Joe's eyes widened. "Your friend's a lion?"

Marisee nodded. "Partly."

"And you said he was made long ago?" Joe added. "How long ago?"

"I don't know exactly when it was," Robert said. "But it was definitely more than a hundred years ago."

Joe looked from Robert to Marisee. "You have strange friends," he said.

"More than a hundred years ago," Marisee repeated softly. "Variegates live very long lives. Do you know what that means, Robert?"

Robert nodded thoughtfully. The rat-children they'd

seen in the Dragon's memories could be the same ones that were luring children now. But where had they been all this time?

"Did you hear the kidnappers say anything else, Joe?" he asked.

"I tried to listen," Joe said, "but some of the mudlarks were crying and praying, so it was hard to hear everything. They said that there's a woman in the Tower. She's like a sorceress that does the Goldsmith's bidding."

"The Goldsmith!" Robert and Marisee said together.

Robert wasn't surprised that the Goldsmith was mentioned. He was cruel enough to steal children. But why would he turn them into rats?

"And she's like you," Joe finished.

"Like me?" Robert was confused. "How?"

Joe touched his skin. "Like you."

"This sorceress has brown skin?" Marisee asked.

Joe nodded.

Robert thought of the other magical women they'd encountered in the last couple of years. There was the Shepherdess who'd trapped London's poor in their dreams. She'd once been a quiet water spirit until her sadness drove her to violent revenge. Her magic was strong – she could be called a sorceress, but her skin was fair. *And* she'd been destroyed by Lady Walbrook.

The Empress of the Holy Roman Empire had sailed to London when the Chaos Monster rampaged through London. She'd arrived on an enchanted ship to claim back the stowaway Fumi that had stolen the city's music. She could command her Fumi air spirits, but she didn't have any magic of her own, and *her* skin wasn't brown.

The only person with brown skin who could – perhaps – be called a sorceress was Madam Mary-Ay Blackwell, Marisee's grandmother. She dropped down into her well every Friday to meet with the Chad water spirits, but she wasn't magical. Still, Emma and Spindrift were staring at Marisee. Their expressions were suddenly unfriendly.

Marisee must have realized the same thing. She stood up. "Do you really believe that the sorceress is my grandmother?"

Neither Spindrift nor Emma replied.

"It's not!" Marisee said. "It's not Grandma. It couldn't be." She glared at Joe. "Has anyone seen this sorceress? Do they know what she looks like? Or that there even is a sorceress?"

"No," Joe said in a small voice. "They don't."

Marisee crossed her arms. "See. It can't be Grandma."

Robert straightened up to stand besides Marisee. He and Emma were friends! How could she make such accusations?

"This has nothing to do with Madam Blackwell," he said. "Trust us. We'll find out exactly what's going on." He tiptoed back to Garnet and kissed her forehead.

"Don't leave this room," he whispered. "Not until it's safe."

Marisee had already opened the trapdoor, hooked the ladder on to the overhanging eaves and thrown it out of the hole. Without saying anything else, she clambered down. When the ladder stopped wriggling, Robert lowered himself on to the first rung. As he made his way into the darkness, he heard a weak voice.

"Don't forget my medicine, Robert!"

"I'm sure he won't, Garnet," Emma replied. "Now try and sleep some more."

MAKING PLANS WITH GRANDMA

Marisee was ready to hurl herself into a well without even being sure that there was anyone to catch her. How dare Robert's friends blame Grandma for turning children into rats! Grandma would never do the Goldsmith's bidding, especially after the time he'd thrown her into the Fleet gaol. Marisee had really wanted to like the Red Guard Gang because they were Robert's friends. She'd been wrong.

"Those faces!" exclaimed Turnmill, standing on the

corner of Milk Street. "I haven't seen a look like that since the boar couldn't stop sneezing. What happened?"

"They think it's Grandma!" Marisee growled. "How could they?"

"Think your grandma's what?" Turnmill looked confused.

"There's a rumour about a sorceress in the Tower," Robert explained. "Who's turning children into rats."

"From the beginning, please," Turnmill said.

The story rushed out of Marisee with Robert interrupting, until Turnmill held up her hand.

"There's a well round the corner," she said. "We'll be safer underground. Then you can tell me the story properly."

If Marisee hadn't been so angry, she would have smiled at how easily Robert hopped on to a well wall and dropped inside. It wasn't very long ago that they'd jumped for the first time, chased by the Shepherdess's violent Sleeper army. They could have been plummeting to their deaths back then. But she and Robert hadn't died. Instead, this whole new world of Elemental London had opened up to them – the Chad water spirits, the Fumi air spirits and the Dragon fire spirits. The earth Elementals, the Magog giants, were asleep on the Thames riverbed, but they had guardians and spies.

"You can jump now!" Robert called up.

Marisee slid down into the well, landing on a soft watery cushion. Turnmill had transformed back into her water form and the quick, frothing brook carried them through the tunnels. In the pale green glow of Turnmill's water, Marisee could just see Robert bobbing ahead. And from somewhere further along the tunnel, she heard the clatter of boar hooves. Sometimes the noise seemed to be on the roof of the tunnel, then underneath Marisee, then running alongside her on the walls. Marisee was sure she could smell the Fleet Ditch reek that was as much a part of the boar as its great curled tusks.

The stream flowed into a cavern and stopped as if it had hit an invisible wall, landing Marisee next to Robert. She wished so much that she could wear breeches like him. There was no dignified way to be borne along a river while wearing a dress. Robert politely looked away while she smoothed her damp skirts and retied her boots.

Turnmill returned to her humanish shape. She wiped her brow.

"I must be getting old. Carrying you Solids is much more exhausting than it used to be!"

Marisee always wondered how old Turnmill actually was. She'd once said she remembered the Romans coming to London.

Marisee recognized this underground room from their past adventures. It had a low, vaulted ceiling and a floor decorated with fragments of tiles. She walked over to the centre and sat on one of the steps that led down to a small tiled square. Robert sat next to her, hunching over, staring at his feet.

"I'm sorry you didn't meet Elijah," Marisee said.

Robert shrugged. "I'm sure there'll be other times."

But Marisee knew, like Robert, that any person escaping enslavement had to disappear very quickly. There'd already be notices in the City of London coffee houses offering a reward for returning Elijah to the Hibberts.

"He may have left news about your family with someone else," Marisee said. "Perhaps they'll find you and tell you."

"Perhaps," Robert said, though he didn't sound as if he believed it. He breathed in. "Can you smell that?"

Marisee could! Cinnamon and nutmeg! Perhaps a barrel of spices had found its way into the old water tunnels. Many of the old cellars in the tumbledown houses along Chick Lane were used to hide stolen goods. But often the floorboards were damp and rotten, and the boxes and barrels would drop into the River Fleet below.

But not this time. The cinnamon and nutmeg had

been stirred into a jug of hot chocolate and the person carrying it was Grandma. She set the jug down on the step next to Marisee.

"I thought you might need a little warming up," she said.

Marisee was grateful that Grandma cared about her so much. Marisee was starting to worry about her, though. Grandma had been complaining about tiredness for as long as Marisee could remember, but now Marisee could see it. Grandma was wearing her usual wide hat, but there were shadows beneath her eyes. Her hands had wobbled a little as she'd carried the jug.

No wonder Grandma was tired. She'd been Keeper of London's wells for so long, sorting out the Chads' problems and arguing with Lord Mayors, as well as looking after her own well, selling the medicinal water. Marisee really wished her mother was here to help Grandma. She wished her mother was here to help *her*. She longed for Mama to hold her whenever she didn't feel brave.

Marisee glanced over at Robert. He never used to drink hot chocolate because he knew how the cocoa was grown and harvested – work that he and his family were forced to carry out in Barbados. But, over the winter months, Robert had finally been tempted, though he always stared into the mug for a moment before sipping.

"So, what happened tonight?" Grandma asked.

What should Marisee say? Should she tell Grandma what Robert's friends thought of her?

Grandma looked from Marisee to Robert, then back to Marisee. "Whatever it is, you can tell me," she said. "I'm old and tough and have very strong shoulders. I've been dealing with angry rivers and Lord Mayor tyrants since before you were born."

Marisee started the story slowly, from the moment the Dragon came to them, to arriving at Cattle Court. Then she let Robert continue. He'd know what words to choose. But he told it the same way Marisee would have. She heard the anger and betrayal in his voice.

Grandma sighed. "Firstly," she said, "I want to ask you to forgive your friends. They're frightened and when people are frightened they do things that make them feel safe."

"How can thinking that you're a sorceress make them feel safe?" Marisee said. She couldn't hold back the fury from her voice.

"Because it feels safer to believe that it's someone you do know than someone – or even some*thing* – that you don't know," Grandma said.

"No, Madam Blackwell!" Turnmill said from behind them.

Suddenly, Marisee felt giddy, like being caught in an eddy of fast-flowing water. Robert swayed and gripped the edge of the step.

Turnmill's voice was deep with anger. "Frightened people look for the easiest person to blame! I remember the witchfinders," she said. "Those charlatans were prowling the country hunting for so-called witches during the times that Solids call the 1600s. Witches, indeed! Weren't they reported by people they knew? By so-called friends and neighbours, and the people that had come to buy their cures? Those poor innocent women were hung from gallows, or murdered trying to prove that they weren't witches."

Marisee's head was spinning. Her chest was heavy and she couldn't breathe, as if she was struggling against a powerful river.

"Turnmill," Grandma said softly. "Please. Calm down."

"Oh!" Turnmill said, shocked.

The spinning stopped and Marisee reeled backwards in her seat. The room echoed with the gush of water as Turnmill, now a glowing stream, flowed away down a tunnel.

"She once told me that the rivers tried to save the women accused of witchcraft," Grandma said. "Turnmill and Lady Fleet and Westbourne-Tybourne. They surged up to wash away the gallows and flood the gaols and courtrooms, but the Guilds threatened to poison their waters then cover them over. The rivers stopped trying. Turnmill's still angry about it. Are you hurt?"

Marisee slowly breathed in and out. Her chest ached a little, but her body was fine. Marisee knew that Turnmill was powerful – her currents used to heave round the watermills, crushing grain into flour, but Marisee had never felt that power before. She touched the sore place on her chest. It was frightening. Turnmill had always felt like a mother to her. And Turnmill had known Marisee's actual mother. She'd told Marisee how she'd watched her mother play by the riverbank. Marisee had forgotten that Turnmill held the strength of centuries of water magic.

"I'm not hurt," Robert said, though his voice was a little shaky. "I can understand why she's so angry."

Grandma came and sat between Marisee and Robert.

"What you've told me isn't the same as the witch hunts," she said. "No one's hunting me. Robert, your friends are most likely feeling as bad as you are now."

Robert shrugged, keeping his head down so that Marisee couldn't read his face.

"Well," Grandma said, filling the silence. "Let's decide what we should do next. We know that there are kidnappers stealing children and taking them to the Tower of London."

"Yes," Marisee said. "They're taking children from across London. And Joe heard the men say they're turning them into rats. Why would they do this?"

"Lord Gullinn had wanted a battalion of spies," Marisee said. "He believed that the rats could fit into smaller spaces and hide where no one can see them. What if that's what the Goldsmith wants too?"

"We have absolutely no proof that the Goldsmith is involved in this," Grandma said sternly. "Never say anything like that where other people can hear you. He does not forgive anyone who tries to defy him. Don't forget how quickly he threw me in prison before." She shuddered. "And next time, he'll make sure he locks me up where no Chad can save me. And you, Robert..." Grandma gave him a long serious look. "That letter in your pocket will mean absolutely nothing if the Goldsmith decides it doesn't. The new Lord Mayor takes all his advice from the Goldsmith, and if the advice is that you are no longer free..."

Marisee placed her mug on the step. "What do you mean, Grandma?"

Robert thumped his mug down. Hot chocolate spilled on to the stone. "Madam Blackwell is telling the truth – once I'm a slave, I'm always a slave."

"You're not a slave!" Marisee said. "No one is a slave! People are taken and turned into slaves."

"*I* know that!" Robert said. He waved a hand towards the ceiling. "How many people up there do? How many care? Because if they did, everything would be different. If I survive this adventure, I will do everything I can to make sure that no one is enslaved again."

GHOSTS ON THE FORESHORE

Early the next morning, Robert helped Marisee sweep the pump house before heading off to the apothecary shop. Madam Blackwell was preparing water bottles for customers. Friday was always her busiest day.

"I'm sure that the Goldsmith's involved somehow," Marisee said, keeping her voice low.

"I wouldn't be surprised if he's the one who planned it," Robert said. He thought about the Dragon's memories.

"It's too much of a coincidence. Lord Gullinn was a goldsmith too."

"Grandma's right, though," Marisee said. "We have to be very careful. We can't just accuse him of kidnapping children and turning them into rats. We need evidence."

Robert pulled a rag out of his pocket to polish the handle of the pump lever. "Mudlarks have been taken to the Tower, but not all of them. Perhaps some of them have actually seen something that can help us."

"Like the kidnappers," Marisee added. "Real proof that the Goldsmith is part of this."

They fell silent, thinking. Robert stood back to admire the shining handle.

"Let's ask them," he said. "We'll go down to the foreshore tomorrow, as soon as we can." He glanced back towards the cottage. "Shall we tell your grandma?"

Marisee sighed and shook her head. Robert hated holding things back from Madam Blackwell, but they both knew that she would stop them.

The next day, Robert did start to wonder if Madam Blackwell suspected something, because she sent word to Mr Boussay that Robert wouldn't be with him. She asked Marisee to help instead.

As usual, the pump house was busy from early.

Thanks to a sprinkling of Chad magic, the water really did ease red-eye and other similar afflictions. Its success was well known. Robert labelled bottles and wrote sums in the ledgers and filled jugs for hours. He was sure that Madam Blackwell's eyes were on him nearly all the time.

Finally, the last paying customer left and Madam Blackwell herself served the people who came without money. She spent time with each one of them, asked after their families and helped some of the young mothers administer water drops to their ailing children's eyes. Robert knew that this was what Madam Blackwell loved doing.

"Oh my!" Marisee ran panting up the path towards the pump house. "How do you bear that man every day? All he wants to do is study his leeches and leave me to do all the hard work!" She looked around. "Where's Grandma?"

"She's back in the cottage talking to the matron from the Clerkenwell workhouse."

Her eyes met Robert's.

"Now?" she asked.

"Now," Robert agreed.

They sneaked through the door of the pump house, then ran as fast as they could down the hill towards London.

*

The church bells were tolling five o'clock by the time they reached the river. The wet sand sucked at Robert's boots and he kept his eyes to the ground, sidestepping the old fishing nets, bricks and wood thrown out by the tide. He secretly hoped that he might actually see the dull glitter of a coin or lost ring, but the mudlarks were still combing the foreshore. If there'd been anything valuable, they'd certainly already have taken it.

The mudlarks reminded Robert of sparrows as they darted around, calling to each other. Perhaps they should be called mudsparrows instead. Some were so young and couldn't have weighed much more than sparrows. They combed the shore for things to sell and trade – if they didn't, they would starve. Robert knew why many of them were there. He'd heard the sorry tales of the Red Guard Gang – fleeing the workhouse or families that treated them badly.

"I'll start here," Robert said, pointing to a child perched on the bow of a wrecked wherry. "I'll ask if they've seen any of the kidnappings. Or maybe they've found something that's been left on the foreshore."

The mudlark was six or seven years old, wearing a wide straw hat tied beneath their chin by a strip of sack cloth. The child's head was turned as if they were talking to someone, but Robert couldn't see anyone else.

Marisee hitched up her skirt so it didn't drag as she picked her way through the river's debris. She stopped to pull her foot free from the slurping sand.

"I'll ask these two," she said, heading towards mudlarks digging at the edge of the water with a stick.

The child on the boat watched Robert approach.

"I don't mean you any harm," said Robert. "I just want to ask if any of your friends have gone missing?"

The child remained silent. Then they turned sideways and seemed to be listening. Robert still saw no one else. Perhaps the other person was hiding behind the ruined boat.

"Robert?"

Marisee was heading back towards him with the two mudlarks beside her. The tallest one had slung a sagging bag over his shoulder. The other carried a net on a stick. The tall one dropped the bag on to a wide flat stone buried in the sand next to the boat. He wore two jackets and loose breeches that dangled over his shins. He was about Robert's age, narrow-faced with a bare head and bare feet. Didn't he feel the cold? Robert's feet were already going numb and he was wearing boots and stockings.

"I know you," the tall boy said, giving Robert a shy smile. "You're the ones that fought the Thames monster, aren't you? The one that came out of the river by Greenwich?

My little cousin was down on the foreshore that day. If it wasn't for you two, she wouldn't be here at all."

Robert felt a warm glow, in spite of the cold seeping through his boots.

"My name's John," the mudlark said. "What do you want to know?"

"We heard that some mudlarks were taken from here two nights ago," Marisee said. "We want to find out who's taking them and why."

The mudlarks looked at each other. A gull cried overhead as the river shifted itself. Thousands of years ago, the Thames had been a mighty river spirit, but now it was filthy and exhausted and let itself be tugged and heaved by the wind and the sea.

"I heard there were…" Robert searched for the right words. He didn't want to frighten the mudlarks. "Children with red eyes," he finished.

"The ratlings," John said sharply. "That's what they are. The men take us and change us into ratlings. No one cares. It's just one less mouth for the parish."

"Who are the men?" Marisee asked.

John shuddered. Even through the two coats, Robert imagined he could see his bony shoulder blades.

"The catchers." It was the child on the boat. Their voice was quiet and high. "And they bring the ratlings to trick us. The ratlings stand far away so we can't see them properly. They say they've got food or coin. We think they're one of us, and when we go closer, we get caught." The child's face tilted away and their mouth moved. They turned back. "Amyas says this happened before, when the city was silent and the plague came. They took the children to the Tower."

Amyas?

"Maud talks to the ghosts," John said. "There's a few mudlarks that met their ends down here, and some of the ghosts like to hang around and tell their tales."

Robert had met ghosts before, in Hyde Park. Some were friendly and helpful; others were as sad or furious as they'd been when they'd died.

"Can the ghosts tell us more, Maud?" Marisee asked. "We want to rescue the stolen children and stop it happening. But we need as much information as possible."

"I only talk to Amyas," Maud replied. "She says she doesn't remember much, but Mama Tems remembers everything."

Mama Tems? Robert felt a shiver of excitement. His mother had told him tales of Mami Wata, a spirit who ruled the rivers in her homeland. Did the Thames have a spirit like that after all?

"Who's Mama Tems?" he asked.

"She takes care of the bodiless here," Maud said. "She makes sure none of them get hurt."

"Are ... are the bodiless ghosts?" Marisee asked.

Maud nodded.

Robert's excitement grew. "Can we meet Mama Tems?"

Maud shook her head. "Amyas says that Mama Tems doesn't trust no one in this world."

"But she can trust us!" Marisee's voice had risen in frustration. "She has to trust us! We saved London twice! She must know about the Chaos Monster. It was just down the river. If it wasn't for us, more mudlarks might have died!"

Robert remembered something else that Joe had mentioned. It had sounded like a fairy tale, but hadn't he and Marisee already seen and heard so many strange things?

"There might be a magic cauldron in the Tower," he said. "They could be using it to make rat-children. Perhaps Mama Tems knows about it."

Maud consulted with her ghost friend, then said, "Mama Tems doesn't like Solids. You promise to keep the Thames clean, but now it's almost a dead thing. You promise to keep children safe, then you abandon them. Solids are greedy and hurt each other. If she helps you, you might use her words in a bad way."

Robert thrust his cold hands into his pockets. His fingers brushed the letter that protected him, signed by the Lord Mayor. He supposed that Mama Tems was just doing everything she could to protect her ghostly children. How *could* he and Marisee persuade her to trust them? Was there someone who could vouch for him and Marisee? Would Mama Tems help them then?

He asked Maud. She tilted her head, listening to Amyas's answer.

"Amyas isn't sure if there's anyone that Mama Tems would trust," Maud said.

John sighed. "Come on, Maud," he said. "We know these two stopped our friends from being crushed by that Chaos Monster. We need to help them as much as we can."

They waited for Maud again. Finally, she and Amyas stopped talking.

"Mama Tems looks after the bodiless on the foreshore," Maud said. "Amyas thinks that the only person she'd trust is another guardian like her."

"You mean someone who cares for ghosts?" John asked.

Maud nodded.

Robert thanked Maud, and he and Marisee picked their way towards the water steps.

"I don't understand why Mama Tems won't talk to us now," Marisee complained. "Where are we supposed to go from here?"

"We go to someone who cares for ghosts," Robert said. "And I think I know just the person."

MISTRESS AGNES

It was a long walk home back to Clerkenwell through dark streets. Marisee and Robert hurried beside each other, peering into the shadowy corners, checking for the glint of rat-red eyes. A hundred years ago, the doors lining these streets had been marked with red crosses. As a farmer's cart clattered past them, Marisee thought of those doleful cries: "Bring out your dead! Bring out your dead!"

The cottage door was flung open and Grandma ran towards them. Out of the corner of her eye, Marisee spotted Sadler, the sleek fox-like Chad that guarded

Sadler's Well – as well as looking out for Grandma. It was comforting to know he was there when Marisee couldn't be.

"Where were you?" Grandma huffed. She put an arm around each of their shoulders. "Why didn't you tell me you were leaving? I don't think I'll ever stop worrying about you until the day I die, and even then beyond the grave I'll be keeping a watch!"

Marisee shivered. She could never think of Grandma not being here, of being bodiless. She felt Grandma's look on the side of her face, but kept her eyes to the ground.

"We went to talk to the mudlarks," Marisee said.

Grandma frowned. "The mudlarks?"

As Marisee opened her mouth to explain, Grandma said, "It's cold out here. Let's go and get warm."

They sat around the kitchen table. The fire used to be lit with a few drips of Dragon fire from a large jug, but the Goldsmith had refused Grandma permission to replenish it. He'd said that the Dragons were for noble tasks only, not domestic drudgery. Marisee and Grandma had to quickly learn how to use a tinderbox – and they were good at it, because the fire was soon roaring. The village baker had delivered a basket of fresh bread rolls and newly churned butter to pay for a flask of healing water. A bowl of plum jam waited with a spoon, ready.

Marisee hadn't thought she'd be hungry, but she was soon cutting open a roll. Robert always ate slowly, as if each mouthful had to be enjoyed. For most of his life until he'd come to live with them, he'd been nearly starved, or given the dregs of food that other people didn't want. He talked while Marisee ate.

Marisee couldn't stop thinking about how the Red Guard Gang believed that Grandma was a wicked sorceress. The mudlarks had mentioned a sorceress too. It wouldn't take long for rumours to thread their way through London. The Goldsmith would love any opportunity to lock Grandma away. He was likely still angry about the time Turnmill had sprung Grandma from the Fleet prison by blasting water up through the filthy underground cells.

"Mama Tems might know if there's really a magic cauldron in the Tower," Robert finished. "But she won't trust us."

Grandma dropped the jam spoon. "Magic cauldron? You didn't mention that before!"

Marisee and Robert looked at each other. Hadn't they?

"Sorry," Marisee said. "Joe wasn't even sure that there actually was a sorceress or a magic cauldron. He thought it sounded like a witches' tale."

"Maybe it did," Grandma said. "But I think you

should follow every clue you have. There are so many legends about magic cauldrons, though no Elemental I've met has ever seen one. Lady Walbrook would definitely know about any rumours, but she won't talk to Solids. So, yes, Mama Tems… If the cauldron has anything to do with the Thames, she'll know about it."

Marisee laid down her knife. "You know her, Grandma?"

Grandma chuckled. "Every Keeper of London's Wells knows *of* her, though none have met her. Not in this life, anyway."

"Is she an Elemental?" Robert asked.

Grandma looked thoughtful. "Not exactly. She guards no brook or well, though some believe she's all that remains of the Thames spirits that cared for the river in ancient times."

"So she *is* like Mami Wata," Robert said.

"Maybe in past times Mama Tems was like Mami Wata and seized the sailors from their boats," Grandma said. "But now the Thames is so full of filth we can almost walk from one bank to the other. Mama Tems commands the foreshore, not the river itself. If she was Elemental, she'd be of the earth."

"Commands the foreshore?" Marisee asked. "Like a queen?"

"No," Grandma said. "As you know, the foreshore is a treacherous place. Many who lost their lives there still remain. She watches over the ghosts."

"So she's like Mistress Agnes in Hyde Park," Robert said.

Grandma nodded.

He smoothed a pat of butter across a roll and spooned on some jam. He held it to his mouth but didn't bite into it.

"Then we should ask Mistress Agnes to vouch for us," he said.

Marisee hadn't visited Hyde Park since London had fallen under the Shepherdess's enchanted sleep. So much had happened there; her stomach clenched just thinking about it. Robert had been seized by the plague monster in the Serpentine and almost drowned. They'd been chased by an army of sleepwalkers, stumbling through the darkening park. And there were the ghosts...

The triple tree gallows of Tyburn stood right next to the park wall – the ghosts of the hanged had fled their bodies, seeking refuge in the park. In the far north, just by the wall next to the gallows, was a dark, cold space haunted by the ghosts of soldiers who'd been shot for deserting the army. They'd been so sad and confused.

But there'd been one ghost who was very friendly and helpful: Mistress Agnes.

Marisee glanced over at Robert. He was staring at the roll, lost in his own memories. The plague beast's tentacles had dragged him beneath the murky, weed-matted water. Did he *really* want to go back? Watching him more carefully, she saw that his hand was shaking a little.

Grandma took the roll from Robert's hand and placed it back on the plate.

"You don't have to come to Hyde Park, Robert," she said.

"I want to!" Robert snatched up the roll and took a big bite. "I'll be fine!"

Marisee and Grandma swapped a look. Robert saw it.

"What else am I supposed to do?" he asked. "Just sit here while children like Garnet are being turned into rats?"

"No, Robert," Grandma said. "I want you to do something that only you can do. Ask the statues what they know."

He took another bite of roll, but he was chewing very slowly, as if he wasn't hungry at all.

"There are so many statues," he said. "I wouldn't

know where to start. And they don't always talk to me." He dropped the roll on to the plate. "And I don't like walking around the streets by myself, even with the Lord Mayor's letter."

"I understand," Grandma said.

They all understood – in spite of the letter, Robert was still at the mercy of kidnappers looking to claim a reward for returning enslaved people who'd escaped their terrible lives. How could a letter help him if he was imprisoned on a ship heading back to the West Indies?

"Perhaps you *should* stay home, then," Grandma said.

"No," Robert said. "I need to return to Hyde Park. I need to…" He took a deep breath. "I'll never forget the plague monster, how it held me underwater, how I couldn't breathe. But I don't want to be frightened all my life. If I don't come with you now, I'll never go back."

Grandma sighed. "The three of us will go together," she said firmly. "*Together.* So no running off."

The lodge keeper was just unlocking the gates to Hyde Park as they arrived the next morning. He gave them a suspicious look but returned to the lodge as soon as he'd flung the gates open. Grandma put an arm around Robert's shoulders.

"You can wait here…" she said.

Robert took a deep breath and strode ahead. "No," he said. "I'm coming with you."

It feels like a different park, Marisee thought, though Robert's gaze kept flitting towards the west and the Serpentine. The last time they'd seen the lake, it had been on fire, and the water spirits had come together to extinguish the flames. Had the plague monster survived? Would its tentacles break the surface and grab her or Robert if they walked too close to its water?

They hurried along the avenue of elm trees, past the reservoir and towards the northern end of the park. It was a sunless morning and Marisee felt the chill as the trees reached further over the path, branches touching each other above her head.

Suddenly, she was sure that they were being watched. Robert and Grandma were the only other humans she could see – it was too early for the lords and ladies to come and parade. There were other creatures, though, Elemental and bodiless, who hid in the park's shadows.

"Can you feel it?" Marisee asked.

Robert nodded. "They know we're here."

"Of course they do," Grandma said, quickening her stride. "The ghosts make it their business to know everything that happens within the park walls. My mother told me that the ghosts used to hide in the trees and leap out to terrify midnight trespassers."

"Such a false affront from one who should know better!"

Marisee jumped. It was a woman's voice, which sounded almost real, except that it seemed to ride on the air towards them. It was also a familiar voice. Grandma laughed.

"Mistress Agnes!" Grandma called. "Are you calling my mother a liar? Because, if that's so, you should be glad that she didn't remain bodiless in this world or she would come and have strong words with you."

"Madam Mary-Ay Blackwell!" Mistress Agnes replied. "So good of you to find time to attend your humble bodiless friend!"

The last time Marisee had met Mistress Agnes, the sky had been darkened by an enchantment and the ghost had been easy to see. Even though the trees were casting shadows, Marisee could not make out even the slightest ghostly shape.

"Can you show yourself and make it easier for my grandchild here?" Grandma asked with a smile in her voice.

"I *am* showing myself!" There was humour in

Mistress Agnes's voice. "It's just your grandchild isn't looking properly!"

A movement caught Marisee's eye, as if the shadows were flickering against the tree. It was the actual tree trunk – a person seemed to be part of the trunk! Among the whorls and wrinkles of the wood, Marisee could definitely see Mistress Agnes in her apron and bonnet, sitting on her stool as if she was still by the well that she cared for before she died. She pressed ghostly spectacles up her nose.

"Thank you," Grandma said. "That's better."

"Well, Madam Blackwell, I'd hate to call your mother a liar," Mistress Agnes said. "To what do I owe this pleasure?"

Grandma waved her hand towards Marisee and Robert. "I think they'll be better at explaining than me."

Marisee and Robert took turns telling the story. Neither of them mentioned how worried they were about Grandma being accused of being the sorceress.

"We think Mama Tems can help us," Robert said. "She sees what happens on the foreshore."

"Indeed," Mistress Agnes said. "She's been the guardian of those who pass there for centuries. Perhaps even longer."

"But she won't speak to us," Marisee said. "She needs proof that we can be trusted."

"Oh, does she now?" Mistress Agnes said.

There was a silence. What did that mean? Should Marisee say something else? Did Mistress Agnes understand what was being asked of her?

Grandma spoke first. "Can you help them, Agnes?" she asked.

"You're asking me for a letter of introduction." Mistress Agnes sighed. A breeze whispered through the leaves and the shadows shifted again. "It comes at a high price, Mary-Ay."

Further west in the park, hooves thudded against the bridleways.

"We can't stay much longer, Agnes," Grandma said. "We don't want everyone to know our secrets. Will you help us?"

"I could help you," Mistress Agnes said. "But I will not."

"Why?" The question burst out of Marisee.

"I'm sorry," Mistress Agnes said. Perhaps it was Marisee's eyes, but the ghost seemed to fade even more. "It will cost too much."

"We'll pay it," Marisee said quickly. "However high, we can find a way."

Grandma stepped towards the faint shape. Marisee wasn't even sure if it was Mistress Agnes or the bumps and ridges of the tree.

"What is the price, Agnes?"

"Trust is hard won." Mistress Agnes's voice was still strong, even though Marisee could no longer see her. "There are few who guard the bodiless. We have promised never to betray one another. I must be fully assured that you will not bring harm to Mama Tems or any that she guards. You must give me what is most precious to you."

"I have a gold ring," Grandma said. "It's in my cottage, but I can bring it at nightfall. It was a gift passed from my grandmother to my mother and then down to me. I believe that there are no others like it."

"I can't accept what's precious to *you*," Mistress Agnes said. "It's not you that's doing the asking."

"I am!" Grandma sounded cross. "I've asked for your help and will happily pay your price."

"The ring is precious to *you*, Mary-Ay," Mistress Agnes said. "I know that. If you give it to me, you'll be sad, but you'll continue with your life. There'll be no ... consequences."

Marisee didn't understand. "It's important to Grandma!" She pulled off her bonnet. "But if that's not good enough, you can take my hair! All of it!"

"Your hair will grow back," Robert said quietly.

He wasn't helping!

"It might not." Marisee touched a short patch of hair above her forehead. The tithe-master had taken a tenth of Marisee's hair to allow her to pass through his tunnel. That hair had never regrown.

Robert reached into his pocket. He slid out the Lord Mayor's letter and offered it.

"No, Robert," Grandma said firmly. "We'll think of something else."

"We will!" Marisee said, grabbing Robert's arm.

He quickly switched the letter to his other hand.

"This is a letter signed by the Lord Mayor that confirms my ... my freedom from enslavement," he said. "If someone tries to take me, I can show them this letter and they should free me."

Should, Marisee thought bitterly. It didn't mean they would. But it was still the only protection that Robert had.

"Put that letter back in your pocket, Robert!" Grandma ordered.

"I can't, Madam Blackwell," Robert said. "If this is what we need to save the imprisoned children, then take it. Is it the correct price, Mistress Agnes?"

"It is, Robert," Mistress Agnes said. "It's precious because there will be consequences if you no longer have it."

"Then take it, Mistress Agnes. Please."

"No," Marisee whispered.

"Are you sure, Robert?" Mistress Agnes's voice was loud.

"Yes." Robert's voice was clear and strong. "Take it!"

A sudden gust of wind snatched the letter from his fingers. It flew towards the tree and disappeared. Marisee wanted to shout at him. Why had he been impatient? Surely there was another way. She caught Grandma's warning look.

"Do we just wait here?" she said crossly.

The letter reappeared and floated back to Robert. Marisee grinned. Mistress Agnes wasn't keeping it! Then her smile faded. It wasn't the same letter. The paper was darker and older. It glowed a dirty yellow, as if the magic was stained.

"What does it say?" Marisee asked.

Robert tried to unfold it, but the paper was rigid and stiff, as if the layers were stuck together.

"I suppose it's only for Mama Tems to see," he said.

Marisee squeezed down everything she wanted to say. How could this be fair? Robert had given Mistress Agnes the only thing that stopped him from being seized off the streets and sent to a plantation in the West Indies. At least he should be able to read what Mistress Agnes had written about him!

Grandma linked arms with Marisee, pulling her away.

"Thank you for your assistance, Agnes," she called back.

Both Marisee and Robert stayed silent.

MAMA TEMS

Robert and Marisee headed straight back to the Thames foreshore. Madam Blackwell had wanted to come with them, even though she had a meeting with the Lord Mayor. They persuaded her that they'd return home as soon as they'd spoken to Mama Tems.

Eastwards on the river, the boats were jammed so close together Robert reckoned that he could walk from one riverbank to the other across them. The incoming tide lapped at a ragged heap of broken barrels on the shoreline. Robert imagined mudlarks rifling through them, searching for their treasures, all the while knowing that they risked their lives from the tides – and now from the kidnappers too.

Marisee scooped up her skirts as they picked their way around the usual debris – frayed rope, bricks, scatterings of nails. Robert kicked at a square of wood, flipping it out of its sandy dip. Further along the foreshore, a merchant's ship was moored, waiting for a lighter boat to offload its cargo. The ground behind had fallen into shadow as the boat's sails blocked the sun.

"What should we do?" Marisee asked. "Wait for Mama Tems to find us? How would she know that we're here?"

"If she's a guardian, I suppose she's always watching."

"The river's too busy!" Marisee said. "She won't show herself when there are so many people about."

That was true. Robert had never felt safe around people he didn't know. Now he was without his letter, it was especially dangerous. He'd longed for freedom all his life and he might have traded it away. But if that meant he would save children from a terrible fate, then it was a good thing to do. He had to squeeze down his fear.

"Let's find somewhere quiet," he said.

Robert and Marisee scrambled over the debris to the darkness beneath the wharf, where the river wall was spotted with moss. Twilight was the time when the veil between the different worlds was at its thinnest. Robert reckoned that this gloom, with the sun's light dampened by the canvas sails, was as close as they were going to get.

"I'll keep a lookout for passers-by," Marisee said, planting herself in front of him.

"Thank you," he said, though he had no idea what he was supposed to do.

Robert plucked Mistress Agnes's letter from his pocket. His fingers tingled like he'd brushed past nettles. He held the letter in the air.

"Mama Tems!" he called out. "I bring a letter of introduction from Mistress Agnes! We need to speak to you."

Further down the river, a ship's bell sounded and a wherry man argued with customers over a fare. The merchant ship bobbed in the water and, for a moment, sunlight slid between the sails and lit up the shadows before the cold darkness returned. Robert waited, closing his eyes. Did anything feel different? A wind blew across the river, stinking of rotten fish. No, it didn't.

"Try again," Marisee said.

Robert took a deep breath.

"Mama Tems!" he called out once more. He heard the edge in his voice. "Children are being taken from the foreshore. They will be turned into rats. We have to stop it, but we need your help."

Perhaps she was already here, watching, waiting, deciding. Was there anything else Robert could do to convince her? He clutched the letter tighter. His fingertips seemed to glow in the darkness. He dug back through his memories. He felt a twinge of sadness knowing that all the precious moments with his brother were lost to him forever. He took a breath and squeezed his eyes closed. His mother and his aunties had taught him stories passed through generations in their birthplace.

"They are part of us," his mother had said. "They can't take stories away from us."

"I know you're here, Mama Tems," he murmured, opening his eyes. "I know the tales of your sisters commanding the rivers in my family's homeland. I had hoped against hope that your kind would be here too, but I gave up that hope. I can't honour you with rich gifts, but" – he waved the letter – "I've forfeited my freedom, the most precious thing I own. Please help us."

The light flickered over Robert as if the ship had moved again, but the river was completely still. Strangely still and strangely quiet. The air was thicker and he could smell spice, cinnamon and nutmeg.

Suddenly, it was very cold. Robert's skin felt too tight

to hold his whole body. Mist skimmed the surface of the water, rippling across the foreshore towards him.

"Mama Tems?" he whispered. "Is that you?"

Marisee backed towards him. "I don't think so," she said.

They stood shoulder to shoulder. It was comforting knowing she was so close.

"Mama Tems?" he called again into the mist.

The mist split apart in a blur of red.

"Wrong!" a man hissed. "Remember me?"

Robert pushed himself back against the river wall as the red curled through the mist like blood in water. It hung in the air, weaving together into something nearly solid.

"I have longed to torment you!" The man's voice sounded almost familiar. "I am forbidden to leave this shore, but now you have come to me!"

The red smudge became a long banyan coat and above that a pale circle of a face. Were there eyes, a nose, a mouth – or was Robert imagining them? But then Marisee jolted next to him.

"Mr … Mr Dross?" she stuttered.

The figure lifted his arms and slowly twirled round. Robert saw right through him.

"Mr Dross?" The man laughed. It sounded like a carpenter's saw on wood. "Yes, I am Mr Dross, the animateur extraordinaire! Mr Dross whose exquisite clockwork creations were seized by the Lord Mayor and his parasites. Mr Dross who you two children murdered in this very place!"

"We didn't murder you!" Marisee shouted. "It was a cannonball! And you were trying to summon the Chaos Monster to destroy London!"

Marisee was always so brave! She was shouting at a ghost! Robert's voice had burrowed down inside him.

"London was already dying," the ghost of Mr Dross said. It flickered and faded, flickered and strengthened. One moment it was stained air, the next almost as solid as Robert himself. "I was just hastening its demise. It was time for this filthy city to be reborn."

"By killing everyone in London?" Marisee asked.

Just like the Shepherdess and the enchanted sleep, Robert thought. *How do people become so vengeful that they want to destroy a city full of people?*

"London has survived plagues," the ghost answered. "It has survived fire. Each time it grows anew, but rarely does it learn from its mistakes."

Mr Dross's ghost became so solid that Robert was sure he could hear the swish of the fabric as its arms brushed the coat. Its face grew bigger and wider and brighter and paler. The air was so cold it burned Robert's skin where it touched. His own breath was a fog that hovered in front of his face like silent words.

"But you and that boy destroyed everything!" Mr Dross's ghost bellowed at Marisee. "Now *I'll* destroy *you!*"

"You're wrong!" Marisee tried to shout back, but her voice was muffled by the mist. "We didn't—"

The ghost shrieked. It rushed towards them, icy cold, a furious blur of red, folding itself around Robert until his eyes stung and he couldn't breathe.

"Stop!" he gasped. "Please, Mr Dross! We didn't…"

Then Robert couldn't speak at all. The ice spread through his body, clutching at his heart, freezing his tongue to the roof of his mouth.

Mama Tems! Robert hoped his thoughts were so loud that they could be heard outside his head. *Help us!*

Something banged against his shoulder. He realized that it was Marisee staggering backwards. She turned to face him, her eyes wide with fear but still flashing with anger. Her mouth moved – she was saying his name.

His mouth tried to move too. He wanted to say he was sorry for bringing her here. His body was so heavy, but too solid to sag. He would topple over and crash like a statue. He wanted to close his eyes. The weight on his eyelids was like river stones, but if he let them slip shut, he was sure they'd never open again.

"Ghost!" a woman's voice yelled. "You have no place here among my children! I have warned you before. Now be gone!"

The Dross ghost shattered, the mist bursting apart like fireworks, specks of red and bright white. Robert's head filled with the smell of damp rope and oakum, the sharp tang of tanning factories and every spice that he had ever known – nutmeg, cinnamon, cardamon ... and oranges. Why did the scent of oranges make him wipe back tears? The answer had to be in his lost memories.

As the cold oozed away, Robert sank to the ground, next to Marisee.

"Are you hurt?" he gasped.

She shook her head. Robert didn't believe her. It felt like there were bruises inside him from where the ghost had tried to crush away his life. He staggered to his feet, then helped Marisee to stand.

"It's ... it's different," she said. "We're by the quay, but we're not."

Robert nodded. The ground felt solid beneath him, but he had to squint to see the stones and old nails. The mossy wall looked like a reflection in flowing water.

"Mama Tems?"

And there she was, dark-skinned like his aunties, her hair cut short and lying slick against her head. Her eyes were dark grey. So many trinkets hung from her ears that Robert couldn't see the skin beneath – tiny golden hooks and jewelled anchors and thin bars of gold shaped like oars. She wore the dress of a rich lady – a dark grey skirt that shimmered without light and a bodice embroidered with intricate rippling silver. A lace cloak was held together by an oyster shell around her neck.

"You want my help?" she said. "I don't trust Solids."

"Mistress Agnes vouches for us," Robert said.

She held out her hand. "Give me the letter."

Robert winced as the magic surged from Mama Tems, yanking the letter from his grasp. She plucked it from the air, opened it flat and ran her finger along the paper. She nodded and the letter shattered, just like Mr Dross's ghost.

And that was it. Robert could never walk the streets of London in safety again.

"It was a false belief, Robert," Mama Tems said, as if reading his mind. "The Goldsmith would make the Lord Mayor renounce you as quickly as a Dragon riddles."

Secretly, Robert had always known that, but the letter was all he'd had. Now he had nothing. He swayed. It was hard not to fall over when the world felt askew.

He blinked, trying to steady himself, but everything still wavered around him. He felt Marisee's calm hand on his shoulder.

"Where are we?" he asked.

Mama Tems smiled. Her teeth were as sharp as a pike's.

"Can't you see?" she asked. "You're in our world."

Our world? Oh, yes! He could see them now! Ghost children crowding around Mama Tems. Some were peering out from beneath her cloak; others were huddled together, their eyes wide and wary. Three children stood beside her, fists clenched like they were ready to fight. They were dressed in clothes too big or too small, so ragged that Robert couldn't tell what the garments had originally been.

"Be quick with your questions," Mama Tems said. "I can't hold the Solid world at bay for long."

"Have you seen who takes the children from the foreshore?" Marisee asked.

"I see little in the Solid world," Mama Tems said, "though my children have told me that their friends were taken before, during the time of the plague."

"And that was Lord Gullinn's orders?" Marisee added.

"I believe so," Mama Tems said.

"Robert? Are you there?"

A familiar voice was pulling him out of the ghosts' world. Not yet! Mama Tems hadn't told them anything they didn't already know.

"Mama Tems," he said. "We heard a rumour about a sorceress in the Tower of London and a magic cauldron. Can you tell us more?"

Her face furrowed. "The weight of your world presses so heavily. I must be quick. Many centuries ago, labourers were digging by the foreshore to widen the wharf by the Tower of London. Their picks hit a chest buried in sand and stones. It contained the head of a giant—"

Marisee gasped.

"And the shards of a cauldron," Mama Tems continued. Her voice was weaker.

"Who was the giant?" Marisee's words tumbled over themselves. "Was it a magic cauldron? What did it do?"

The ghosts had disappeared. The ground beneath Robert's feet hardened, and the shapes of the rope and bricks sharpened.

"The giant was Myrr." Mama Tems's voice sounded like the tap of thin rope against stone. "The guardian. And the cauldron..."

Her voice faded away. Robert couldn't hear her answer.

"Please!" he begged. "Say that again, Mama Tems!"

But she was gone. Only the lingering scent of cinnamon remained. Marisee was leaning against the damp river wall, breathing heavily.

"Are you down there, Robert?" The voice came from above. It was Emma. She was on the quay. "Answer me if you are!"

Robert's legs were wobbly, as if he'd had to run between the two worlds. The merchant boat had shifted and the sun shone brightly. There were no more shadows.

"Robert!"

"I'm here!" he called up.

Emma appeared at the top of the water steps.

"Robert!" Tears ran down her face. "Garnet has gone!"

GARNET

As Marisee watched Robert run up the stairs towards Emma, she suddenly felt as invisible as the ghosts. She understood why Emma meant so much to Robert, but hadn't Marisee been his first friend? Hadn't she and Grandma also helped him at great risk to themselves? How could he go racing to the Red Guard Gang after they'd accused Grandma of being an evil sorceress!

"Marisee!" Robert was beckoning her from the top of the steps. "Didn't you hear? They've taken Garnet."

Yes, she had heard! Did he think that she was

deliberately lagging behind? Marisee was the one who'd had to persuade Robert to investigate the stolen children in the first place. Garnet hadn't done anything to hurt anyone. *She* hadn't accused Grandma of being a sorceress. Of course Marisee would do anything that she could to find her.

"I'm coming," she said, and she wound her way through the foreshore debris and up the slippery steps.

Emma explained quickly. The young child had sneaked out, following Turpin and Duval to Covent Garden. The boys had no idea that she was there until they'd heard the scream behind them.

"They took her from an alley off Fleet Street," Emma said.

"Did the boys see who took her?" asked Marisee.

"It was so quick," Emma replied. "They were in uniform. They looked like soldiers." She fought back tears. Without thinking, Marisee moved forward to comfort her, but Emma stepped back, her face blazing with fury. "The boys saw a child with red eyes!"

Robert insisted that they go to the alley where Garnet had been seized, even though Emma had assured him that the Red Guard Gang had searched every part of it. Marisee was grateful that Grandma always made her carry a few pennies for emergencies. They were the only passengers on the boat ferrying them back to the north bank.

The wherry man looked at them with curiosity. There were countless poor people in London. Marisee knew that many of them would happily collect a reward for returning an escaped "slave". When she spoke to the wherry man, she made sure her voice was loud – she wanted him to hear that she was English, born in London. She didn't want him to have any ideas about rowing her and Robert out to the ships that sailed the kidnapped African people to the plantations. Robert kept his gaze on his boots and said nothing.

Once they'd landed, they made their way towards Fleet Street. The alley was next to a tavern called Ye Olde Cheshire Cheese and, even at this time of the day, Marisee heard the sounds of merriment from inside. Had anyone in there seen what had happened to Garnet? Perhaps she should go in and ask.

The tavern door opened and a man was hurled into the alley. His face was smeared with coal dust, his eyes rolling.

"And don't come back until you can hold your beer!" a man yelled from inside.

The coal man picked himself up and staggered towards Fleet Street.

No, Marisee decided. She was certainly not going in there.

The alley was nothing but an alley, stinking of all the things that usually made Marisee hold her nose when she passed them. She followed Robert as he walked to the end and then back again, crouching to stare into cellar windows and up towards the roofs that grazed each other on either side of the passage.

Marisee touched Robert's shoulder. "Garnet's not here, Robert. Let's go back to Grandma's before she starts worrying. We can decide what to do next from there. We will find Garnet."

Robert nodded but said nothing.

In the early evening, when everyone was well rested, Grandma brought out chairs from the cottage. Robert paced back and forth. Turnmill sat on the well wall, her feet scuffing the bricks.

She said, "We know for certain that in 1666 Lord Gullinn wanted to create a human-beast army so he could rule London."

"Then when he discovered the rat-children, he wanted a battalion of spies to join that army," Marisee said.

"Ah, spies," Turnmill said. "A hundred years ago, the

docks were like they are now, full of ships bringing cargo from around the world. The merchants had to pay tax at Custom House, but some cheated and didn't pay what was due. I can imagine greedy Lord Gullinn planning to send out his spies. They'd lurk on the docks, between the bales and barrels, and in the shadowy nooks of the Custom House, listening to every conversation, watching the goods being unloaded from the ships and then reporting back to their master."

Marisee looked around her. It would be so easy for rat spies to hide in the shadows of the pump room or behind a tree.

"Lord Gullinn would know everyone's business," Turnmill continued. "Everyone's secrets. He'd demand they pay him to keep him quiet. Then perhaps he'd build his own quay and warehouses that the merchants *must* use, paying him a fortune to do so, or, once more he'd threaten to spill their secrets. Every Solid has secrets. So no one would dare challenge him. He would build his empire, secret by secret. London one day, England the next, and afterwards, anywhere in the world that Lord Gullinn chose."

"But his plan didn't work or we'd have known about it," Marisee said.

"Mr Pipes must have defied him," said Robert. "Even

though Lord Gullinn was sure that Mr Pipes had made … had turned the children into…"

Marisee knew that he couldn't finish because he was thinking of Garnet.

"Do you think he used the magic cauldron?" she asked Turnmill. "And if he did, what happened to it?"

"And the giant's head," Grandma said. "Please don't forget the giant's head."

Marisee was sure that she'd never, ever forget a giant's head.

"Mama Tems said the giant was called Myrr," she said.

"Myrr?" Turnmill looked up. "I've forgotten my Norse. I wish Ditch was here – he's still fluent. But I think it means 'mud'."

"So perhaps the giant was made of mud or came from the mud," Grandma said.

Robert stopped pacing. "Earth magic," he said. "Like Gog and Magog."

"You sound very certain," Turnmill said.

Robert shrugged. "I just feel it."

Turnmill frowned, but said nothing.

"So if the Goldsmith's kidnapping children to make … make rat spies." Marisee glanced at Robert before continuing. "Is he carrying on Lord Gullinn's plan?"

"We have no proof that it's the Goldsmith," Grandma said firmly.

"Who else would be so cruel?" Marisee protested.

"Marisee!" Grandma hissed. "You know that he uses his ravens as spies. You have no idea who may be lurking in those trees or on the chimney stacks listening to us! So please don't make unfounded accusations!"

Marisee clamped her mouth shut. She was right, though! It had to be the Goldsmith!

Grandma sighed. "So what do we know now? Children are being taken and there may be a magic cauldron that, perhaps, can be used to make them into spies."

"It wouldn't just be children," Turnmill said. "Surely it would be used to make other Variegates. I haven't heard of other Variegates, but London is a harsh place to be alone. Variegates may try to find each other. If there are any new ones, someone like Henry might know."

"So even if the Gold— If the cauldron *is* in the Tower of London," Marisee said, "no one knows how to make it work. Otherwise, there'd be new Variegates." That was hopeful, wasn't it?

"The cauldron might not be working, but children are being stolen," Robert said bitterly. "That means someone must be very sure that the cauldron will be ready soon."

"With a sorceress to help," Grandma added. She turned to Turnmill. "Can you ask the Chads inside the Tower of London if they know anything more about the cauldron?"

Turnmill kicked the well a little harder. "No," she said. "I can't. The Tower was built as a fortress for humans. Now it's a prison for us too. The Chads who care for the wells and springs there can never leave."

"They're prisoners?" Marisee asked, shocked.

"I believe so," Turnmill said. "The tunnels are blocked."

"Blocked?" Grandma frowned. "How?"

"A binding. Made from threads that hurt Chads," Turnmill said. "But perhaps the Chads inside the Tower have no wish to leave. Maybe they've been weakened."

Robert started pacing again.

"The answers to all our questions are inside the Tower," he said. "One of us has to find a way in."

Turnmill jumped down from the wall. Marisee's head was filled with the grinding of mill wheels and she was doused in invisible fresh river water. Then the magic washed away.

"Find a way into the Tower?" Turnmill repeated. "One does not simply walk into the Tower of London, Robert. It holds too many secrets to risk being invaded. It's impossible to enter without permission or reason."

"I know," Robert said.

There was something in his tone that made Marisee stare at him.

"The Tower of London is a fortress and a prison," he continued, avoiding her eyes. "The obvious way in is as a prisoner."

"A PRISONER?" Marisee, Turnmill and Grandma shouted together.

"Nobody is being taken as a prisoner to the Tower of London," Grandma spluttered. "Especially not you, Robert. Forget that idea right now!"

"Then how do we find out about the cauldron?" he asked. "And the giant? And rescue Garnet and the other children? There isn't time to wait around hoping for a better idea if children are being turned into rats."

Grandma glared at him. "*Nobody* is being taken as a prisoner to the Tower of London," she repeated.

Robert scowled into the evening.

"Are there guards we can bribe for information?" Grandma asked.

"The guards won't talk to outsiders," Turnmill said. "Not for all the gold in the king's pocket. There are rumours of a spy network – everyone watching everyone and claiming a reward if they report a wrongdoing. For those who divulge the Tower's secrets, punishment will be harsh, especially if there are cruel experiments happening in there once more."

Robert was pacing again, even quicker. It was giving Marisee a headache.

"Can we fight our way in?" Grandma asked. She sounded a little desperate.

"It's a fortress, Grandma," Marisee said.

"We'll think of something," Grandma said. "We will! But absolutely no one is going to be a prisoner in there." She struggled to her feet. "Oh," she groaned. "I'm really feeling my age now. I'm going inside to make supper. Perhaps I'll have some inspiration while I'm cutting up carrots."

"And I'm supposed to report to Lady Walbrook," Turnmill said. "Not that she'll help. She still hates you Solids."

She hopped up on to the well wall, waved, then stepped into the mouth. Marisee listened even though she knew there'd be no splash.

Marisee waited until Grandma was far along the path before planting herself in front of Robert to make him stop moving.

"Don't do it," she said.

He looked at her as if to say *What?* but then sighed. "Can you think of any other way of getting into the

Tower? The last time Haakon captured me, he told me that's where he was taking me. Someone in the Tower definitely wants me alive." He ran his hands through his hair. "Marisee, I can't just sit around waiting. We could be running out of time already."

They stared at each other.

"You're going to do it, aren't you?" she said.

He nodded.

Marisee glanced towards the well, lowering her voice just in case. "Then I'm going to come with you."

"No," Robert said with certainty. "That won't help. I need you on the outside."

"But we always go on adventures together!"

"Not this time."

"Why?" The word came out louder and harder than Marisee expected.

"Because you have to make sure that I can escape," Robert said. "It's too dangerous for us both to be trapped inside the Tower. And what's stopping the Goldsmith from stealing more children? You must do everything you can to protect them." Robert lowered *his* voice. "And I need you to protect me too. What if the Goldsmith tries to send me back to the West Indies?"

He would try. Marisee knew that. The Goldsmith's revenge would be swift and harsh.

"While I discover as much as I can inside the Tower," Robert said, "can you do the same out here? Find out everything about Mr Pipes and the cauldron. Did Lord Gullinn ever have an army of Variegates? *Are* there other Variegates that we don't know about? How were they created and what happened to them? So much of this traces back to the Goldsmiths Guild, but Madam Blackwell's right. We need to prove it."

Marisee felt sick. Was she really going to let her best friend walk into a place that so many people had never left?

Robert touched her shoulder. "We know that the Goldsmith wants power. What if he does have a magic cauldron and finds a way to control the whole of London? What would happen to people like me – the ones that have escaped? And the ones still enslaved in London? Or your Grandma? He'd want complete power over the Chads. There'd be no more Well Keepers."

Or Elementals, Marisee thought. The Goldsmith already controlled many of the city's Dragons and used ravens to spy for him. He was always threatening to cover many of the rivers too. And Marisee was sure that he wouldn't be content with London. He was exactly the same as Lord Gullinn – he wanted everything.

She took a deep breath. Unless she could think

of another plan, Robert was right. They had to follow different clues.

"Where do I find out more without making the Goldsmith suspicious?" she said, half to herself.

Robert answered with the same two words that had been itching in the back of her mind. "The Dragon."

Marisee knew that the Mary-le-Bow Dragon had wanted her to see more memories, but Marisee had pulled away, terrified by the heat of the fire. Could she make herself stay longer? She would have to! It would not be nearly as dangerous as Robert's mission.

"How will you become a prisoner?" she asked him miserably.

Robert looked away from her. "I think it's best that you don't know," he said.

BETRAYAL

Robert waited until the first morning light before leaving Madam Blackwell's cottage. He'd been awake all night trying to decide the best way to be taken prisoner. Though an hour or two had been spent wondering if there was still another way to rescue the children, he hadn't been able to think of one. So what *should* he do? He couldn't knock on the Tower of London gates and ask to be let in. That would be very suspicious. It had to seem like he was there against his will.

It was ridiculous that he'd once fought Haakon the capture-creature to *prevent* himself from being taken to the Tower of London, but now he was looking for a way to get inside. But … what if somehow Robert crossed paths with Haakon again? Haakon was a ruthless hunter. He'd been a member of the Guild of Variegated Assassins. He would not be satisfied until he caught Robert and delivered him to his master, whoever that might be – although Robert was sure now that he knew who it was, even if he dared not say it aloud.

How could he find Haakon? Even thinking about it made Robert's stomach churn. But Robert did have another enemy – one who'd betrayed him to Haakon before for money and would definitely do it again. Robert didn't know where he was, either, but he had a good idea how to find out.

When Robert went downstairs, Madam Blackwell was simmering porridge in a pan on the fire. She held out the pan, offering him some. He shook his head. His stomach was now churning so hard it felt as if his insides were turning to butter.

Madam Blackwell gave him a sympathetic smile. "An early start with Mr Boussay?"

Robert gave her a tiny nod. It felt like less of a lie.

She gave the porridge another stir. She always added spices to make it smell and taste wonderful.

"I'll make sure there's a good supper later," she said. "And we'll talk about what we should do next."

Robert almost ran to the door. He couldn't look at her.

"Robert! Wait!"

Had Madam Blackwell discovered magic that would help her see what was in his head? He was tempted to really run, but then she'd definitely be suspicious!

"I've filled some water flasks for Mr Hissop," she said. "He's a tailor and treats his apprentices well, but they've all caught red-eye. Can you deliver it? He lives in White Horse Yard, not far from Mr Boussay."

"Yes, Madam Blackwell," he said. "Of course."

Robert grabbed the basket of flasks from the pump house and walked away quickly. A few carts passed him. He could have called up to one of the drivers and asked for a ride for some of the way, but he wanted to be alone with his thoughts.

It was strange. He was always trying so hard to be invisible, but now he had to make sure that one of the people he'd never wanted to see again found him.

First, he had to find out where that person lived.

The church bells had rung the hour twice by the time he reached the Red Guard Gang's den. As he turned into the yard, two shadows darted towards the wall and remained still. If Robert didn't know better, he'd have assumed they were part of the wall itself.

"Turpin?" he whispered. "Duval?"

The shadows didn't move.

"I've come to help you find Garnet," he said.

The shadows twitched and pulled away from their hiding place. Even in the gloomy yard, Robert saw how tired the brothers were. Their eyes were sunken, their arms criss-crossed with scratches, as if they'd been squeezing themselves into tiny spaces searching for their friend.

"We've looked everywhere," Turpin said.

"Everywhere," Duval echoed.

"We even went to the Tower of London," Turpin said. "Because that's where they took her. But there's big gates and soldiers with guns."

"I have a plan to rescue her," Robert told them. "But I need your help."

The boys drew closer.

"Rescue her?" Turpin said. "We can help!"

"Can you tell me where to find Steeple?" Robert asked.

"Find Steeple?" Turpin's eyes widened in shock.

Steeple had once been a member of the Red Guard Gang. When he was a small child, his family had sold him to a master sweep who'd made him climb up chimneys to scrape away the thick soot. He'd run away and found the gang, but he'd broken their rules and betrayed Robert, not once but twice. He'd been expelled from the gang and was working as a nightman, helping his cousin clean London's privies. It was a dangerous job, climbing into the toilet cesspits and scraping out the stinking waste. Robert didn't feel sorry for him.

Robert also knew that Steeple wanted revenge. He blamed Robert for his misfortune.

"But he betrayed you to the capture-creature," Turpin said.

"You mustn't let Steeple know where you are!" Duval agreed, just as alarmed. "He'll send people to hurt you!"

Robert couldn't tell the boys that he was relying on Steeple's revenge – they'd tell Emma. She was already upset about Garnet. He didn't want to worry her even more.

"If I know where Steeple is," Robert said, "I know where to avoid. If he catches me, I'll never be able to rescue her."

Duval and Turpin looked at each other, their expressions less certain.

"Does he live with his cousin?" Robert pressed.

Duval shook his head. "He's got a room in the tavern where the nightmen go."

"Most of the tavern keepers don't like the nightmen

drinking there because of the stink," Turpin said. "But the Barrel and Hook on Rotten Row don't mind them. Mr Robinson, the landlord, used to be a nightman himself."

"Thank you." The Barrel and Hook? Robert let the map of London unscroll in his mind. Rotten Row was off Goswell Road, north-east from here and a long walk from Covent Garden. Were there alleys he could creep down without being seen by too many people? And when he arrived, what should he do? Wait by the door of the tavern until Steeple came out? That could be any time, because Steeple worked at night and must sleep during the day. Robert would definitely attract too much attention if he just stood there.

"Every morning, Steeple goes to the chop-house on Lemon Street," Duval added. "He has sardines and bread and coffee, then he goes to sleep."

Robert couldn't help smiling. "You know a lot about him."

"Spindrift said that we must keep our enemies close," Duval said. He touched Robert's arm. "Will you really find Garnet?"

Turpin blinked back tears. "Will she still be Garnet, or will they turn her into…"

"I'll find her," Robert said. "And she will still be the

Garnet we know." *I hope!* He gave them a confident smile. "And, you two, please be careful."

The boys dipped their heads and flitted away.

It took Robert nearly an hour to walk to the chop-house, keeping his head down and looking at no one. For every step he took forward, he wanted to take two more backwards. He made himself remember that Garnet was imprisoned in the Tower and the Goldsmith wanted to turn her into a rat. Those thoughts forced himself onward.

The chop-house was a shabby building that must have been falling down for over a hundred years. Its windows were grimy with dust and soot clung to the inside of the windows as if every meal cooked there had been burned. Was Steeple already inside? It was impossible to see into the room beyond.

The church bells rang half past eight. If nothing happened, Robert would have to leave for Mr Boussay's and try again tomorrow. But tomorrow might be too late for Garnet…

Robert had come this far. He couldn't – mustn't – walk away without checking if Steeple *was* eating his breakfast. He clutched the basket tight, making the bottles clang together. Madam Blackwell had given him an excuse to enter the chop-house without knowing it.

What was the tailor's name, again? Mr Hissop, that was it. Robert took a deep breath, crossed the road and entered the rundown, dirty building.

Yes, he thought as soon as he stepped through the door. *Every meal cooked here must certainly have been burned.* The room was low-ceilinged and the air so thick with beer fumes and smoke from the men's pipes and the hearth fire that it could almost be cut into a pie. Everything looked singed, as if the Great Fire had licked at it before guttering out.

Every head in the room turned to look at Robert. Even the serving boy paused as he thrust an empty tankard beneath the ale barrel. Robert felt himself blush. He rattled the basket, peering through the gloom at the dirt-smeared faces. Turpin and Duval were right about the stink. Robert and Marisee had pretended to be nightmen to find a way into Mr Dross's house when they were investigating the Chaos Monster. He knew that stink first-hand – he hadn't thought that it could get any worse. But this was a whole room full of nightmen. His eyes watered and his nostrils twitched as if they were trying to seal themselves up. He had to keep his expression friendly, though. His eyes darted around the room. *Steeple! Are you here?*

"I'm … I'm … looking for Mr Hissop." Robert rattled

his basket again. "I have a delivery of Madam Blackwell's healing eye water."

"Healing water?" The chop-house owner grinned, then banged the ale barrel. "This is the only healing water we care about!"

The customers roared with laughter. Robert made his mouth chuckle too, although all he wanted was to race back out. Every single person was still looking at him. Even the ragged cat uncurled itself on the counter to fix its eyes on him.

"He's a tailor," Robert said. "Perhaps you know where I can find him?"

"Tailor?" the man sitting at the table by the door grumbled. "You think tailors are going to be chewing their bread with the likes of us?"

The other men shouted agreement. A few swore. The chop-house owner's grin widened. He only had one tooth at the front of his mouth, like a snake fang.

"But some of my good friends here do have eye-itch, true?" he said to his customers.

There were grunts of agreement.

The nightman closest to Robert stood up quickly. His chair hit the floor with a bang. "It's on account of our calling," he said. "We don't get no fresh air at the bottom of the privies."

Another man stood up. He was tall, wide-shouldered and angry. "So why don't you leave those bottles for us, lad? As a thank you?"

"Thank you for what?" Even as Robert said those words he knew he should have stayed quiet.

Chairs clattered as more men stood. Another wave of privy smells hit Robert. He held his breath.

"As a thank you for letting you leave here – alive!" the chop-house owner said.

The wide-shouldered man moved so that he was standing between Robert and the door. A short man in a torn coat and sagging tricorn reached out to grab Robert. As Robert jolted away, the basket slipped from his arm and crashed to the floor. Water seeped from cracked flasks. A couple of men snatched the ones that were still intact, but most of them weren't interested in that. They were advancing towards Robert, their faces snarling with laughter.

"There's a reward for a boy that looks like you," the chop-house owner said. "Look!" He pointed to a stained notice nailed to a post behind him. "Lord Pritchard. He lost a boy." He squinted at Robert more closely. "Same height. Same weight. You're his boy, aren't you?"

"I'm not anyone's boy!"

What are you doing, Robert? Keep quiet! Just get out!

"If we hand you in," the man in the torn coat said, "we'll have enough coin to be eating dinners here for the next month!"

A yell went up and hands tugged at Robert. They were like rats fighting for a piece of bread. His arms flailed as he tried to push them away, his palms smacking into their jaws and elbows. It made no difference. His jacket was ripped apart. A blow landed on his ankle. He crumpled.

Why didn't you stay outside? Why didn't you come back tomorrow? Why did you even think that this plan could ever work?

Robert was hauled to his feet. Rough hands brushed him down.

"Can't send you back to the lord looking shabby," the man in the torn coat said. "We don't want no pennies deducted."

"I am not Lord Pritchard's boy!" Robert's voice was weak – he didn't want to breathe in the rotting air. "The Lord Mayor gave me a letter. It proves that I'm free."

"Pardon my mistake," the chop-house owner said with a smirk. "We didn't mean you no harm. Show us the letter and we'll let you go."

Robert dug his hands into his pockets, even though he knew they'd be empty. Mama Tems had made his letter disappear.

"It… I don't have it with me," Robert stuttered. "But if you go to the Lord Mayor…"

"*Go to the Lord Mayor.*" The chop-house owner tried to imitate Robert's voice. He sounded nothing like Robert, but the other men found it very funny. "He won't let us anywhere near his grand mansion unless it's to clean out his privy!"

There were more cheers.

"Tie the boy up!" the chop-house owner ordered.

Robert's hands were yanked behind his back and bound together, the rope digging into his skin. He kicked out hard, felt his boot land. A man cursed and a rope was looped around Robert's ankles, then pulled tight. He almost toppled over, but his captors stopped him.

"Don't damage the goods!" the wide-shouldered man warned.

Robert was lifted like a sack of coal and flung over the man's broad shoulder. The air was crushed from Robert's lungs and he gasped for breath. That was worse. The coat reeked, as if the wearer used his own coat to clean his nightman's tools. Sweat prickled along Robert's forehead. He blinked it from his eyes, but he still couldn't see. The world was wavering around him. If he fainted, he couldn't fight back. He had to stay awake! He wriggled, trying to drive his knees into his carrier's chest.

The chop-house owner came out from behind the counter. He was brandishing a thick wooden staff.

"We don't want to damage him," he said. "But maybe there's somewhere we can smack him that doesn't show."

"And we can say he was trying to escape," another man said. "His owner's going to be grateful whatever way."

I don't have an owner. Robert wanted to say it out loud, but even if his mouth'd had the strength to form the words, his body didn't have enough air.

The chop-house door opened. The breeze did little to lessen the stink.

"You got your cart, Ebenezer?" the man carrying Robert asked.

"It's in the yard!" Ebenezer said. "Drop him next to the barrels! Or even in 'em!"

Those barrels were filled with privy waste. Robert squirmed harder.

A crash came from back further inside the chop-house.

"Oi!" the chop-house owner yelled. "What d'you think you're doing?"

The man carrying Robert muttered a curse word and turned. Now all Robert could see was the street beyond the door. He wished he had confided his plan to someone. Turnmill and the Fleet Ditch Boar would have saved him.

This stinking place definitely needed a strong surge of river water to clean it out. But no one knew where he was or what he was doing.

Robert felt his carrier's shoulders stiffening, as if he was readying for a fight.

"You just broke my chair!" the chop-house owner bellowed at someone.

The other person chuckled. "Are you going to fight the Goldsmith and all the Lord Mayor's yeomen?"

Robert's left ear was jammed against the smelly coat, but he definitely recognized that voice.

It was Steeple.

"I'm saving your life, Mr Bertram," Steeple added. "The boy was telling the truth. He got a pardon straight from the Lord Mayor – and we all know who's whispering in the Lord Mayor's ear, don't we?"

Robert heard the man carrying him mutter, "That Goldsmith."

"How d'you know all this, Steeple?" the chop-house owner asked. "I reckon you just want to claim Pritchard's reward yourself."

"Because I know this boy," Steeple said. "That right, Robert?"

Robert tried to nod, but there was no room for his neck to move. His "yes" came out as a grunt.

"He was living with some street children in St Giles when I first met him," Steeple said.

And you were one of them too, Steeple! Robert screamed in his mind.

"I befriended him," Steeple said. "Helped him hide from his enemies, even though I knew there was a reward for him."

LIAR! But Robert had to keep his mouth shut, had to ignore that Steeple was taunting him. There was only one reason why Steeple would save Robert from the nightmen – to betray him again and get paid for it. And that's what Robert had wanted. But now he was slung over a nightman's shoulder, he wished he was anywhere else.

"I don't care about none of that," the chop-house owner said. "We still haven't seen no pardon."

Steeple looked Robert right in the eye. "This boy and his lying friend took all the credit for getting rid of that river beast last year," he said. "The Lord Mayor was so grateful he made the Goldsmith pay Pritchard for the boy's freedom. Isn't that so, Robert?"

Robert gritted his teeth and gave him a nod, though he had no idea if that second part was true or not.

"You'd better not be lying," said the man carrying Robert.

Steeple clutched his chest. "Swear it on my heart!"

Robert was swung from the man's shoulder and dropped on to the filthy floor. He winced at a kick to his thigh that couldn't have been an accident. He lay there, furious faces peering down at him, muttering.

"Out of my way!"

Steeple pushed through the men and stood over Robert, grinning. He crouched down and unknotted the ropes that bound Robert's wrists and ankles. Robert scrambled to his feet. The room was still wavering and his chest felt as if it was full of Dragon fire. Steeple slung an arm around Robert's shoulders. Robert staggered. He felt like his body was made from smoke.

"Happy to see you again, my friend," Steeple said cheerfully. The grin was big, but Steeple's eyes were hard. "And I'm sure you're pleased to see me, aren't you?"

Robert nodded and attempted a smile. He *was* pleased, though Steeple would have no idea why. Steeple nudged Robert through the door and out into the street. Robert was sorry that Madam Blackwell's flasks had been broken and her basket trampled into the puddle. It felt as bad as lying to her.

As soon as they turned the corner of the building, Robert braced himself. Steeple grabbed Robert's wrist, squeezing the skin grazed by the ropes. His smile stayed fixed, his eyes stayed hard. He was thinner than before, his face gaunt.

"They could have hurt you badly," Steeple said. "But I saved you."

"Thank you."

There was a silence. Steeple was watching him, waiting.

"Who sent you?" Steeple said at last.

"No one! I was looking for Mr Hissop—"

Steeple shoved Robert against the wall. Robert gasped with pain. His breath flurried, before gathering again. Steeple pushed his face close to Robert's. Grime drew a map across Steeple's forehead.

"You could walk into any tavern, any chop-house in London, at any time of night or day!" he spat. "But you find yourself here at the same time I'm here! I haven't stayed alive this long by being stupid."

No, not stupid, but not brave or loyal to anyone but yourself. Robert's last memory of Steeple was him fleeing, terrified, as the Chaos Monster rampaged through the centre of London. Steeple had left Robert and his friends to die. Steeple was a coward, but he was also a clever coward. Robert had to think quickly.

"Who sent you?" Steeple yelled.

"The gang!" Robert gasped. "Spindrift! He's heard that you might be here. He wanted to be certain."

Another shove. Robert's spine banged against a jagged brick. "Why?"

"Because ... because ..." What had Duval said? "Because he says you should keep your enemies close. He's worried that you'll ... that you might do something that puts them in danger."

Like you did with me! You betrayed me to the capture-creature!

Steeple smiled. "Ah, so he realizes that I'm not a man to be treated badly." He frowned. "I was loyal to the gang. Still, they chose you over me." He stepped away from Robert. "But that's forgotten now, isn't it? I'm fine and you seem fine. You're living with that well woman, aren't you?"

Robert wanted to rub his sore chest, but he wasn't going to show Steeple he was in pain. Should he admit where he lived? Though it *was* common knowledge. Only yesterday, he'd been helping customers.

"Yes," he replied. "I live with Madam Blackwell."

Steeple looked thoughtful. "But you can't stay there *all* the time." He forced out a laugh. "You're not in prison, are you!"

Robert forced out his own laugh. "No. I assist an apothecary."

He watched Steeple's face closely. The false smile had returned, even wider.

"An apothecary…" Steeple repeated. He shoved the sleeve of his jacket up his arm and prodded a long scab. "This should be healed by now. I think I need a salve."

"Mr Boussay recommends a plaister of onion and calendula for healing," Robert said.

Steeple let his sleeve drop down. "Mr Boussay? Is that your apothecary?"

"Yes." Robert didn't want to say the next words, but this was why he was here. The capture-creature had to know where to find him. "His shop is on St John Street. If you visit, I'll mix a salve for you." He made himself meet Steeple's pebble eyes. "It will be payment for saving me this morning."

"Mr Boussay … on St John Street." Steeple dipped his head. "That's very kind, Robert. And helpful too. Thank you. You'll definitely receive a visit later."

Steeple turned and walked back to the chop-house.

Robert waited for a moment. Then he ran as fast as he could to the apothecary's shop.

MR PIPES

Marisee watched Robert leave from her bedroom window. She hoped he'd turn round and look up at her, but he was lost in his own thoughts. He'd have hated not being fully truthful with Grandma, especially as he'd also collected water from the pump house. She must have asked him to run an errand. Marisee wished that he'd told her his plan, but she understood why he couldn't. He didn't want her to lie to Grandma as well.

Marisee lay back on her bed. Hadn't she wanted another adventure with Robert? *With* Robert, though. Not an adventure where they both go off and do different things. Her plan for today meant doing something that she particularly didn't want to do, especially on her own. She wasn't frightened of the Dragon, but she was *very* frightened of where the Dragon's memories were going to take her.

And she was supposed to find a way to help Robert escape from the Tower. How? No one escaped from the Tower. They should have planned this better, but Robert had refused to delay. Marisee sighed to herself. She had to believe that Robert *would* rescue Garnet and the other stolen children, or she'd bury her head under her blanket and stay there all day.

"Marisee!" Grandma was calling her. "Can you get the marmalade from the top shelf? My ankles are too swollen to climb ladders today."

"Yes, Grandma!" she called back.

She swept the blanket away, but the air was so cold that she wrapped it back round herself and went down to the kitchen.

Marisee lingered in the cottage more than she needed to. Grandma had a busy morning, but didn't really need her help. Still, Marisee swept the kitchen floor twice, brought in some firewood, scrubbed a pan and hammered back a loose nail in the front room's shutter. Her mind was heaving. Was Robert already in the Tower? How would she know?

Perhaps Marisee should tell Turnmill after all. She needed advice from someone! But Turnmill would tell Grandma, and Grandma would probably march to the Tower to try and find Robert. What if Grandma went through those gates and never came out again? No. Marisee couldn't tell Grandma. She couldn't tell Turnmill. If Mama was here… Marisee wished she wasn't so alone. She had to find out everything she could about the cauldron and the giant's head *and* help Robert escape, all by herself. But at least she knew what she had to do first. She needed to head into the City of London, to the Dragon of Mary-le-Bow.

Cheapside was loud! Marisee let the city's music wash over her – the clatter of coach wheels on the cobbles, a young child shouting at its mother for attention, an oboe player whose reedy notes fought with the shrill calls of an orange seller. A hundred years ago, when the plague had spread fear and death through the city, many of the streets had been silent. And while London was weak, Lord Gullinn had kidnapped children to build an army of spies. Now it seemed to be happening again. Why?

Had the cauldron been rediscovered? Had it ever been lost? Did the Goldsmith know how to use it?

Turnmill hadn't heard of any more Variegates, adult or child. Marisee hoped that the Dragon's memories could give her answers. She dodged round the people crowding Cheapside and looked up at the golden Dragon on the weathervane of St Mary-le-Bow Church. Did no one else notice how it often spun in a different direction from the wind?

She pushed open the door to the bell tower. The stone cherubs were lifeless. Would they have spoken to Robert again if he was here? Marisee wished that he was here. She didn't want to have this adventure on her own. She made herself run up the steps to the bellringers' room.

"Dragon!" she called softly. "Can you hear me?"

She waited.

"I'm ready now," she said. "Please show me the rest of your memories."

Black and gold specks trickled through the boards in the ceiling above, each speck a tiny creature that joined others to make the Dragon. Her head emerged first, a blur becoming a high, broad forehead, deep-set eyes, a jaw that could open wide and crush Marisee if she so chose.

"You wish to return to my memories?" the Dragon said.

"Yes," Marisee replied. "Please. To Mr Pipes and Lord Gullinn."

"Very well."

Marisee stiffened as the specks swarmed her. She wanted to thrash at them, but she made herself keep her arms by her sides, even as the swarm brushed against her ears then curled inside them. Her lips pressed tight together as they settled on her face like her mask. Her fingers, her wrists – they were mottled black and gold. Soon, she closed her eyes, her lids too heavy to open.

Heat blazed all around. She took a breath, and then a deeper one. The air was scorched, but she reminded herself that it wasn't real. It couldn't hurt her. But it could hurt all the other people running, shrieking, from their homes, carrying sacks and children and loose clothes in their arms.

A shadow skimmed through the blazing thatch of the roofs. It was so quick that Marisee wasn't sure that she'd seen it. She squinted into the smoke – yes, there was a shape she recognized. It was a Dragon. A ball of fire looped out of the smoke and hit another roof. Instantly, the flames shot upwards and another house burned.

Marisee didn't understand. "Did Dragons start the fire?" she wanted to ask. "Is that what you wanted me to see?"

And then the fire was gone. She was back in Mr Pipes' room but this time the creatures that made the Mary-le

Bow Dragon were hiding in the shadows of the ceiling beams, so Marisee was looking down from above. The candles threw light upon an open ledger. Its pages were covered with spidery, ink-smudged writing and drawings.

She could make out some notes: *Rats have great flexibility of body. Squeeze through small spaces. Will make excellent spies.*

"He never guessed, did he?" It was Mr Pipes' voice, but Marisee couldn't see him yet. He was in the room, out of the Dragon's line of vision. The Dragon must have shifted, because now Marisee saw Mr Pipes by the pot that had contained the octopus. It didn't seem much larger than a soup tureen, but, peering down from above, Marisee could see no bottom – only darkness, like an endless tunnel.

The dome of a head rose up through the darkness, but remained just below the pot's rim. Was that the same octopus as before? How could it fit in there?

"He thinks you hold a small octopus," Mr Pipes said, tracing a finger down the pot's side. "Nothing more. If only he knew how long it took me to put you together again. If only he knew what you can do."

Mr Pipes was talking to the pot… The pot! But it wasn't just a pot. It was a cauldron! Why hadn't she noticed before? Could it be…?

Mr Pipes continued talking.

"But therein lies my dilemma," he said. "The Great Fire has left London in ashes, but Lord Gullinn is more insistent than ever. He says he wants *ratlings*..." Mr Pipes uttered the word with disgust. "Such a terrible name for those unfortunate children. He wants rat-children to search the cellars for hidden treasures. And to work as his spies. He will discover more secrets, perhaps even the Lord Mayor's own. He will demand the right to rebuild London. He will control the warehouses and shops and homes and charge a terrible rent for them."

A candle flickered. Mr Pipes glanced towards the door, then back to the vessel.

"Even that won't be enough for greedy Lord Gullinn," he said. "He'll build between and below his properties, cellars and tiny secret alleyways, all designed for his rat spies to scuttle through the city, gathering secrets for him. Should I help him with this terrible act? If I deliver him nothing, he will harm those two unfortunate children. What to do?"

Mr Pipes flicked the vessel. It chimed like the tenor bell in the Mary-le-Bow belfry. The sound was too deep for such a shallow-looking pot, thought Marisee. It was definitely a magical sound.

He walked over to the ledger spread open on the long

table. He turned the pages and paused on a page covered in diagrams of jagged shards. The writing was smudged, but, even so, it didn't look like letters. Were they symbols? Marisee peered at it. There were letters in tiny script below the symbols, as if he'd been untangling a code.

"How I always longed to discover a cauldron of coalescence," Mr Pipes said sadly. "And now I have one, built from shattered pieces. Who knew that those old necro-alchemists' musings would prove so accurate? I wish they'd had the foresight to warn about the evil too. Lord Gullinn must never know your power. I must destroy you."

Mr Pipes straightened up, listening.

"He will arrive soon," he muttered. "*Do* I have time to destroy you?"

Marisee felt a stab of excitement. Mr Pipes *had* found a magic cauldron! And he'd discovered how it worked. Had he created the rat-children then changed his mind? He had said nothing about a giant's head, though. Was that part of the story just a legend?

Marisee squinted at the pages harder. One shard had been coloured in with dark ink or paint. It looked like a gap in a mouth full of teeth.

"What should I do? What should I do?" Mr Pipes muttered.

The water in the cauldron churned. Two tentacles flopped over the side, one so long it nearly reached the floor. Each sucker was the size of a guinea, squelching against the side of the cauldron. A pool of water gathered on the desk.

The octopus had definitely not been that big last time.

"Pipes!" a voice shouted from outside. "Do not think to hide from me!"

"*You* must hide from *him*!" Mr Pipes told the octopus. "I dread to think what terrible orders he will give me if he discovers that a caterpillar fell into the cauldron and melded with another beast."

Caterpillar? This was an octopus-caterpillar Variegate? Marisee had always thought of Variegates as being part human, but this cauldron could create any creature. She studied the octopus more closely. Its tentacles were covered in tiny spines, just like a caterpillar's.

The tentacles withdrew into the cauldron, back into the magical darkness. Mr Pipes slammed the ledger shut.

Lord Gullinn stormed in. He strode up to Mr Pipes, shoving him hard. Mr Pipes stumbled, his flailing arms knocking his ink across the table.

"Where are my ratlings?" Lord Gullinn bellowed.

"You … you only visited me yesterday, Lord Gullinn," Mr Pipes stuttered. "I have made no progress since then. I have been helping the apothecaries mix salves for the poor folks wounded in the fire."

"Salves!" Lord Gullinn's hand clenched the hilt of his sword. "I have provided you with children aplenty. The Tower of London is like a workhouse now, filled with the noisy brats. Forget the salves. Your work now is to create ratlings. I know that you've found the formula." Lord Gullinn's eyes narrowed. "Perhaps I should ask the necro-alchemists to examine your little ratling friends to find out exactly what they are – though both you and I know that necro-alchemists prefer their subjects to be dead… Whatever the ratlings suffer, it will be your fault, Pipes."

"But, Lord Gullinn!" Even in the dullness of the candles' light, Marisee saw the sly expression on Mr Pipes' face. "The goldsmiths instructed the necro-alchemists to make the Variegates last time," he said. "The master of your guild stood with necro-alchemists in the laboratory as they combined the hearts and brains of lions and bears with the bodies of the most ruthless and dangerous men. When the old king and queen discovered the experiments, they were disgusted. The necro-alchemists were driven from society. Do you believe that our King George will look favourably on your experiments now?"

Lord Gullinn scowled. "Are you threatening to betray me to the king, Pipes?" he barked.

The water in the cauldron bubbled. Marisee's heart beat hard.

"No, Lord Gullinn," Mr Pipes said calmly. "You are such a powerful man. A mere alchemist could never harm a great man like you."

"Remember that!" Lord Gullinn said. "You'd be nothing without me."

He swept his arm around. "All this is paid for by my gold. Everything belongs to me. Even this."

He walked over to the cauldron. Mr Pipes became very still. The tip of a tentacle appeared over the edge.

"An octopus is such an ugly beast," the lord sneered. "Though I've heard that it makes a good stew!" He turned back to Mr Pipes. "You *have* discovered the secret," he said. "You have created human beasts. Rat-children."

A second tentacle flopped over the rim of the cauldron.

"Tell me the secret!" Lord Gullinn yelled.

"I cannot, Lord Gullinn." Mr Pipes' voice wobbled. "You will do nothing good with it."

"Good?" Lord Gullinn smirked. "I have already done good. I've cleansed this city of plague."

"But ... there is no known cure," Mr Pipes said. "Every apothecary, every alchemist, every mountebank has been searching for one."

"I know," Lord Gullinn said. "Which is why I burned it away."

"Burned?" Mr Pipes whispered. "The fire? That was an accident! Farryner the baker…" He stared at the lord, his face creased in horror. "You … started it deliberately?"

Lord Gullinn smiled. "Do you think we protect the Dragons for their beauty?" he said. "They must work for their keep."

"You ordered the Dragons to burn the city?" Mr Pipes looked distraught. "The summer has been dry. The houses are made from wood and straw. So many homes destroyed! Hundreds more people could have lost their lives!"

Lord Gullinn shrugged. "That was the price to be paid. Now we – *I* – can start again."

He unsheathed his sword – an action so quick that Marisee barely saw it. The tip poked Mr Pipes' shoulder. He cried out and clutched the wound.

"I have no more patience," Lord Gullinn said. "Tell me how you made the ratlings!"

"I will not!" Mr Pipes' voice did not sound as strong as his words.

Lord Gullinn raised his sword. His eyes suddenly fixed on something behind Mr Pipes.

"What is that?" he asked.

"N-nothing, Lord," Mr Pipes stammered.

Lord Gullinn, sword raised, stepped closer to the ledger.

"Is that not the Guild of Goldsmiths' arms engraved here?" He tapped a faded symbol on the cover. "Pipes! What lies within this book?"

"Salves. Potions. Incantations..." Mr Pipes said weakly. "I found it in a forgotten pantry deep in the cellars."

"And you told me nothing of this?"

"It escaped my mind, My Lord!" Mr Pipes said plaintively. "My daughter and grandchildren live on Old Swan Lane. They only just fled their house in time, but everything they possessed was consumed by the fire."

Lord Gullinn ignored him. He swiped back the cover and turned page after page. He stopped on the diagram of the shards, studying them. "What is this, Pipes?"

Mr Pipes' gaze swung between the ledger and the cauldron. "It's nothing but the ridiculous scribblings of old men," he muttered. "I believe that it refers to a vessel to be used for combustion."

"You lie, Pipes!" Lord Gullinn waved his sword in anger, but then returned his attention to the ledger.

Another tentacle flopped over the side of the cauldron.

"Cauldron of coalescence." Lord Gullinn read the words with gathering excitement. "To coalesce… To combine, to meld, to blend…" His head jerked up. His eyes blazed with fury. "Where is it?" he demanded.

"Lord Gullinn … I don't understand…"

"Do not insult me!" The sword whistled through the air, but Mr Pipes leaped away in time. "These shards are a puzzle. They fit together to make a vessel that creates Variegates! That's how you made the ratlings. Where is it?"

Lord Gullinn whipped round to peer at the room.

"Surely you cannot hide a vessel so enormous that it contains both man and beast!" His gaze settled on the octopus's tentacles. "Oh," he said. "I am a fool not to have noticed this before, such a large beast in such a small vessel." He bent towards the cauldron. "And this is like no sea beast I have seen before. I see hair. No – spines, like…" The candles lit up the confusion in his eyes. "This is a beast of your own making, isn't it, Pipes?"

"No, my lord." Mr Pipes' eyes stayed on the sword. "It was a mistake. I rescued the small octopus and then … a caterpillar must have crawled into the cauldron and…"

Lord Gullinn held up a hand to silence him. "I wish

you had been honest with me from the beginning, Pipes. I would have rewarded you handsomely for your assistance. But I know now that I can never trust you."

Lord Gullinn's sword swung forward. It didn't land. A tentacle whipped out and coiled round Lord Gullinn's upper arm. The sword clanged to the floor and Mr Pipes kicked it away from the lord's reach.

"Release me!" Lord Gullinn pummelled the tentacle. A second tentacle wrapped round the lord's other arm. "Pipes!" he yelled. "Order your beast to let me go!"

Mr Pipes shook his head. "It is your beast, Lord Gullinn. Remember, everything in this room belongs to you," he said. "But I will not let you take the cauldron. It has already caused too much harm."

Mr Pipes stood back and watched as the octopus lifted Lord Gullinn in the air. The lord squirmed and kicked, but the octopus grasped him tighter. The billowing silk of Lord Gullinn's sleeves bunched around his flailing arms.

"You will pay with your life for this treachery, Pipes!" he gasped.

Mr Pipes took a timid step closer to him.

"My life? Your life?" Mr Pipes asked. "Or the lives of all those children you wish to make half-beast? Better that it's you or me that pays the price."

He shoved Lord Gullinn in the chest. The lord shrieked as the octopus drew him up and into the cauldron. Lord Gullinn was a terrible man, but Marisee couldn't let him die! She tried to jump forward, but the Dragon's memory restrained her.

Suddenly, Lord Gullinn seemed to be looking straight at her.

"Dragon!" he croaked. "I see you hiding in the crevices! I order you to save me!"

Marisee felt as though she was being taken apart, surging through stone and time and air, then she was back lying on the floor of the bellringers' room. The black and gold specks streamed from around her, clustering and strengthening into the shape of the Dragon's head. Her chest hurt and her mouth was dry. Her heart hammered.

"A Dragon started the Great Fire of London." It was strange saying those words when Marisee had always believed that it was the fault of Mr Farryner the baker. "And Mr Pipes killed Lord Gullinn."

"You have seen my memories," the Dragon said. "Now you must save the children."

The head split apart once more, and a ribbon of black and gold specks slipped through the gaps in the ceiling, up towards the weathervane.

EMMA

Marisee stumbled down the stairs and out of Mary-le-Bow Church. She imagined the cherubs over the door staring at her back as she ran through the churchyard. She collapsed on a patch of dry grass next to a gravestone. Her brain was so full that the ideas might pour out of her ears. She needed to piece it all together.

She knew now that the Great Fire had not started in the bakehouse. Lord Gullinn had ordered his Dragons to burn down London so he could create a new city that was under his control. He wanted rat-children to spy on his enemies and find out their secrets. Mr Pipes had completed the magic cauldron. Somehow he had created rat-children but vowed never to create another child Variegate.

What had happened next? Had Mr Pipes been imprisoned? Executed? What happened to the cauldron and the ledger? And she had learned nothing about the giant's head. Marisee wanted to scream with frustration. Now she knew for certain that there was a magic cauldron, but she had no idea what she should do next. She had to stay calm. Was there anything else she'd seen or heard that could help her? She screwed her face up tight, hoping it would force her thoughts to straighten themselves. She wished she could tell Grandma everything. She couldn't hold all this by herself. She felt so lonely, and no matter how much she tried to make sense of everything, she ended up with that big question: *What should I do now?*

Marisee heaved herself up. She was so weary, but she couldn't let herself be tired. Every minute she delayed, more children might be stolen. Robert was probably already in danger. She supposed that there *was* one person she could confide in, one person who would do everything they could to help her, because they cared about Robert as much as she did and certainly wanted to rescue the children in the Tower. Marisee didn't want their help. But, for Robert's sake, she had to ask.

Marisee hoped that the Red Guard Gang were still in Cattle Court. Since Steeple betrayed them, they moved around all the time, but perhaps they would stay put for a while in case Garnet somehow escaped and came looking for them. Milk Street was only a few minutes' walk away from Cheapside. Marisee had no excuse not to try.

She made her wobbly feet walk out of the churchyard on to the street. Just before she crossed the road, she let her gaze linger on the brick roofs of the shops and houses, the stone steeples of the city's many churches with their array of weathervanes, the fiery golden orb of the Monument to the Great Fire of London. Through the Dragon's memories, she'd seen a time when none of this was here. It was strange and frightening.

Marisee dashed across the road in front of a speeding hackney carriage, ignoring the rude shout from the driver, and ran on to Milk Street. It was busy with a market in full swing. Rows and rows of sellers called out their wares – chicken necks, lamb shanks, ox hearts, fresh pollock… Street children begged for scraps from the butchers and coins from the scullery maids carrying out chores for the cooks and housekeepers. It seemed that some things didn't change.

At first, Marisee couldn't see the narrow passageway leading to Cattle Court, but then realized it was hidden behind a stack of barrels of salted pork. She squeezed past the barrels, ignoring the suspicious glances from the butcher. The sounds of the market fell away as she entered the dark alley. There should be an old fence – yes, there it was. Marisee pulled aside the loose panel and tried to replace it exactly as it had been. She looked across the yard, past the tethering post to the ruined house. It seemed even more deserted than before. The door was hanging off the hinges and the glass was missing from all the windows. A broken shutter was propped against the wall. Marisee was surprised that it hadn't been taken for firewood.

She walked towards the house, studying the upper windows. They were dark, as if shuttered from the inside. A thought wormed its way through her mind. What if the Red Guard Gang had gone but the house wasn't empty? What if kidnappers were waiting for her? She studied the windows even more intently. She couldn't see anything in them. Robert always thought of her as the brave one. She *had* to be brave now.

She reached the door and peered into the shadowy hallway.

"Hello!" she called. "It's Marisee!"

Her voice seemed to sink into the rotting wood and decaying walls.

"Hello!" she shouted again, stepping into the hallway. "It's Marisee. Is anyone here?"

The trapdoor in the ceiling flipped open and legs dangled over the edge.

"Can you be any louder?" Emma asked. "You're even noisier than the market."

"You didn't answer the first time," Marisee snapped back.

Emma scowled down at her from the trapdoor. "Is Robert with you?"

"No," Marisee said. "He's a prisoner in the Tower."

She could have softened the blow – but why should she? Marisee was still cross that Emma thought Grandma was a sorceress making ratlings. Emma's legs disappeared and the rope ladder was thrown out. Marisee stepped towards it, ready to clamber up the twisting contraption, but Emma slid down without touching the rungs. She was far more graceful than Marisee could ever be.

"Tell me what happened!" She clutched Marisee's arm. "Did the capture-creature find him? Robert was sure he'd be safe with you and your grandmother!"

Marisee wriggled her arm free. "Safe with the grandmother you think is the sorceress!" she retorted.

The two girls glared at each other.

"Stop shouting at Emma!" came a voice from above.

Duval's face appeared in the trap doorway. "She shouldn't shout at Emma, should she, Turpin?"

"No, Duval." Turpin peered down. "She shouldn't."

"Sorry," Marisee said. "It's just that—"

"Robert's a prisoner in the Tower," Emma finished.

The boys gasped. They too barely touched the ladder as they dropped to the floor.

"We saw Robert this morning," Duval said. "He was asking about Steeple."

Emma's scowl deepened. "Why was he looking for Steeple, Marisee?"

Marisee looked away. "I don't know," she said. "He wouldn't tell me his plan, except that he wanted to find a way into the Tower of London to rescue Garnet and the other children."

"Turpin. Duval." Emma's quiet voice was even more frightening than her shouting. "Tell me everything that happened this morning. And" – her voice dropped even lower – "I mean everything."

The boys explained how Robert had found them here earlier while Spindrift and Emma had been out trying to find any news of Garnet. They admitted that they'd told Robert where to find Steeple.

"He said he needed to know where Steeple was, so he could avoid him."

Duval was close to tears. Marisee wanted to comfort him, but Turpin wrapped his arms around his brother.

"Go back upstairs," Emma said softly. "Spindrift has hidden a packet of sugar plums in the dress trunk. Go and find it."

The boys nodded and were up the ladder and through the trapdoor before Marisee had blinked twice.

Emma blew out her cheeks. She glanced up towards the trapdoor as if imagining the boys with their ears pressed against the wood, listening. She nodded towards the yard. Marisee followed her outside. They sat down, their backs leaning against the tethering post.

"Surely there must be more to the plan than finding a way into the Tower?" Emma said. "What did your grandmother say?"

"We didn't tell her," Marisee said. "She would have stopped us."

She braced herself, ready for Emma to say something unpleasant about Grandma. There was silence, so Marisee carried on. "We know the Goldsmith is—" She looked up at the sky and the clusters of chimneys. Were raven spies listening? "We're sure we know who's ordering the kidnapping, but we don't know why. The Dragon on the Mary-le-Bow steeple showed me her memories. I thought it would help, but I still don't know what to do."

"Dragons." Emma sighed. "Even after shard beasts and Chaos Monsters and the enchanted sleep, it's hard to believe that there really are Dragons in London. What did she show you?"

"A man called Lord Gullinn ordered Dragons to start the Great Fire of London," Marisee said.

Emma shifted so she was sitting beside her. "Showed you? How?"

Marisee winced, remembering the scorch of the flames against her face. "Dragons have memories and they can … *wrap you* in them so it's like you were there."

She tried to describe everything – though she couldn't put the feelings into words: the suffocating heat, the overwhelming helplessness, the tentacles, the splash, the scream, the cauldron.

"There's a magic cauldron!" Emma said. She jumped up. "Does that mean that the Goldsmith's already changed children into … into… I can't bear to think about Garnet becoming like those red-eyed ratlings! We have to do something!"

Emma had said "we". Marisee and Emma did not trust each other in the same way that Marisee and Robert trusted each other, but at least with Emma, Marisee was no longer on her own.

"Is there anything else that you remember?" Emma

asked. There was urgency in her voice. "Anything at all?"

Marisee rubbed the sides of her face. Everything was blurring together inside her head. Was there anything else? Was there…?

"No," she said at last. "Nothing."

Emma sunk down again. "If the Goldsmith was using the cauldron, there'd probably be new Variegates, wouldn't there?"

Marisee nodded. That's what she had thought.

"How can we find out if there are?" Emma continued.

"Turnmill said that Variegates would find each other," Marisee explained. "We have to ask another Variegate."

Emma made a face. "You mean the capture-creature?"

Marisee stood up. She brushed down her dress and knocked out a small pebble that had stuck in the sole of her shoe. She offered her hand to Emma, who paused for a moment, then took it and jumped back up again.

"We need to speak to Henry," Marisee said.

THE CAPTURE

Robert wanted to go home. He wanted to be sitting by Madam Blackwell's pump house feeling safe. But if his plan was to work, he had to be where he'd told Steeple he'd be – at Mr Boussay's apothecary shop.

Even though he was running there, he would be so late starting work! Robert hoped that Mr Boussay hadn't sent a message to Madam Blackwell to enquire about his whereabouts.

He slowed down as he turned into St John Street. He sniffed the air and studied the shadow underneath the shop's street sign. No, Haakon wasn't here – yet. Would

Steeple send the capture-creature after him again, or come himself?

Robert hurried across the street to the shop. He pushed the door – it was locked. It was never locked at this time of the morning! Lord Frant's footman was always here first thing for alkermes for his master's stomach. And the barber from Fleet Street always came to collect a salve to heal skin wounds. What if Haakon had already been here and Mr Boussay was wounded or … dead? Robert had never wanted kind Mr Boussay to be hurt.

He banged on the door. "Mr Boussay! Are you there? Mr Boussay! Please, let me in!"

A key turned inside. A bolt was drawn back and the door opened. Mr Boussay peered around, looking confused.

"Robert! Why all the noise? You know I lock the street door when I'm busy in the back room. You should have come through the yard."

Of course! Robert had forgotten! Saturday was a delivery day. Mr Boussay would be organizing boxes of snakeskin and Armenian clay and buckets of stinking liquids that made Robert hold his nose when he had to measure them into bottles and jars. The apothecary was usually so engrossed in his new purchases that he had no idea what else was happening around him. He certainly wouldn't have noticed that Robert was late – or if a capture-creature was prowling around outside.

"Have you … have you had any unusual visitors today?" Robert asked.

Mr Boussay frowned. "The young lad who delivered the powdered mummy. His left ear was much bigger than his right ear … but you know that I make it my business not to look too closely at the purveyors."

That was true. Mr Boussay chose not to ask where many of his strangest ingredients came from. The apothecary opened the door to let Robert in and stomped back to his boxes and buckets. Robert wanted to slam the door shut and bolt it. But he didn't. Haakon would find a way in, no matter what, so it would be better that the capture-creature entered without damaging the shop.

Robert flipped the sign in the window to "Open". He needed to distract himself. He'd clean down the counter. Mr Boussay wasn't good at wiping away the drips and powders that spilled there. Robert was careful not to touch anything, though. Mr Boussay was sometimes asked to mix hemlock and mercury and other poisons.

The bell jangled as a customer entered the shop. Robert's heart thumped as he looked up. It was Lord Frant's footman, Godfrey.

"Have you got the old man's powders?" he called.

"I'll make them fresh," Robert said, reaching for the jars of wormwood and dried red beetles.

"His chest sounds like the bellows too," Godfrey said. "He wants something to ease his breathing."

"Of course."

Robert would need capsicum and ginger. He'd have to tie a cloth over his nose or he'd be sneezing for days.

Godfrey liked to talk. Lord Frant demanded total silence from his servants and would often go down to the kitchen in the evenings to berate them for being too noisy. Godfrey settled down on a stool and began to regale Robert with tales about the lords and ladies that visited Lord Frant's townhouse. Robert was happy to let the words wash over him. He always felt that Godfrey treated him like an equal.

Robert prepared the powders for Lord Frant's stomach and handed them to Godfrey. He scanned the shelves. The jar of capsicum must be in the back room with Mr Boussay.

"One moment," he said to Godfrey.

Godfrey nodded and carried on talking as if Robert was still in front of him. Mr Boussay had disappeared, though the door to the stairs leading to Mr Boussay's room above the shop was open. The apothecary often crept away for a late-morning nap. Robert stood on a chair to reach the jar of capsicum powder. The ginger was there too. He might as well make up the paste in here.

He weighed out the ingredients carefully, holding his breath, and mixed them together. Why did it look as if there was so little of it? He didn't want Lord Frant to complain that he'd been cheated. The capsicum powder *was* quite powerful. Any more and Lord Frant might sneeze his nose right off. Robert scraped the plaister on to a square of paper and carefully tied it with string.

"Will you pay now?" he asked Godfrey, as he walked back into the shop.

Something was wrong. It wasn't just the silence; it was the thick, rancid weight of the air. Robert had to force himself to close the door to the back room and carry on into the shop.

Haakon was waiting. He stood with his back against the shop door. The sign had been flipped to "Closed". Now Robert knew what Haakon truly was, how could he have ever thought Haakon was only human? He was dressed in human clothes – white leather breeches, white stockings and boots trimmed with fur. But the shoulders beneath the long, tattered coat rippled with bear-like power. His hair was grey, almost white – like a pelt – beneath a knitted cap. He was the capture-creature. A Variegated assassin created more than a hundred years ago from a man and a polar bear to relentlessly hunt criminals.

Robert wanted to run, as fast as he could. But he had to let himself be captured. That was his plan. But now it was about to happen, he wanted nothing less.

"Where ... where's Godfrey?" he stuttered. "You haven't hurt him, have you?"

A growl of laughter. "He excused himself and left as I entered."

There were no more words. Haakon pounced. One massive paw scooped Robert towards him; the other dropped a hood over Robert's head, plunging him into darkness. He was spun round.

"Arms behind your back!"

Robert obeyed. His wrists were lashed together with rope, digging into the wounds from the chop-house. For a moment, everything was still. The only sound was Robert's own breathing inside the hood. Haakon clutched Robert to him, pulling the flaps of his greatcoat over Robert and quickly buttoning them. As Haakon stood tall, Robert's feet were lifted from the floor.

Haakon ran, hunched over, with Robert squeezed between the hook of his arm and his chest, the greatcoat buttoned around Robert like a sling. Sometimes Haakon bent so low that his hands almost touched the ground – this was when he was at his fastest, the wild animal muscles flexing beneath his tunic.

At last, Haakon slowed, then stopped. Robert heard muffled voices – men's voices – and Haakon's arm dropped. Coat buttons were loosened and Robert fell. He landed on something soft, hands still tied. His hood was whipped away. He was in a high-sided handcart filled with bolts of cloth. Haakon stared down at him from alongside another man wearing a dark tunic and waistcoat.

"Clear off now," the man said. "Get your coin from the Goldsmith."

"The Goldsmith does not keep his promises," Haakon growled.

The man shrugged. "That ain't my problem. You're lucky that he lets you abominations keep living."

Haakon stalked away, the hood dangling in his fingers.

"I don't know why they still use that beast!" the man muttered. "He gives me the creepings every time." His voice changed. "Lie down!" he ordered. "If you shout out or try to escape, you're pig swill – do you understand?"

Robert lay down. The man piled fabric over him until there was only a space left for his face. The threads tickled his nose, but at least he could breathe. The man grunted as he lifted the handles of the cart. It tipped down a little, but Robert was jammed between the bolts of cloth. As it rattled and jiggled its way through the narrow streets, Robert was grateful for the padding.

London's noisy business carried on around him. Women called from the windows in the houses above them. A bucket was emptied from a garret on to the street. The cart driver shouted and the women laughed. Dogs yipped and Robert was sure he could hear cows lowing. Would he pass by Cheapside? He wondered if Marisee had returned to the Dragon of Mary-le-Bow. He'd hated being unable to escape from the Dragon's memories. That moment when the thatched roof burst into flames, when the heat had scorched his skin… He was sure that he had shrieked. Would *he* have been brave enough to return? He wasn't sure, but he knew for certain that Marisee *was* that brave.

Robert could hear the river now. The driver was greeting people, the handcart weaving as if hurrying through traffic. Yes, he was definitely on a river wharf. The porters were calling to the lightermen, the stink of rotting fish seeping through the cloth. If he was close to the Billingsgate fish market, the Tower wasn't far away.

No, not far away at all, because suddenly Robert felt cold fear and hot anger. It leaked through the Tower walls, pressing against his skin like a seeping, invisible poultice.

And there was a wildness that was not human – the terrified, trapped animals he'd seen in the Dragon's memories.

The handcart gathered speed again, then halted. The driver called out, a gate opened and then a portcullis squealed above him. As Robert glimpsed a brick archway, another portcullis clanged behind them. The fear, the fury, the terror – it was like a cloak dropped across the whole Tower.

The handcart stopped once more, voices muttered and the cart was tipped sideways. Robert's knee knocked painfully against the wood as he fell. Luckily, the cloth softened his landing.

"What are you doing!" the cart driver yelled. "That cloth's going to Mr Hector's! It's for the Lady Goldsmith's jackets! There mustn't be a single speck of dirt on it."

The driver cared more about the cloth than about Robert.

Robert was pulled out of the tangle of brocades and lifted to his feet. Two guards looked him up and down.

"You sure you got the right one?" the guard asked. "He's too well fed. Most of them orphans are so thin you can almost see through them!" He tugged Robert's shirt. "These ain't no rags neither."

"The creature caught him," the driver said. "So he's bound to be the right one."

"The creature!" One of the guards grasped Robert's right elbow. "Ah! Well, that's different. He must be a special one. The creature only gets sent out for the special ones." He shoved Robert in the back. "Move!"

Robert's legs were stiff after being bent in the same position for that juddering journey. The guard had no patience for his slow hobble and dragged him, staggering, along the cobbled paths. The second guard followed, holding a gun. Robert had assumed that he'd be led to a prison at the heart of the Tower of London, but he was taken to a squat tower just inside the walls. He was thrust at a different guard who caught him with a look of disgust.

The new guard took a burning candle from a small table inside the door and pushed Robert ahead of him, up the stone steps. Robert walked in a pool of darkness, the weak flame flickering across the walls. They stopped at a thick door.

Was this where they kept the children? Was Garnet behind that door? Or something truly terrible? He tried to stand up straight and thrust back his shoulders as Marisee would do when they were about to face danger.

The guard reached for a key hanging from his belt and, holding the candle close to the keyhole, jammed the key in and twisted. The door opened.

For a moment, the candle's light flickered across rows of cages lining the walls. *This must be the Menagerie where the animals are kept,* Robert thought. But there were no animal sounds.

The guard gave him a hard shove and he fell to his knees. The door slammed shut and he could see nothing at all.

Until the red eyes flashed in the dark.

Breath brushed his skin.

"Don't hurt me," he pleaded. "Please! I'm here to rescue you."

"Rescue us?" a voice whispered in his ear. "You are too late for that."

HENRY AND THE SQUALL

Marisee hadn't seen Henry or the Squall since they'd conquered the Chaos Monster. The Squall was a Fumi air spirit who'd angered the Council of Fumi Elders many years ago. He'd been exiled to a ruined windmill near the Greenwich peninsula. Henry was a combination of lion and man – one of the original Variegated assassins. He should have been a predator, enjoying the hunt – but he'd hated it. Like the Squall, he'd managed to escape and live secretly on the Isle of Dogs. When the Chaos Monster had risen, the Goldsmith had burned down their old windmill, but now Henry and the Squall lived in an even better windmill, at the end of a row of mills grinding grain for the bakers and spices for the apothecaries. The other millers chose to ignore the strange residents because, since their arrival, the millers' sails would turn every day, even when there was no wind.

The rowing-boat ferry dropped Marisee and Emma by the water steps on the Isle of Dogs. Marisee breathed in. *One of the mills must be grinding nutmeg*, she thought. Grandma loved to sprinkle nutmeg in their cocoa – perhaps Marisee could collect a small bag of spice for her. She sighed to herself. How could she be thinking such an ordinary thing when her best friend was in danger and children were being turned into rat-like creatures just around the bend of the river?

"This way," Marisee said to Emma.

The windmill was as dented as the hat that was usually perched on Henry's head. The paint was peeling off, but the sails were well tended, with no tears in the canvas. They circled steadily in the breezeless morning. The front door had been sealed, with several planks of wood nailed across it.

"How do we get in?" Emma asked.

"Let's check the other side," Marisee said.

The back of the windmill faced an overgrown field. The crown of a battered hat was sticking up over the grass.

"Henry!" Marisee called out.

The hat didn't move. Suddenly, a breeze whirled about them, whipping her hair around her head. Emma sneezed as the air turned white with flour. She jammed her cap firmly in place.

"Squall?" Marisee laughed. "Is that you?"

The Fumi appeared, with the pole-like body and shovel-shaped head of all Fumis. While most London Fumis were dark from absorbing the filthy smoke, the Squall was pale with the flour dust of the windmills.

"I'll go and sweep him over to you," the Squall said.

Every Fumi that Marisee had ever met had a voice like a creaking weathervane. The Squall was no different.

The grass blew aside, carving a path to where Henry sat on a rocking chair, a book in his lap. He glanced back, saw Marisee and Emma, and smiled. He lived a peaceful life, but his wide mouth and pointed teeth were a sharp reminder that he was part lion.

He heaved himself out of the rocking chair. The book fell from his lap, but the breeze swooped it up and dropped it back on to the chair.

"Thank you, Squall," Henry said.

He leaned backwards so far that Marisee thought

he'd topple over. He hung like that for a moment before being propelled forward, his feet brushing the grass. He landed in front of Marisee and Emma, wobbling as he caught his balance, but then righted himself.

"You're not getting any lighter," the Squall complained.

If Emma thought Henry was strange, she hid it well. His bright round eyes were black-rimmed, and his nose protruded, snout-like. He wore an oversized threadbare greatcoat and furry boots.

"Where's Robert?" Henry asked, squinting at Marisee through pale lashes. He straightened himself and suddenly seemed much taller and broader. "Why isn't he with you? Is he in danger?" he roared. "Where is he? Tell us where to go! Me and the Squall will be there!"

"He's... It's a long story," Marisee said quickly. "We do need your help, though."

Henry shrank back to his original size. "If it's a long story, we'd better sit down."

There was another gust of Squall, and three chairs flew through the air and landed on the ground. Henry gestured for Emma and Marisee to take a seat. He stretched his back and lowered himself with a wince.

"What do you need from us?" Henry asked.

Marisee told him the same story she'd told Emma, and Emma added her own thoughts.

Henry lifted a hand. "Wait!" he said, leaning forward. "Tell me about Mr Pipes and that Lord Gullinn again."

As Marisee repeated the Dragon's memory, Henry's lips drew back from his gums in a snarl.

"I know about Lord Gullinn," he growled, holding up his hands so that the sun caught the fine sand-coloured hair covering his skin. "Even before him, the Guild of Goldsmiths had been paying a group of necro-alchemists from Europe to create Variegate folk for a long time. All their abominable experiments failed until, eventually, there was us." He closed his eyes and carried on talking. "Me and Haakon and the others we lost along the way. We were created to have the logic of humans and the murderous instinct of wild beasts. We have unusually long lives." He opened his eyes. "Long lives in a world where no one wants us. The king and queen and the bishops called us abominations. The necro-alchemists that made us were punished. It should never have happened again."

"But it did," Marisee said softly.

"Yes, it did." Henry scratched his head beneath his hat. His nails were long and thin, like claws. "There will always be greedy people – greedy lords, greedy necro-alchemists." He scratched his ear next. "There were rumours ... that Lord Gullinn wanted to make Variegate children." The ex-assassin took a deep breath and a tear dangled from his long eyelashes. "It's cruel enough making us from full-grown people, but children…"

"We've heard about two children," Marisee said gently. "Were there more?"

Henry paused to think. "I believe not."

"But you don't know for certain?" Emma checked.

"Us Variegates always seem to sniff each other out," Henry said. "Marisee, you remember the Breach near our old windmill, don't you? Where the Thames pushed through the river wall and made a lake?"

Marisee nodded.

"Well, it wasn't only the river that poured through," Henry said. "One day, I ended up face to tentacle with an enormous old octopus that had got stuck in the gap. Me and Squall helped him get free. He didn't speak much Human. His mouth ain't made for those sounds. But Squall knows some basic Cephalopod and translated for me. The poor thing had been found in the Thames when he was just a small fry and kept in a cauldron. One day, a caterpillar fell in and, before he knew it, Octo was getting bigger and bigger – so big he thought he'd burst out of the cauldron. Somehow, though, there always seemed to be room for him."

"I saw him!" Marisee said. "The Dragon showed me! The octopus… Lord Gullinn…" She shuddered at the memory. She had hated feeling so powerless to stop it.

"Yes," Henry said. "He told Squall that too. Lord Gullinn didn't come to the best end, did he? Though I didn't feel sorry for him. He was cruel and greedy."

"What else did the octopus tell you?" Marisee asked, trying to forget Lord Gullinn being pulled into the cauldron.

"He said that after Gullinn... Well," Henry said, "you know what happened to him. Mr Pipes promised to destroy the cauldron and the ledger. He threw the ledger down a well near the White Tower and the octopus in the moat."

"Did Mr Pipes definitely destroy the cauldron?" Emma asked.

"He carried Octo in a tub so the octopus couldn't see anything, but when he was leaving the chamber, Octo managed to see bits of broken cauldron on the table."

"And after that?" Marisee urged.

"Octo didn't know," Henry said. "He was too busy swimming to freedom. But he was sure that Mr Pipes would never let the cauldron be used again." Another tear splashed on to his cheek. "There should never be another Variegate, ever. Every day I feel like the two parts of me are fighting each other – the man and the lion. I fear that they'll devour one another. Imagine a child not knowing if they were human or rat."

Emma said, "Mr Pipes may never have used it again, but perhaps he didn't destroy it properly."

"Or the Goldsmith may have a different cauldron," Marisee suggested.

But it was hard to believe that there were two magic cauldrons of coalescence.

"Did the octopus know how the cauldron worked?" she asked.

"No," Henry said. "But Mr Pipes had a ledger where he wrote down everything and sometimes he'd talk as he was going about his work. Octo thinks that Pipes was the one who'd fixed the cauldron in the first place. It was in pieces before that."

"I saw it," Marisee said. "In the ledger. There was a diagram of the shards." She looked at Emma. "What if the Goldsmith really does have Mr Pipes' cauldron? Or pieces of it? Perhaps he hasn't used it yet because it's not complete."

"We need to find those pieces and destroy them properly," Emma said.

"How do you destroy a magic cauldron?" Marisee wondered. The answer came to her as she spoke. "We have to find Mr Pipes' ledger. In the Dragon's memories, he was reading it when he was talking about destroying the cauldron. I think there were instructions for making it and breaking it up again. Did you say that Mr Pipes dropped the ledger down a well, Henry?"

"That's what Octo told me," Henry replied.

A squawk came from high above. A black blur of feathers shot across the sky.

Henry squinted upwards. "Is that a raven?"

Down a well, Marisee thought. Where did the ledger go from there? She had an idea, but they'd have to move quickly. It looked like the Goldsmith had sent out his spies.

RATLINGS

Robert shoved at the darkness in the cell. His hands met thin air. The animal smell was strong in here, but there wasn't the same suffocating terror and fury that had overwhelmed him earlier.

"Leave him alone!" came a voice from somewhere above him. "The guards'll hurt you if you harm him."

"I don't care," said a wispy voice right by Robert's ear. "How can they punish me more than they have already?"

"They'll find a way." Another voice in the gloom. "And I'll help them because of what you've done to us!"

Robert heard the scrape of a tinder flint and finally

saw the flicker of a candle. The meaty smell of tallow wax filled the air. As his eyes became used to the half-darkness, he saw a room filled with open cages. They were lined up on shelves and scattered across the floor. A blanket twitched in the cage in front of him. A small hand emerged from beneath its folds. The blanket was pushed down and a head appeared. All around him, the same thing was happening: blankets shifted; feet, arms and heads poked out.

"I know you!" A voice high up, on his left. "You came down by the river, didn't you? You were asking questions."

It was hard to see her properly. He was sure that he recognized the voice. Was it the mudlark with the ghost friend?

"Maud?" he said. "They took you too?"

"They came back after you went," Maud said. "I was talking to Amyas and didn't see them."

"I'm so sorry," said Robert. He wished he could tell her that he had planned to be taken prisoner so he could rescue the children, but who knew who might be listening?

"My friend Garnet was kidnapped too. Is she here?" he asked hopefully.

"I haven't met anyone with that name yet," Maud replied.

If Garnet wasn't in here, where could she be? Robert took a deep breath to ask a question, but he dreaded the answer.

"Have they done…? Are you…?" What words should he use? "Have they changed you?"

"Do you mean, is she one of us?" the wispy voice said. "Is she a ratling? Not yet. The Goldsmith doesn't know how. But soon."

Not yet. There was still hope!

A second candle was lit. Even in the weak light, the rat-child's eyes flashed red. She was a girl. Her face was narrow, and whiskers sprouted from her cheeks. The round ears on the top of her head twitched. The shadow of a tail curled up from beneath her skirt. Was she the same girl Robert had seen in the Dragon's memories? Those memories had been made over a hundred years ago, but hadn't Henry lived even longer than a hundred years?

A boy darted towards the girl – a boy that was also part rat. He too looked like the rat-child in Mr Pipes' room.

"Who are you?" Robert whispered.

"What do we look like?" the boy said with disgust.

"Tommy," the girl pleaded. "Please. We promised each other that we wouldn't hurt the children."

"Liar!" a voice shouted from a cage on a high shelf. "You help those men take us!"

"'Cause the Goldsmith said he'd fix us," the girl said. "If we help him, he'll help us."

"But *he's* the one they really want." Tommy jabbed a thumb at Robert. "The Goldsmith's got something special lined up for him."

The cell filled with whispers. As Robert's eyes adjusted to the gloom, he saw faces peering out from the cages. So many children! All looking at him!

"How do you know?" he asked.

"Because that's our business," Tommy said. "We were spies. I heard the Goldsmith's horrible daughter talking about it. You're his special ingredient."

Robert remembered what Joe had said about the cauldron. Children and rats were mixed together like a soup. "Special ingredient?" he said. "I don't understand."

"Look around you," Tommy said. "You see any other ratlings? The Goldsmith's been getting everything ready but he hasn't made none yet. It looks like you're the thing he needs to make it happen."

"You're going to help the Goldsmith turn us into rats!" The captured children's voices were high with fear.

They crawled out of the cages – waifs in rags with terror in their eyes.

Tommy tipped up his head to talk to them. "The Goldsmith reckons this one's got special powers."

A loud laugh escaped from Robert before he could stop it. "I haven't got special powers!" he said. "If I did, I wouldn't have let the Hibberts bring me to England!"

"Special powers," Tommy insisted. "They need you to help the Goldsmith. Maybe he wants to change all the orphans in London into rats."

Robert backed away. "I don't know what you're talking about! I came to rescue my friend, Garnet! Every one of you too. I want to stop the Goldsmith!"

"Oh," Tommy said. "Garnet! You've come to rescue Garnet!"

"You know her?" Robert said, full of hope. "She's safe?"

Tommy called out. "Garnet? Garnet? Are you here?"

Robert squinted in the shadows, longing for her to reply. No answer came.

"The Goldsmith keeps the children here," Tommy said. "There's no one called Garnet. You're lying."

Robert ran towards the cages so he could search for himself. "She was taken by the kidnappers," he said. "I'm sure of it!"

Was she safe and sound back at the den? Or had something even worse happened to her?

"Stop it, Tommy!" the rat-girl said. Her voice clicked in her throat, as if she was struggling to use her human voice.

"I won't!" Tommy grinned, his lips shrinking back to show four long, sharp teeth.

The girl clutched his arm and pulled him away.

"Don't," she said softly. "If they take you, I'll be all by myself. We promised to stay together, remember?" Her head cocked to the side. "Listen. The guards are coming."

The rat-children hurried back into the shadows. As the door opened, a woman was speaking.

"He was to be taken to the solitary cell! If any harm has come to him, you know to whom you'll be accountable!"

"No one told me, Miss Amelia," the guard said. "I've just started my watch."

He entered the cell, carrying a lantern. As the light was cast along the walls, Robert saw the chamber more clearly. Cages were stacked on the floor and shelves, each cage containing at least one child. The doors were open, but the children huddled in the back, clutching blankets and one another. Somewhere among them were the rat-children.

"And do you really believe that my father cares about who was on watch?" Miss Amelia barked back.

The guard grabbed Robert's arm and looked him up and down. "I can't see no blood nor bite marks," he said. "Nothing happened. Come and look for yourself."

Miss Amelia stepped into the room. She was around sixteen or seventeen years old. She wore a rich plum-red velvet dress embroidered with golden thread – the colours of the Goldsmith's coat of arms. She had a sharp, angry face.

"Hurry up!" she ordered.

The guard pulled Robert out of the cell, and the door slammed behind him. In the passageway, a second guard stepped out of a recess in the wall. He was much taller than Robert. He gripped a sword and fell into step behind them.

"Where are you taking me?" There was a wobble in Robert's voice.

Were the rat-children right? Did the Goldsmith want Robert because he believed Robert was a "special ingredient"? Because the Goldsmith was going to be very disappointed.

Miss Amelia ignored his question. They left the tower and marched across the walkway that formed the outer walls of the castle. Then over the moat – the water looked so deep and dirty – into the main castle. The day was cool and misty, the air heavy with the tang of tar and stagnant water. The wind blew in the smell of boiling meat from the east. Madam Blackwell had told him that the Victualling Yard in Deptford prepared supplies for the Navy; you could always tell the rations by the smell.

People rushed past him – maids carrying baskets, and immaculately dressed footmen, guards and soldiers in different uniforms. The Tower of London was like a village! But in the very middle of this village was the White Tower. Fear and fury surged from its walls, almost knocking Robert over. He staggered. Miss Amelia shot him an annoyed look.

"Get moving!" the guard snapped.

Miss Amelia strode ahead across the courtyard. Robert's body ached. The day had taken its toll. The guard behind him shoved him forward.

"Who are you?" he said, stumbling after her, even though he was almost sure that he knew. "Where are you taking me?"

She stopped suddenly. Her smile was wide and cold. "To assist my father," she said, and raced on.

So Tommy the rat-boy had been right, Robert thought. But how would he, Robert, help someone as powerful as the Goldsmith?

He was hurried up rickety timber steps towards a door. Two guards immediately strode out.

"Good morning, Miss Amelia," the taller one said. "We must search him."

"Lift your arms," the other guard grunted.

Robert obeyed. The guards kneaded his arms, his

legs, his chest as if somehow he'd magically stuck weapons to his skin. Though perhaps in a place like this, where there had been centuries of magic, it could happen. Their fingers thrust into his pockets. If they'd asked, he could have saved them the effort – his pockets no longer held anything important at all.

"What is this?" the guard asked, holding up a lump wrapped in paper, bound in string.

Robert had forgotten about the cold remedy he'd mixed for Godfrey. He must have slipped it in his pocket when Haakon seized him. The guard held it to his nose and immediately sneezed.

"I help Mr Boussay, the apothecary," Robert said. "It's medicine to clear the nose."

The guard sneezed again and threw the package back at Robert.

"Enough," Miss Amelia said, pushing past the guard. "We have work to do."

The guard scowled, but stood aside, letting them through. Miss Amelia nudged Robert towards a narrow flight of stairs that led downwards. He sniffed. He could smell… What was it?

"Gunpowder was stored here," Miss Amelia said proudly. "The gunpowder that won many wars. But my father has discovered an even better way to win at war."

"Stealing children and turning them into animals?" Robert said.

"Oh, much better than that," Miss Amelia replied with a laugh.

They passed through a narrow entrance into a basement. A few pale shafts of light fell through high half-windows. Candles dribbled wax from candelabra on to the flagstone floor. The walls were crowded with shelves and, like Mr Boussay's apothecary shop, the shelves were crowded with bottles, jars and urns with finely written labels hanging from their necks. Two animal skeletons had been posed as if they were running. *Lions, perhaps*, Robert thought, *or tigers*. A third skeleton – could that be a monkey? It was pinned to the wall, to look as if it was climbing. There were piles of ledgers and giant glass bowls filled with phials of powders and liquids. Bunches of dried flowers and herbs were pinned to the edges of the shelves. Robert brushed them with his fingers as he passed, breathing in the familiar scents of rosemary, thyme and lavender.

A woman stood with her back to them, staring at a large map hanging from the wall. She wore a silver silk dress that moved like water, and midnight-blue gloves. A wicker hamper hung from her arm. Her head as far as Robert could see was bare – of hat or hair.

"Get out of here!" Miss Amelia snapped. "Servants are forbidden from this room without my father's permission."

The woman pointed to a place on the map. She didn't turn round.

"I visited that island," she said softly. "Many years ago. It's where I found the sphagnum weed."

"I don't care where you went or what you found," Miss Amelia said. "You have duties."

The woman didn't answer. A guard pushed Robert onward.

The room was divided by a wooden fence, splitting it in two. The fence reached from the stone floor to the vaulted ceiling, with a central gate guarded by two yeoman. One held a pike longer than he was tall, the sharp edges of its axe-like head gleaming in the candlelight. The other yeoman wore a belt hung with an array of daggers. His hand rested on the heavy-jewelled hilt of a blade as thin as a spike.

Both yeomen stared ahead, taut and upright. Robert sensed that they didn't only use their eyes – their whole bodies were on watch. They reminded Robert of mongooses in Barbados.

Miss Amelia strode towards the gate. A key stuck out from the lock.

"What's through there?" Robert asked.

"You will see," she replied, her eyes glinting like the yeomens' weapons.

She turned the key. Robert expected the gate to open towards him like a door, but it slid sideways, overlapping the fence.

In some ways, both halves of the basement were the same. The ceiling was high and vaulted, and the walls were stone. This half of the room was lit by so many guttering candles – in candelabras, in sconces, in lanterns – that the air seemed to flicker. In the middle of this part of the room was a well, wider than the one in Madam Blackwell's pump house, but with no wall around it. The water that lapped at its sides glowed white. Robert could see no pump or bucket for collecting it.

This side of the basement was filled with cages, just like the chamber he'd left. The cage closest to him seemed empty until he studied it closer. Dark smoke swirled within, then settled into the shovel-shaped head and pole body of a Fumi. Drops of colour erupted from around it. It was speaking – perhaps shouting or crying for help.

"Is that Fumi imprisoned?" Robert asked. "Why?"

"Wrongdoing," Miss Amelia said shortly.

How had Robert not seen it straight away? More cages filled with churning smoke threaded with the city's smells – fumes from the brewers and tanning factories, the reek of the abattoirs, the harshness of smouldering sea coal.

Robert turned to Miss Amelia. "Do ... do the Council of Fumis allow their spirits to be held like this?"

"A rogue air spirit almost destroyed London," Miss Amelia said. "My father has convinced the Council that London is safest if their wrongdoers are here."

"Did your father use Dragons to *convince* the Council?" asked Robert.

Miss Amelia smiled that wide, cold smile again. "We don't protect Dragons just for their beauty." Her smile widened. "They must work to earn our protection."

"But it wasn't even a London Fumi that raised the Chaos Monster," Robert protested. "It had stowed away from Salzburg!"

"Why should that matter?" Miss Amelia said. "One small Fumi almost caused the destruction of London. The London Fumis should have foreseen the danger and stopped it. My father – and the Dragons – persuaded them to pass the responsibility to us."

And what was the Goldsmith doing with that *responsibility*? Robert imagined the bullying Goldsmith demanding the prisoners from the Council of Elders or threatening to destroy every Fumi. His Dragons were powerful enough – and so was the Goldsmith. No one or nothing could stop him doing as he wished.

Except for Robert and Marisee. They had to stop him.

Why were there so many cages? The Tower of London had always served as a prison, but surely not for Elementals? As he passed the well, he noticed that the water was slightly dented, as if something was pressing into the centre. He looked harder and saw the outline of thin bars. Suddenly, a watery silver hand shot up and then disappeared again.

"Is that well a prison too?" he said.

"That's none of your business," Miss Amelia said, marching on.

"Move!" the guard barked from behind, trying to shove Robert through the door. But he couldn't move. He'd heard something! Singing! He knew the song. He knew the voice, even though it was weak.

"Do you know the muffin man?" the voice croaked. *"The muffin man, the muffin man..."*

That was the favourite song of a child he knew so well.

"Garnet!" he shouted. "Garnet! Are you here?"

The singing stopped. "Robert?" the child squealed. "Robert! Robert! Where are you? Have you come for me?"

"Garnet!" He ran towards the voice. "Where are *you*?"

"Robert!"

She was somewhere above him. She must be locked in one of the cages on a high shelf. *Garnet, in a cage!*

"Is Emma with you, Robert? Can you see me? I can't see you!" Her voice faded, as if she'd run out of breath to speak. "I'm sick, Robert! Did you bring me the medicine? You said you would."

"Garnet! Where are you?" The room was too high to see into the upper reaches. "I'm coming!"

The guard pushed Robert so hard that he was sent sprawling on to the stone floor. His jaws clicked shut and he tasted blood from his bitten lip.

"Please, Miss Amelia!" he said as he tried to stand up. "Garnet's my friend! I need to make sure she isn't hurt."

"She won't be hurt," Miss Amelia said with a smirk. "My father promises – as long as you do what he says."

Robert crossed his arms. "I want you to free her now!"

Miss Amelia sighed and nodded over Robert's shoulder. Two more guards appeared. They each grabbed one of Robert's arms and lifted him off the floor, carrying him after Miss Amelia.

"Robert!" Garnet called. "Are you leaving me? Don't go! Help me!"

The guards dropped Robert in a heap by Miss Amelia's feet. She was facing a door that slid open silently.

"Go down the steps, Robert," Miss Amelia said.

He looked back towards Garnet, but found himself staring at the guards' pikes and swords pointing at him. The woman in the rippling dress was standing behind them. She caught his eye and looked away.

"Down the steps, Robert," Miss Amelia ordered.

Steps. How could there be more steps? He was already in the basement. What was below a basement? He peered down the winding staircase. The steps were thin, tapering timber planks that seemed to become smaller as they descended.

"Why must I go down there?" he asked.

"To assist us," Miss Amelia said.

Robert frowned. "And if I don't want to *assist* you?"

Miss Amelia's eyes narrowed.

"Warder!" she shouted. "The prisoner is being obstinate!"

Behind him, the door slid open again. Robert heard the tap of a pike handle on the stone floor, the sound of footsteps, the jangle of keys, the screech of a cage door. A voice.

"Robert! Have you come back for me! Are they letting me go?"

Garnet was brought to him, flanked by two yeomen, their hands on her shoulders. Robert felt a flash of rage. She was so tiny that they had to bend to hold her.

"Let me go!" she wailed.

She swung her foot back and kicked at a guard's ankle. He wore boots and she was barefoot, so it must have hurt her more than him. He crouched, thrusting his sour face close to hers.

"Do that again, brat, and I'll throw you into the moat," he growled.

"I don't care!" Garnet swung her leg again, ready. "I have other friends who'll rescue me."

"Please, Garnet," Robert said quickly. "Don't make them angry."

She glared at him. "I thought you were here to help me escape! I don't need you. I can escape on my own." She swung her leg once more and aimed a kick at Miss Amelia.

If the two yeomen guarding the gate had reminded Robert of mongooses, Miss Amelia was the snake. Mongooses were famous for battling snakes, but they didn't always win. Sometimes the snake would writhe and seem to weaken, then lash out, sinking its fangs into the mongoose's neck, releasing deadly venom. Miss Amelia looked like she'd lash out with poison.

She lunged towards Garnet. "How dare you!"

The snake's uncoiling. Be careful, Garnet!

Suddenly, the woman who'd been staring at the map was standing between Miss Amelia and Garnet.

"Your father promised to keep the child safe, Miss Amelia," she said.

Miss Amelia looked furious. "It's none of your business!"

The woman didn't move. "If you harm this child, why should Robert help you?"

Miss Amelia grinned – the snake about to swallow a mongoose whole. "We have other ways to ensure his assistance."

"You are right, Miss Amelia," the woman said. "But perhaps you should step away from the child. She's sick. Who knows the nature of her illness?"

"I *am* sick," Garnet groaned before slumping. "I'm hot and I'm cold and my stomach hurts. Robert was supposed to bring me medicine."

"Sick?" Miss Amelia jumped back. "Take her from me! Lock her away!"

A guard picked up Garnet and carried her off. She squirmed so she could face Robert.

"So you aren't going to rescue me?" she muttered.

The door slid shut. Robert held himself back from

lurching towards it as it closed. At least he knew Garnet was alive.

"Now get down those stairs," Miss Amelia ordered him.

The woman touched Robert's arm. "You'll achieve nothing by arguing with her," she said.

It was the first time that Robert could see her face properly, away from the shadows and flickering candlelight. Her skin was light brown – much lighter than his own. Had she been stolen from her homeland and brought to England like him?

Or – hadn't Joe the mudlark mentioned a rumour of a sorceress in the Tower with brown skin? Was the rumour real?

"Why?" he asked. "What's down there?"

"Move!" Miss Amelia yelled. "I won't tell you again!"

Robert stepped on to the first stair and gripped the rope that was clamped along the wall. The woman followed behind him, then he heard the swish of Miss Amelia's gown and the thump of the guards' boots as down, down, down they climbed.

MR PIPES' LEDGER

London's rivers flowed under the ground and over it. Few Solids knew about the criss-crossing channels, tunnels and streams several feet beneath the streets. Even fewer ever saw them. Now Marisee was going to show them to Emma.

Marisee wanted to slip into a well, but how could she expect Emma to follow her? Why would anyone jump and expect to live? And what if Emma did jump but the Chads weren't ready to catch a Solid they didn't know? Instead, Marisee decided to trace her way back to the old furrier's cellar where she and Robert had emerged that evening.

It seemed so long ago that they had been on their way to meet Elijah at St Bride's Church and Robert had been full of hope for news about his family. Now, he was a prisoner in the Tower and Marisee had no idea if he was still alive.

She had to have hope.

"So, what happens if we find the ledger?" Emma asked.

"Then we find the cauldron and destroy it."

Emma stopped walking. "I think we may need more of a plan than that."

"I know!" Marisee realized she was shouting. "But I can't think of one. Can you?"

"I'll try," Emma said. "Because Robert's already walked into the Tower of London without a plan for getting out again. I don't understand why he'd do that."

"Because of Garnet!" Marisee was shouting again. "That's why!"

They stood staring at each other. Maybe there was a well nearby that Marisee *could* jump down. At this moment, she would be very happy to desert Emma in the street. But if Marisee wanted to rescue Robert, she would need Emma's help. She had to remain calm. She started walking again.

"Let's find the ledger first," she said evenly. "I believe that the Goldsmith needs it to make the cauldron work.

Then perhaps ... perhaps we can use it to bargain with the Goldsmith."

Emma stopped walking. "*Bargain* with the Goldsmith? You mean there's a chance that we'd actually give him the ledger?"

"No! Yes!" Marisee's head was all muddled up. "I don't know! But he must need it. We could tell him to release Robert and the other children and then…"

"Then we'd give him the instructions for making children into rats?" Emma looked disgusted.

"We could tear out those pages," Marisee suggested, knowing that the sly Goldsmith would probably check every single page before agreeing to bargain. "And we'd know how to destroy the cauldron. We'd find a way to do that before he uses it again."

"I don't think that's a good plan," Emma said gently.

"Then what *is* a good plan?" Marisee was close to tears.

"Shall we think again if we find the ledger?" Emma said. "It's been missing for more than a hundred years. It probably fell apart long ago."

Marisee stalked away, Emma following a couple of steps behind. They turned off Fleet Street into the narrow alleyway close to St Bride's Church. It took a little while for Marisee to recognize the right door and the two half-windows that cast a tiny amount of light into the cellar. Marisee and Emma had to push together to force the door open, glancing up and down the alleyway to make sure no one was watching. A shadow skimmed between the leaning buildings. Was that a bird? A big one, like a raven? *Was* the Goldsmith spying on them?

They fumbled through the dark room and down the flights of steps. The way became darker and darker, the smell of the rotting pelts stronger and stronger.

"It really stinks," Marisee said, her fingers brushing against the walls of the pitch-black cellar.

"I've smelled far worse," Emma said. "Once, I lived next to a factory where they boiled beef fat to make soap."

"Have you lived in many places?" Marisee asked.

"We're not all lucky enough to have a grandmother with a cottage," Emma replied.

Marisee frowned into the darkness. Was Emma being rude? Marisee wasn't sure. She just sounded sad.

Down and down, Marisee's outstretched fingers prodded the walls, searching for the plank of wood. Was that its edge here? Or here? She couldn't tell. She rapped on the wall.

"Turnmill?" she called. "Sally? Can you let us through?"

She could hear Emma's breathing behind her,

waiting. The darkness seemed heavier, the rotten smell thicker. Marisee knocked again.

"Sally! It's Marisee."

"Who's Sally?" Emma asked. "And why is she behind that wall?"

There was a click and Marisee felt a rush of clean air as the plank lifted and a square of silver appeared in front of them. Emma gave a little surprised gasp. Marisee smiled to herself – for once, she'd be the confident one who knew where she was going!

"Through here," she explained to Emma.

"Yes," Emma said. "That's what I supposed."

Marisee quickly clambered into the tunnel before she said something rude back. She felt the tangle of Sally Fleet's magic before the young Chad rose from a puddle at the end of the tunnel. Emma drew in her breath.

"Who's this Solid?" Sally Fleet asked, looking Emma up and down. "I thought Auntie Turnmill has to give permission for Solids to come down here."

"Her name's Emma," Marisee said. "She's Robert's friend."

Emma was pressed against the wall, staring back at Sally. Sally did look strange – partly a girl of around thirteen years old, partly a water spirit with large dark eyes and sharp narrow nails like a burrowing animal. She had recently started dressing in clothes from the Room of Lost Things. Today, she wore a ragged jacket over woollen breeches. She'd tied a silk scarf around her neck and jammed a milkmaid's bonnet over her long hair.

"Robert's friend?" Sally said. "Well, you're my friend too."

She reached out for Emma's hand. Emma fixed a smile on her face, stepped forward and took it. Marisee thought that it was just as well that the Fleet Ditch Boar hadn't come to greet them.

"We need to find a big leather-bound book," Marisee said. "It was thrown down a well many years ago and is very important. Where can we start looking?"

"Go to the Mithraeum," Sally said. "Lady Walbrook keeps many books there."

"But she might not have this one," Marisee said.

Marisee had no intention of visiting Lady Walbrook unless she really must. The first time Marisee had met the powerful riverhead, Lady Walbrook had punished a Chad by turning it into dust. Marisee would never forget the pony-shaped water spirit trying to break free up until it finally disintegrated. Lady Walbrook especially hated humans. She had bound Marisee's wrists with burning magical thread when Marisee had tried to protect the terrified Chad.

"It would have fallen into the tunnels about a hundred years ago," Marisee added.

As Marisee said the words out loud, she realized how hopeless this search was. How could paper and leather survive in these tunnels for a century? Except ... wasn't there one place where discarded things did survive?

"What about the Room of Lost Things?" she said.

"Yes!" Sally spun round. "Let's go and look there. I want some new boots anyway."

As they hurried along the tunnels, Marisee knew that Emma would be bursting with questions, but Marisee didn't want to talk to her. It would be embarrassing to have an argument in front of Sally. The tunnel was becoming more cluttered. They stepped across broken roof tiles and over iron barrel-hoops, heaps of sacking and broken crates, until finally the tunnel opened up and they'd arrived.

Emma turned to Marisee, stricken. "How can we find anything here?"

It did seem as if everything lost in the river had ended up in this room – from Roman millstones to the animal bones thrown from the Smithfield slaughterhouses. There were heaps of rags, shelves of flasks and bottles, and a column of different-sized trunks balancing against the far wall.

Emma sat down on the hull of an upturned rowing

boat. "What's the point?" she said. "There's so much of everything."

There *was* a point! Mr Pipes' ledger would tell them everything they needed to know about the cauldron – how it was made and how to destroy it.

"We have to try," Marisee said. Emma was staring at the ground, but Marisee knew she was listening. "Robert's risked his life to try and save the children in the Tower. We must do everything we can to help him."

Emma gave her a little nod and stood up.

"What if I start over there?" Marisee pointed at a row of barrels. "And you go through the rags?"

Emma gave that little nod again.

"I'll help too," Sally said, heading towards the trunks.

Emma shifted a pile of rags from a warped three-legged table. "You've been here before," she said to Marisee. "Do you know how this place works?"

"I don't think it works in any way," Marisee said, starting to sift through the objects in front of the barrels. "It just collects things. Some flow in on the river. Other stuff's been dropped down the wells and brought here by the Chads. That's what I'm hoping happened to the ledger."

It was hard to stay hopeful. Marisee had looked beneath a sack of men's leather boots, behind a row of cow skulls and under a ship's sail. The sail had been neatly folded into a square, but was too heavy for her to lift. She crawled across it, patting it as hard as she could to feel if there was anything hidden within it.

Emma was searching around the broken boat. She emerged with her face smeared with pitch.

"This is impossible," she said.

Still, they carried on, peering into corners and barrels, sweeping aside piles of clothes and emptying boxes of shoes.

Sally squealed, and Marisee felt as if she'd been dropped into a slow, stagnant river.

Emma grimaced and cleared her throat. "What … what happened?"

"The Chads hold the memories of their rivers," Marisee said. "When they have strong feelings, *you* sometimes feel their rivers too."

"Please can you ask her to keep her memories to herself." Emma sounded annoyed.

Sally was balancing on the column of trunks. A trunk lid had been thrown open. Her head was buried inside the trunk, but her hand was in the air, holding up a heavy-looking leather-bound book.

"What does it say on the cover?" Marisee said, excited.

Sally straightened herself. "I don't know. I can't read."

She kept her human shape but still seemed to flow as she descended the stack of trunks, clutching the book. She gave the book to Emma. Emma? Didn't Sally realize that Marisee could read too?

Emma squinted at the faded writing on the cover. She groaned. *"The Compleat Housewife."*

Marisee slumped down against the trunks. She couldn't quite meet Emma's eye, because Emma was right. They were never going to find the ledger in here. It had probably fallen apart or been swept into the sea a hundred years ago.

"If he dropped it in a well near the White Tower..." Emma said. "That's in the Tower of London. Maybe we should look closer to there."

"The Tower of London?" Sally Fleet's head emerged from behind a cart wheel. "You should have said that. Not much comes out of the Tower nowadays, but the moat used to wriggle through the old tunnels and bring lost things to us. Lady Walbrook took them."

"So Lady Walbrook may really have the ledger," Marisee reluctantly agreed.

Sally gave Marisee a doleful look. "I told you to go to the Mithraeum, didn't I?"

Marisee closed her eyes, trying to find the courage

inside her. It was hidden deep. But if she was to help Robert, she had to ask for Lady Walbrook's assistance. She certainly couldn't risk taking Emma there, though.

As it was, Emma wanted to return to the Red Guard Gang den, just in case there was the tiniest chance Garnet might find her way back home.

"What if she finds the den empty and wanders off again?" Emma said.

She had to know that Garnet wouldn't be coming home unless Robert was rescued. But, like Marisee, Emma was holding on to hope. If Emma left, Marisee wasn't sure that she could hold on to hope by herself.

"Please wait here for me," Marisee pleaded. "I have to visit Lady Walbrook without you because she hates humans. The only reason she might see me is because she respects Grandma. She could have the ledger, Emma. That's what we've come here to find."

Emma blew out her cheeks, but sat down on the upturned hull of the rowing boat.

Sally Fleet hurried Marisee through the tunnels towards the Mithraeum, Lady Walbrook's palace.

Lady Walbrook was waiting for them in the tunnel outside the entrance, as if guarding it. She was tall, and her dress and skin shifted from pale brown to slate grey to silver. Her hair was twisted into plaits on top of her head. Her face was still, her nose bridge chipped as if it was porcelain. Her cold eyes stared at Marisee.

"Solids are not welcome here," she said.

Marisee certainly didn't want to *be* here, but she clamped her lips together and bowed.

"I've come to request…" *No, it has to be more than ask.* "To beg for your help," she said.

"Are my rivers in danger?" Lady Walbrook asked.

"No," Marisee admitted. "Not exactly, but—"

"Then I have no interest in helping you," Lady Walbrook said, turning away.

Marisee had to think quickly to persuade Lady Walbrook to help her.

"They *are* in danger, Lady Walbrook!" she said. "Or they most definitely will be, from the Goldsmith. He's trying to take control of London. You know that he's no friend of the Chads, or any Elemental except the Dragons."

"The goldsmiths have been trying to control London for centuries," Lady Walbrook replied. "They have failed."

"I believe he has a cauldron," Marisee said. "A cauldron of coalescence that—"

"Cauldron of coalescence?" Silver, grey, brown – the colours shifted through Lady Walbrook. Her stony eyes fixed on Marisee. "Tell me."

"Children have been kidnapped and taken to the Tower, Lady Walbrook," Marisee said. "The Goldsmith wants to create an army of rat-children spies. We think he has a magic cauldron that belonged to a scholar called Mr Pipes – a cauldron of coalescence."

Lady Walbrook said nothing. It was like talking to a statue.

"The Goldsmith is ruthless," Marisee finished. "Imagine what else he may use the cauldron for. He could create any beast he wished."

Lady Walbrook's skin shimmered silver. Marisee stepped back. That was the colour of her anger. The silver faded into flint grey.

"What do you want?" Lady Walbrook asked.

"Mr Pipes' ledger, please," Marisee said. "If you have it."

"What will you do with it?" Lady Walbrook asked.

Marisee couldn't mention bargaining with the Goldsmith. Grandma had told her that sometimes you had to be diplomatic, even though that sounded like a long word for "telling a lie".

"We want to know how to destroy the cauldron," Marisee said simply.

The colours shifted again – grey, silver, grey, silver. Lady Walbrook stared at her, and for a moment Marisee heard the creak of wooden waterwheels and the slap of oars against a river's current.

"I do not care about the children," Lady Walbrook said. "They will only grow older and disrespect our streams and rivers like their forebears. But I have read it. I fear an army of Variegates. He will meld together creatures that we cannot fight. You must stop the Goldsmith."

Then suddenly Marisee was standing by herself. A large ledger lay on the ground by her feet. Marisee picked it up and leafed through it. She instantly recognized Mr Pipes' spidery writing.

Sally Fleet silently appeared by her side.

"Is that the lost thing you wanted to find?" she asked.

Marisee nodded.

With the ledger clutched tightly under her arm, Marisee ran back through the tunnels to the Room of Lost Things.

"Look!" She waved it at Emma. "We have it."

Emma stood up. "It's definitely Mr Pipes' ledger?"

"Yes!" Marisee said, thrusting it at Emma. "Look."

As Emma held out her hands, something in the air changed. At first, Marisee thought that it was magic, seeping from the ledger into the tunnel.

Sally Fleet gasped. "No, no, no, no," she said. In the next second, she was gone.

"What's happening?" Emma asked, eyes wide.

Marisee held the ledger tight to her chest.

"I don't know," she said. "But something feels very wrong. We have to get out!"

It was too late. The stink of rotting meat oozed down the tunnel. A ribbon of black and orange dots swarmed towards them, already forming into its Dragon shape. The head hovered above them, the ribbon hardening into a tail that coiled around Emma and Marisee, drawing them into its loop. As the scales clicked into place, a man strode in behind it. Marisee recognized him instantly.

"You have no permission to be here!" she shouted at him.

A ship's rudder was leaning against the wall but just out of reach. She couldn't even arm herself.

"There is nowhere in London that I am not permitted to go," the Goldsmith said coolly. "You know what I want. Give me the ledger and I will leave."

Marisee tried to wriggle free, but the loop of Dragon tail tightened. The Goldsmith reached forward. His fingertips brushed the leather cover of the ledger.

"She will give you nothing!" Lady Walbrook appeared in the room.

She opened her mouth and a silver web sprang towards the Goldsmith. Marisee knew that it stung humans and could destroy other water spirits. The Dragon roared, a stream of black and orange sparks flying from its mouth. They threaded through the web, slicing it. Silver dripped on to the piles of rags and driftwood before turning to steam.

A roar echoed from the tunnel, followed by the rap of hooves on flattened earth. The Fleet Ditch Boar charged into the room, gathering speed, launching himself towards the Goldsmith. The Dragon swung its head, batting the boar away. He hit the column of trunks and they tumbled down around him.

Lady Walbrook opened her mouth to shoot another web. Her skin was pure silver now. Sally Fleet was by her side, hands raised, a small silver ball hovering by her fingers.

The Goldsmith raised his hand. "Stop! This is not a fight between me and the Chads." He flicked his thumb towards Marisee. "This girl has found something that was stolen from my Guild many years ago. It was not Pipes' to destroy." He lowered his voice. "Lady Walbrook, I believe that you were hiding my legal property. Isn't that an offence under the Whittington Articles?"

Lady Walbrook didn't reply.

"Is that not so, Lady Walbrook?" the Goldsmith insisted.

Still no answer from the riverhead.

"So the girls must return it to me," the Goldsmith said.

Marisee clutched the ledger tighter. The Fleet Ditch Boar had freed himself from the trunks and planted himself in front of her. He snorted, pawing the ground. The Goldsmith ignored him. His eyes were on Marisee. Why didn't Lady Walbrook defend Marisee? Was the Goldsmith correct?

Marisee thought hard. Hadn't she wanted to use the ledger to bargain with the Goldsmith? It may not have been a good plan, but it might be their only chance now.

"I *will* give you the ledger," she said.

Emma's intake of breath was loud.

"But there's a price," Marisee added.

The Goldsmith raised an eyebrow. "A price to pay to return my Guild's possession?"

The Dragon's tail tautened even more.

"But I'm curious," the Goldsmith said. "What is your price?"

"Free the children you've imprisoned in the Tower of London," Marisee replied.

The Goldsmith laughed. "I have no idea what children you're talking about."

"Garnet!" Emma shouted. "And the other ones you kidnapped from the streets and the foreshore."

"Be careful who you accuse," the Goldsmith said quietly. "But perhaps we *can* reach an agreement."

To Marisee's surprise, the Goldsmith stepped back, his hands hanging by his side.

"Release them!" he ordered.

The Dragon's tail dissolved but the head remained above them, jaws agape, dripping sparks. Marisee rubbed her ribs. Emma flinched.

Marisee moved towards the rudder, but didn't touch it. The Goldsmith's eyes were still on her. She made herself look right back. There had to be nail marks in the ledger from where she was holding it so tightly.

"I *can* pay you, Marisee," he said. "But with something that you really want."

"I don't want anything from you!" she batted back.

A smirk played around the Goldsmith's lips.

"I will take you to your mother."

Her … her … *mother*? Marisee suddenly lost all her strength. She could barely keep hold of the ledger.

"She … she's alive?" she managed to stutter out.

"Yes," the Goldsmith said. "Your mother is very much alive." He beckoned towards Marisee. "Give me the ledger and I will take you to her."

MYRR

Robert walked down the staircase that led below the basement. It ended in a narrow archway lit by a lantern hanging from a hook. The corridor widened beyond it. Rows of hanging lanterns threw light across the walls. As Robert moved forward, an iron portcullis plummeted down in front of them, crashing to the stone floor. If Robert had been standing beneath it, he would have been crushed. He looked down at the metal points denting the stone.

"Tell it to lift the gate," Miss Amelia demanded.

"Tell what?" He squinted at the gate. "I don't understand."

"My father knows the statues talk to you," Miss Amelia said.

"The ... the statues?"

"Don't think about lying to me," Miss Amelia replied. "My father has spies. The ravens, the Dragons... He even has a Fumi that has promised to do my father's bidding rather than end up in a cage. My father is certain that you possess the same abominable trait as Pipes." She pointed to the archway above the portcullis. "We believe that Pipes blocked the way to stop us from taking back what's rightly ours. You *can* open it and you *will* open it."

What abominable trait? According to Mistress Hibbert, where he had lived before – when he had first arrived in England – Robert had many abominable traits. What could he share with Mr Pipes, who lived so long ago and whose life was so different from Robert's?

He glanced up to where Miss Amelia was pointing. The stone above the portcullis had been carved into the shape of a face – round, bulbous eyes like a toad, a pig snout, small ears like an owl – that stuck out from the wall. The archway was its giant mouth, the portcullis its vicious teeth.

"You mean talking to statues?" Robert said. Miss Amelia made it sound easy. It might have been for Mr

Pipes, but it wasn't for him. "*They* talk to me. I can't control it."

The first time it had happened was during the enchanted sleep. The statues on the steeple of St George's in Bloomsbury had stepped down and run towards him. The king who usually perched atop the steeple had told Robert, *I see you!* Robert had been terrified. Now, he stared at the portcullis and the strange animal face above it. There was no sign that it could hear him or had any intention of doing anything Robert asked of it.

"I don't know what I'm supposed to do," Robert said.

"Open it!" Miss Amelia tapped her foot. "*Now* – if you want your little friend Garnet to be safe."

But how? Robert looked up at the face. "Open up!" he shouted.

Nothing happened. He turned to the woman. Her eyes darted away from his.

"Do you know what I should do?" he asked.

"What happened when the other statues talked to you?" she replied. There was an edge of urgency in her voice.

What *had* happened those times? It had been during the moments when London had crackled with the strength of Elemental magic – the Shepherdess's water magic, the Fumis' air magic. Perhaps that was the ingredient he needed.

"There was extra magical power," he said.

"If you want to see that brat again, open the portcullis." Miss Amelia sighed, and her cold smile returned. "But if you have lost interest in your little friend," she added, "then I'm sure you must worry about your mother and sisters, Robert. My father and Lord Hibbert are good friends. He says that your sisters are good workers and Lord Hibbert will get a good price for them if he's persuaded to sell them." Her smile widened. "My father knows many willing purchasers, far away from the Hibberts' plantation."

Hatred bubbled through Robert. How dare they threaten to take his sisters from his mother! She'd already lost her sons. And they'd sell his family as if they were cattle. But he was here to rescue the children – he had to do whatever he must to survive.

He glanced up at the stone head. He felt no power at all.

Then he saw a blur of movement to his side – the woman was flicking liquid from a curved glass bottle towards him. This sorceress was dousing him with a magic potion! He tried to blink it from his eyes, but the liquid seemed to stalk across his skin, roaring and shrieking like an angry animal imprisoned in the Royal Menagerie. Was that sound real or only in his head? The animal was drowned out by the blast of trumpets, the stomping feet of soldiers marching to war, the quiet sobbing of a young queen awaiting her death.

What had the sorceress done? Robert's knees buckled and he collapsed to the floor. But ... at the same time, he felt power bubbling up inside him.

"The portcullis, Robert," came Miss Amelia's chilling voice.

It didn't seem impossible now. He could do it!

"Open up!" he wheezed. "Open! Up!"

Through the blur of the stinging potion, Robert watched the portcullis lift.

Miss Amelia clapped her hands. "At last! My father was right! You *are* like Pipes!" She lifted the hem of her luxurious dress and stepped carefully past him. "Pipes thought he could keep his secrets from us. He was wrong. The ratlings told us everything."

She started down the passageway, the woman – the sorceress – just behind her. *Was* Robert just like Pipes? Miss Amelia was so certain. Where was she leading him? And what did she plan to do with him when they arrived? Every part of Robert's body wanted to stop walking. But if the sorceress didn't bewitch him with her potions, the guard would force him onward with a sword. He followed.

The passageway was long and narrow, like a secret corridor running alongside a room.

"No one has walked here for more than a hundred years." Miss Amelia turned round to Robert. "But now we have you, the time has come."

Robert looked her in the eye. "For what?"

"Don't question me, boy!" she replied as she faced straight ahead once more.

The passageway ended at a wall. At first glance, it was a dead end, but there was a wooden door set into the wall. It was painted the colour of stones, smooth, without handle nor lock – so easy to miss. Robert swallowed. He could feel it – something behind that door, something ancient and enormous.

"Open it!" Miss Amelia ordered him.

Robert didn't want to know what was on the other side. He glanced back at the guards – their weapons were raised. He ran his fingers across the wood, searching for a hidden handle. There was none. He lay his face against the door, as if he was whispering to whatever lay beyond.

"Open," he whispered.

There was a click and the door swung open. Was the door a living thing, to obey him like that? He had no time to think about it, because he was thrust forward.

Two lanterns glowed on a low platform, but there were no candles inside, lighting them. Robert's eyes moved quickly from the lanterns to the thing in the centre of the platform. It was a head, bigger than Robert was tall. Its neck was swathed in a coil of red velvet. Even by the flickering candleless lanterns' light, one thing was clear – the skin was as smooth as stone and as pale as a statue, yet its tumble of hair looked as real as Robert's own. Although it was still, Robert sensed an alertness, as if it was listening and waiting.

The guards gasped. "So it is true," one of them murmured.

Miss Amelia gave them a triumphant look. "Of course it's true. My father wouldn't lie."

It took Robert a moment to find his voice.

"Is it one of the earth giants?" he asked. "I thought Gog and Magog were sleeping on the riverbed."

"They are," the sorceress replied. She was staring at the head too. "This is Myrr. He was the first creature to emerge from the Magogs' cauldron of coalescence, created from a drowning sailor and the living earth at the bottom of the river."

"The cauldron of coalescence," Miss Amelia said breathlessly. "*Our* cauldron of coalescence." She gave Robert a defiant look. "Pipes offered the shards to the

Guild of Goldsmiths in exchange for his life. No one dared to assemble it because the kings and queens hated Variegates. They vowed to execute anyone who even tried to make Variegates without a trial, and then pass their body to the surgeons for dissection."

The giant's head, Robert thought. *The cauldron of coalescence. Just as Mama Tems had told us.*

"But your father *is* assembling it," Robert said.

"My father fears no one," Miss Amelia replied. "Not even the king. He will soon be more powerful than all of them."

Robert took a step closer to the giant. The thick brown hair was long and streaked with white. The shadow of a scar crossed one of Myrr's cheeks. A long, thick moustache hid his mouth. His chin was covered by a heavy beard that flowed down the red velvet and across the platform. His eyes were closed. Robert wanted them to stay closed.

"He was a guardian of the Magogs," the sorceress said. "And perhaps of the cauldron too. His severed head was wrapped in a shroud inside a chest, with the shards of the cauldron and a sword of Roman making. It was found by Norman labourers building the Tower."

Robert didn't understand. If there were stories about giants on the Thames riverbed, surely there should be stories about a real giant's head in the Tower of London?

"Why doesn't everyone know about him?" Robert asked.

"Think about it, Robert," the sorceress said. "What do you think the Norman conquerors wanted?"

"I don't know," Robert said. "I wasn't born here."

"But you know about conquerors," the sorceress said. "How do they keep their power?"

Robert thought of the guns and cudgels and evil punishments used on his friends and family on the Hibberts' plantation. Even here in England he wasn't safe.

"Through fear," Robert said. "They keep people afraid."

The sorceress nodded. "The Normans wanted English people to believe that nothing was more powerful than their army. They wanted the English to stay afraid. Imagine what could have happened if Londoners had known that a giant's head had been found in the Thames? Maybe they'd believe that they were descended from giants and that they could fight the Normans after all. Or maybe they'd go hunting for giants to be their champions."

"Champions?" Miss Amelia nodded scornfully towards the giant, though Robert noticed that she kept her distance. "It's just a head! My father says that the

Elementals — earth giants, water spirits, Fumis, even Dragons — are inferior to us. Humans are and always will be the rulers."

"Aren't the Dragons powerful too?" Robert asked.

"The goldsmiths have taught Dragons their place." Miss Amelia gave him a sly look. "But with the cauldron, *all* the Elementals will know their place."

Although the Goldsmith had never hidden the fact that he despised the Elementals, Robert still shuddered at the confidence in her words.

"Why am *I* here?" Robert asked.

Miss Amelia jabbed her thumb in the direction of the giant. "Tell him to give me the last shard."

"Of the cauldron," the sorceress explained. "Mr Pipes destroyed the cauldron in this chamber."

"And my clever father has assembled it again," Miss Amelia said. "But there is a piece missing. That giant will know what became of it."

Robert's eyes were drawn back to the giant. "Why do you think it will talk to me?" He moved closer. "It's not a statue," he said.

"*He* is not a statue," the sorceress said. "But there are statues in this room that might talk to you."

Robert hadn't noticed two recesses set in the wall behind Myrr's head. Each contained a stone bird.

"They're crows," the sorceress said.

The statues were larger than the crows Robert had seen in the farmers' fields near Madam Blackwell's cottage. One was carved with its wings and legs tucked underneath its body, head curled to the side. It looked as if it was sleeping. The other statue's wings were outstretched as if about to land. Its beak held a dead mouse. The mouse was not carved – it was real.

"You think they'll talk to me?" Robert said.

"You must try, Robert." There was a hard edge to the sorceress's voice.

Their eyes met. *Why are you helping the Goldsmith?* he wanted to ask her.

"Do it," she replied, as if answering him. "Or they will hurt the people we love."

The people "we" love? Who can a sorceress that aids the Goldsmith truly love?

Robert walked towards Myrr. Even with his back to her, Robert felt Miss Amelia watching him closely. Was it the wavering candleless lanterns or had Myrr's stony skin twitched? Robert made himself keep walking.

"Hurry up!" Miss Amelia hissed. "My father will be waiting for us."

Robert stepped on to the platform and stood in front of the sleeping bird. It had not been sculpted with skill. It didn't fit together properly, as if the wings, body and head had been carved by different people and were for different-sized birds. There were few details of feathers – it looked like a misshapen crow covered in a smooth hide.

The other statue was the same. Although the mouse in its beak looked fresh, Robert couldn't smell decay.

"Will you speak to me?" he asked that stone bird quietly.

The beak snapped shut and the mouse disappeared. Robert jumped back. No one else moved. Hadn't they seen it?

"If you can hear me," Robert said, "tell us where to find the last shard of the cauldron."

There was a soft coo from the sleeping crow.

The sorceress whispered, "Keep trying, Robert."

Clouds of dust bloomed from both recesses. The crows seemed to ruffle their feathers, even though their bodies remained smooth stone. They were statues and living birds at the same time.

The crow that had swallowed the mouse cackled.

"You want the shard?" it said.

No! He didn't want it, not if it made the cauldron complete for the Goldsmith to use. But he had no choice but to ask them.

"Oh, tell him!" A rough sleepy voice came from the

other crow. "I don't care if he fixes the cauldron." The sleeping crow uncurled itself and stared at Robert with its hard stone eyes. "It doesn't make any difference to us."

"Make them answer you!" Miss Amelia insisted. "Stop wasting time."

Robert spun round to face her. "They *are* talking! Can't you hear them?"

Two faces looked back at him – Miss Amelia's furious, the sorceress's confused.

"If they are talking," the sorceress said, "only you can hear and see it."

"How can it be only me?" he asked.

"Earth magic," the sorceress replied. "It was in Mr Pipes and it's in you. Earth to earth, magic to magic."

Earth magic! Inside me! He wanted to laugh. He was just Robert! Sometimes magical things happened to him, but it was nothing that *he* could control.

Behind him, the crows squabbled about the cauldron shard. They were so loud, but clearly only Robert heard them! So … that meant that he could lie. He would say that the birds had no idea about the last shard. Miss Amelia might threaten him as much as she wanted, but if he held on and insisted that he didn't know – what could she do?

"Well?" Miss Amelia demanded.

"They don't know anything," Robert said.

Miss Amelia's eyes narrowed. "I don't believe you."

The sleeping crow rose from its perch and glided towards the platform. It settled next to the giant's head, stroking his right cheek with the tip of its wing. Its companion flew to the giant's other side, its wing brushing the giant's left cheek. The skin seemed less pale now.

"Remember the promise we made to Mr Pipes," said the crow on the right.

"And to Myrr," the other crow added.

"What promise?" Robert asked.

Both crows turned to face Robert, opening their beaks.

"We promised Mr Pipes not to help, not to hinder," they said together.

"But no one's entered this room for a long time," the first crow said.

Steps clopped on to the platform behind Robert. It was Miss Amelia, accompanied by the guards.

"Remember your little friend Garnet," she said. "Speak to this abomination and get that last shard, or else."

The crows cawed and rose up, towards Miss Amelia. She couldn't see them, but she looked about, as if sensing the air moving around her. A crow pecked her ear.

"What's happening?" Miss Amelia shrieked, clutching her ear. "Stop it, boy! Stop it!"

"I'm not doing anything," Robert protested.

"Yes, you are! You're using magic! I'll tell my father!"

She raced out of the room, flailing at the invisible crows. The guards hurried after her.

Robert turned to the sorceress. "It wasn't me," he said.

They stared at each other. Her face…

"Do what you must," she said. "Before the Goldsmith becomes impatient."

"So what? Why *should* I ask for the shard?" Robert demanded. "Won't it be used for terrible things?"

The sorceress gave him a quick, sad look and walked away. The door swung shut behind her.

Robert returned his attention to Myrr and the crows, which had settled next to the head.

"Rude, rude humans," one of the crows said.

The birds cawed, a sound like raucous laughter, louder and louder. A cloud of dust rose around them until there was nothing but dust and noise. Then silence again.

The dust cleared. The statues had cracked apart like eggs, the stone shells scattered across the platform. The crows were now glossy black, their feathers fluttering and twitching. One stood as if on tiptoe. It spread its wings, flapping hard, then folded them to its side. The other tucked its legs beneath its body.

They both stared at Robert, their dark eyes seeming to pin him in place.

"Myrr wants you to find the shard," the resting crow said. "We're all weary of this place and want to be free."

"Is it true that Myrr was the Magogs' guardian?" Robert asked.

"It is," the resting crow replied. "Though perhaps more a guardian of their cauldron. He was lazy, though, and fell asleep. The Romans found him. He fought hard but there were too many of them. He wasn't a very good warrior. He'd had no battle training."

"But he smashed the cauldron," the other crow said. "Before the Romans took it and worked out its power. They suspected the magic and willed Myrr to tell them. When he refused to answer, they cut off his head and threw his body in the river. They kept his head in a trunk with the shards, which they also threw into the Thames when they left England."

"And who are you?" Robert asked. "Did the Magogs make you too?"

"Most certainly not," said the resting crow, ruffling its feathers. "We were carved out of the finest marble for a lady's chamber, long ago. Then we were abandoned down here and forgotten. Only you see us as birds."

"Does Myrr talk?" Robert asked.

Neither crow replied.

Robert studied Myrr's face. He still believed that the giant was listening.

"Do you know where to find the last shard?" Robert asked him.

Silence.

"He will not break his promise to Pipes to protect the last shard," the standing crow said.

"But if you've come this far," said the other, "you can take it."

From where? Robert wanted to yell at them. Why couldn't they just tell him where it was? He made himself calm down. The sorceress had claimed that he held earth magic. He *had* opened the portcullis and the giant's chamber door too. Statues talked to him and no one else.

The crows' heads bobbed as if agreeing with his thoughts. He sat cross-legged next to Myrr.

"You know where the shard is but can't tell me," he said to the giant. "The crows can't help me but neither can they hinder me. It's like a riddle." He looked around the chamber slowly. "There's no hiding place that I can see. And if I have earth magic, shouldn't I be able to see it if other humans can't?" He jumped up. "But if I do find the shard, I'll be helping the Goldsmith turn children into rats... I'll say that I tried but it was nowhere to be found."

He strode towards the door. There was no handle on the inside. He shoved it hard with his shoulder, but it wouldn't budge.

"Open!" he yelled. "Open up!"

The door remained locked. He turned away.

"Now you are trapped," the crows said. "Like us."

Robert slumped down with his back against the door. To free himself, he had to take the cauldron shard to the Goldsmith. He had seen too much death on the plantation in Barbados. His mother had reassured him that the family would be together again in the next life. Would it be so terrible to die here, knowing that he had stopped the Goldsmith from completing the cauldron?

But ... how could he be sure that he *had* stopped him? The Goldsmith was determined to rule London by any means. He controlled Dragons who fought for him. If Robert died in here, that wouldn't change and the Goldsmith would find someone else to retrieve the shard for him. And what of Garnet and the other children? They might be punished harshly for Robert's disobedience.

He stood up, wincing. Every part of him ached. He walked over to the platform and stood in front of the giant. The crows fluffed out their wings and hopped, exactly in time with each other. They reminded Robert of the rich people's balls that he'd been forced to attend with Lady

Hibbert, him all dressed up to show off to her friends. The lords and ladies would twirl and hop on the ballroom floor while their servants waited for hours in the kitchen.

"I wish you could tell me where to find the shard," he said.

Robert lifted the red velvet draped around Myrr's neck and peered underneath. Wooden planks, no shard.

"Are you concealing it?" he asked the crows.

Their heads bobbed from left to right. Robert had to do what he had been trying hard to avoid. He had to touch the giant. He picked up one of the lanterns, then took a deep breath and gently ran his fingers through the giant's beard. He was sure that he could feel the giant's breath on him and the warmth from the giant's skin. Was Myrr alive? In a deep sleep?

"If you want to be free," Robert said to him, "tell me where to find the shard."

A strange grunting sound came from the giant's throat.

"Why can't you help me?" Robert said.

The giant grunted again.

Robert thought for a moment. "You can't help me, but you can't hinder me," he said. "Is that because you can't open your mouth? Why's that?" He could barely see the giant's lips beneath the thick beard. "What if you can't open your mouth because there's something hidden inside it?"

Myrr's cheeks pulsed as if he was trying hard to speak, but no sound came out.

"This must be Mr Pipes' final protection..." Robert mused. "He's hidden the shard in your mouth! And you've promised him not to open it. I have to find a way to get it out."

Robert sat down on the floor, staring at the giant. How on earth was he supposed to make him open his mouth? Pull on his beard? No! Robert imagined tufts of beard in his fingers while Myrr's mouth stayed firmly closed.

Robert sat upright. He'd forgotten something important about himself. His mind sometimes played tricks on him. It made him believe that he was still Robert Hibbert, born enslaved, sold like an object from person to person. But that *wasn't* who he was! He was Robert Strong, an apothecary's assistant.

How many times had customers come to the shop looking for a cure for their blocked noses? How many times had Mr Boussay prescribed medicine to make them sneeze? It was one of the first cures that Robert had been taught. And what did Robert have in the pocket of his waistband? He took out the package. It was the plaister he'd made for Godfrey the footman. Would this work on a giant? Could one big sneeze make the giant open his mouth?

He unwrapped the medicine. It had hardened in his pocket and smelled of nothing at all. He wrapped it back up and rubbed it between his palms as he himself had instructed customers to do. Gradually, it softened, and his eyes started to tingle, then water. He returned to Myrr.

"I'm going to give you some medicine," Robert said, trying to ignore his own tickling nose and itchy throat.

He held the plaister under Myrr's nose. Nothing happened. *Be patient*, he told himself. The giant had to breathe in the spicy fumes for it to work. Surely it would take longer with such big nostrils, even though Robert wasn't fully sure if Myrr was breathing at all.

Sometimes Mr Boussay would direct customers to place a dab of the medicine inside each nostril. If the customer was really suffering, they'd do it there and then, inside the shop. It worked. Every time.

Could it work this time?

Robert kneaded the paste to make it softer, then scooped out a lump with his finger.

"I'm so sorry about this," Robert said, before he thrust his finger up Myrr's nostril.

It was soft and warm and a bit damp. Robert quickly

wiped off the paste and, trying hard not to think about what he was doing, dabbed a second lump inside Myrr's other nostril. Robert stepped back and watched.

The crows started leaping and squawking, as if the ballroom musicians had sped up but couldn't keep time with each other. Then Myrr's nose twitched. There was a moment of stillness, then the giant roared. His mouth opened, revealing no teeth at all. Something flew out across the chamber, hitting the opposite wall with a sound like a bell cracking in two.

The room shook, making Myrr's head tip and sway. Robert staggered.

"Thank you!" Myrr shouted. "Free to return to my kin at last!"

His eyes flew open – they were clay-brown. His skin quivered as wind blew through the chamber like a furious Fumi. The crows were shrieking so loudly that Robert had to clamp his hands over his ears. Myrr's head bulged like a toad's eye, then shrank smaller and smaller until it was the same size as Robert's. The red velvet lifted and wrapped itself up around the head like a bag. The platform trembled, and suddenly the red velvet bag holding Myrr's head plummeted downwards, breaking through the platform.

The crows screamed once more – a strangely happy

sound. There was a splash and all was still again.

Robert took a few seconds to steady himself. He went over to the enormous hole in the middle of the platform and peered down to the water flowing beneath it. A flash of red bobbed on the current, then was swept away.

He walked over to the wall and picked up the shard. It looked like any fragment of old pottery that might wash up in the Room of Lost Things. But this is what would complete the weapon that would enable the Goldsmith to rule London.

"Open up this instance!" came Miss Amelia's muffled voice.

The door was shoved hard. The guards barged in, followed by Miss Amelia. The sorceress remained in the passageway.

"That's mine!" Miss Amelia said, snatching the shard out of Robert's hand. "I hope my father has the ledger by now. We certainly have children – and the ratcatcher has a fine few cages of rats. But best of all…" She gave Robert a sly smile. "We have you."

THE SECRET LABORATORY

The Goldsmith's carriage was waiting on Fleet Street. Clutching the ledger, Marisee had kept her eyes to the ground as she left the tunnels, trying to close her ears to Emma calling after her. Lady Walbrook's silence was even louder than Emma's shouting.

The Goldsmith opened the carriage door for her. It wasn't his expensive formal carriage with the coat of arms and footmen – it was small and dark, drawn by one horse. How could she step inside and be so close to this man who had always wished her family and Robert harm?

"I'll sit with the driver," she said.

"As you wish," the Goldsmith replied. He climbed into the carriage and closed the door.

Marisee was thankful that the journey was a short one as she almost jolted from the seat every time the carriage stopped and started in the busy traffic. The driver pointedly ignored her – he obviously didn't like company.

They headed east following the shape of the river, then north as they reached London Bridge. The carriage stopped by the Monument. The Mary-le-Bow Dragon's memories returned to Marisee. At the time of the Great Fire, there'd been a church here instead of this tall column crowned with golden flames.

"But it wasn't the baker," she said to herself. "It was the Dragons, ordered by Lord Gullinn."

And now here she was, riding a carriage with the Goldsmith, who intended to rule London and beyond. What was she doing? In her hands were the very instructions that would make him invincible.

But her mother...

Marisee would meet her mother for the first time! Her heart felt as if it had been sucked out from between her ribs and sent flying towards the sky. *Please, please don't let this be a trick.* Could she try and flee if the Goldsmith was lying? She thought of Emma, left standing in the Room of Lost Things, and Garnet being turned into a rat, and Robert who was risking his life by being taken prisoner in the Tower. Had she really betrayed them all?

Her heart tugged again. Her mother was close – she knew it. The Goldsmith was standing by the Monument, holding open a door. Gripping the ledger tight, Marisee climbed down from the coach and went inside.

Marisee had become so used to London not always being what it seemed, she had expected the inside of the Monument to be much bigger than it appeared on the outside. It wasn't. It was narrow and filled with a spiral staircase, all the way to the top. The Goldsmith pointed to an open hatch in the ground.

"Is it a tunnel?" she asked. Perhaps it connected to water tunnels and there'd be a way to reach Turnmill or other Chads.

"No," the Goldsmith said. "When Hooke and Wren designed the Monument, they wanted it to be a place of learning." He pointed upwards. "They made its column into one big telescope, pointing up to the stars, but the horses and carriages made the ground shake. Down here, we honour Sir Wren's spirit by continuing to use it to advance knowledge."

Marisee looked into the hatch. There were steps leading down. She couldn't see the room below, but it seemed well lit. The book under her arm, though, was filled with darker experiments.

"What knowledge?" she asked.

The Goldsmith started down the steps. "Do you wish to make your mother wait, Marisee?" he called back.

Her mother…

Would Marisee recognize her mother? Would her mother recognize *her*? If Mama had been living in London all this time, why had she never let Marisee know? Perhaps she didn't care about Marisee at all.

Had Marisee betrayed her friends for a mother who didn't care about her?

She followed the Goldsmith down twenty, thirty, fifty, sixty steps, until the staircase opened on to a room that *was* bigger than she'd expected.

It must spread out underground, far beyond the Monument, she thought.

Boxes and trunks were stacked against the walls. Benches were weighed down with beakers and flasks, racks of glass tubes, and boxes with names scribbled on the side. It was like Mr Boussay's back room. The air was heavy with a sharpness that pushed its way under her skin – something magical perhaps?

"It's a laboratory," Marisee gasped. "A secret laboratory."

A door at the far end of the room reminded Marisee of prison doors. Were there tunnels beyond it? Could she escape through them? Was that the door through which her mother would enter, or – she looked back the way she'd come – would her mother come down these stairs?

Marisee braced herself for the Goldsmith to seize the ledger, but instead he picked up a trunk and placed it on a bench. The key was already in the lock – he twisted it and threw open the lid. Marisee jumped back as a flash of heat hit her face, stinging her eyes.

The trunk rattled and rocked as a wave of orange, gold and black surged out, breaking on the laboratory floor. More bright specks followed, forming into columns like soldiers and scuttling around Marisee's feet like a magical rug. The columns twisted into each other until Marisee could no longer see specks – it was becoming one moving beast.

The Goldsmith opened a second trunk. More gold, more orange, more black, smouldering and spinning. And yet another trunk.

"So many Dragons," Marisee whispered.

The smell of rotting meat filled her nose, and her throat hurt from the heat. How come the Dragon at

St Mary-le-Bow didn't stink? Perhaps it was because the Goldsmith fed his Dragons on... The Dragon in the Lord Mayor's cellar had told them that the Goldsmith sometimes gave it humans. Marisee shuddered. She and Robert had almost been a Dragon's meal.

One by one, the Dragons coiled up the steps and through the hatch, claws scraping against the bricks. The Goldsmith watched, face tipped up.

"What are they doing?" Marisee asked.

The Goldsmith clapped loudly. The Dragons roared. Marisee clamped her hands over her ears as the walls and floor echoed their noise back at her. She wiped the sweat from her forehead. The heat, the rancid smell, the ... the waiting. She felt sick to her stomach.

"Where's my mother?" Her voice was smaller than she wanted. "You promised me."

The Goldsmith held his hand to his ear. Marisee heard it too. A *swoosh, swoosh, SWOOSH* followed by the *kraa, kraa, kraa* of ravens. A dark shape grew bigger and bigger – no, two shapes – cawing loudly as they swooped through the hatch. They settled on the bench, staring at Marisee with hard eyes, opening and closing their sharp curved beaks.

"Prepare yourself, Marisee," the Goldsmith said. "The grand reunion is moments away."

Only moments until Marisee saw her mother. *Where is she?*

The door at the far end of the room opened. Marisee's breath caught. She needed air. It must be her mother.

Her mother.

The first person who entered was a girl, slightly older than Marisee. She wore a luxurious embroidered dress and flourished a clay shard in front of her like a sword. She strode towards them.

"I have it, Papa! The missing piece," she said, holding it out.

"Well done, Amelia!" The Goldsmith smiled. "I would expect nothing less of my daughter."

Daughter? Yes, Marisee could see the resemblance in the coldness of their smiles.

Amelia noticed Marisee for the first time.

"And *you* have the ledger, Papa." She grinned.

Before Marisee could move, Amelia jumped forward and snatched the ledger from Marisee's grasp. She handed it to her father.

"I do now," the Goldsmith said. "Thank you."

Marisee stared down at her empty hands. "Mama isn't with you?" Her voice was even smaller. "Was it a trick?"

The Goldsmith shook his head. "Not at all." He lay

the ledger down on a bench, slowly turning the pages. He studied the page covered with drawings of the cauldron shards. The ink was still smeared across the top.

There were more footsteps. Was this her mother? Surely, it must be.

No! It was Robert. *Robert!*

He blinked when he saw Marisee, then quickly looked away. Her heart clenched. She didn't want him to look at her after the choice she'd made. But where was her mother? It was the only thought her head could hold.

A woman followed close behind Robert. Her shimmering gown flowed around her. Her long fingers were covered by midnight-blue gloves. Her head was completely bare. She wore no hat; she had no hair. But her face … her face was the face that Marisee had conjured from her imagination. It was Marisee's face and Grandma's face, but this face too.

The way Marisee's own heart tightened… The way her whole body wanted to dash from the spot where she stood, across to this woman… The way she wanted to reach out her hands and feel their fingertips touch… This woman could only be one person.

"Mama?" she whispered.

The woman's eyes widened. "Marisee? Is that really you?"

Robert looked from Marisee to the woman. His mouth fell open, then his face clouded with anger.

"You're Marisee's mother?" he said. "And you're helping the Goldsmith?"

"Yes!" the woman – Mama – snapped back. "Because I wanted to keep my child safe! She shouldn't be here!" She glared at the Goldsmith. "You promised! If I did what you said, she'd be safe. Let her go!"

The Goldsmith lifted another trunk on to the bench. "She's not a prisoner, Mistress Bee. Marisee, you came with me of your own free will, didn't you?"

Marisee nodded miserably. "He said if I gave him the ledger, I could meet you."

Robert gasped. "You gave the Goldsmith the ledger?"

Mama's fists clenched. "You broke your promise," she hissed at the Goldsmith. "You *did* hurt my child. You gave her an impossible choice."

Mama rushed towards Marisee and folded her in her arms. Her face brushed Marisee's hair.

"I've thought of you every single day," she whispered. "I should never have left you. I'm sorry."

Tears poured down Marisee's face. She was here, at last. Mama was here.

Suddenly, Mama was yanked away from her by a guard. Mama spun towards the guard, eyes full of fury.

The Goldsmith clapped his hands. Up above him, a Dragon roared.

"You haven't completed your duties, Mistress Bee," the Goldsmith said, unhooking the lid from the trunk. "I'm sure that having your daughter so close will encourage you to comply until the very end."

Mama glowered at him and said nothing.

The Goldsmith lifted a vessel from the trunk. Marisee recognized it from Mr Pipes' room in the Dragon's memory. She leaned forward to see it better. It didn't look magical. It was old and patched together from bits of broken pottery. There was a pointed piece missing.

"Amelia?" he said, holding out his hand.

Amelia handed her father the shard. It clicked into place. The cauldron hummed, like the sound after a bell has chimed, then silence. Amelia stared at it in wonder.

"The cauldron of coalescence," she said.

"Indeed." The Goldsmith spread open the ledger. "And we must wait no longer."

"You cannot continue with this!" Mama shouted. "The ideas are untested. It is just a theory from the necro-alchemists of old."

The Goldsmith looked up at her. "The necro-alchemists of old created Variegates without the cauldron.

This…" He flicked the cauldron. It hummed again. "This makes it quick. We do not waste our ingredients."

Mama shouted, "Children are not ingredients!"

"Yes, they are," the Goldsmith said.

The laboratory was starting to fill with people. Two guards entered, holding a glass box between them. It swirled with dark smoke that was spotted with bright colours. Marisee's eyes burned from the stink of burning coal and brewers' fumes, rushlights and cheap candles. It was a Fumi! Why was there a Fumi in a glass cage? More guards brought cages filled with rats, a stoat, a cockerel.

"Let me test my prize," the Goldsmith said.

He took the cage with the cockerel, unhooked the door and tipped the bird into the cauldron. The cauldron looked so small, but the cockerel disappeared. The Goldsmith snatched the cage of rats.

"Open it!" he ordered.

A guard unhooked the door at the top of the cage. The Goldsmith grabbed a rat by the scruff of its neck and dropped the squirming animal into the cauldron. Even the room's walls seemed to lean forward, waiting.

A faint crowing came from the depths of the vessel. Marisee remembered the Dragon's memory of looking down into the cauldron and not seeing its bottom.

A creature sprang out. It was feathered, with a beak,

a cockerel's comb and wattles. Its face was long and thin, like a rat's. It dropped to the bench on four legs, waving stumpy wings.

"Cage it!" the Goldsmith barked.

The guards were staring at it in horror. None moved.

"Perhaps we should place another rat in the cauldron," the Goldsmith said. "Followed by one of you guards."

A guard quickly dropped a pail over the poor animal. A second guard held an empty trunk at the edge of the bench. The first guard slid the pail along the bench, finally pushing the creature into the empty trunk. The lid was slammed shut. The guards were unable to hide the disgust on their faces.

"I think we are ready to proceed," the Goldsmith said coolly.

"No!" Mama protested. "You cannot do this!"

"I can, and I will," the Goldsmith said. "And *you* shall help me."

THE COALESCENCE

The sorceress was Marisee's mother!

Robert should have guessed that! The point of their chins, the rise of their cheekbones – they were the same! But why was Marisee's mother the Goldsmith's sorceress? And why was Marisee here at all? Had she come with a plan to help them escape? How could her plan be to give the Goldsmith the book that told him how to use the cauldron?

Guards brought in barrels that crackled with silvery sparks. They placed them next to Mistress Bee.

"Mama?" Marisee called to her. "What's happening?"

"You were not supposed to see this, Marisee," Mistress Bee said. "You were not supposed to know this. I wish you hadn't found me."

"You wish I hadn't found you?" Marisee's eyes were shiny with tears. "You said you thought of me every day!"

Part of Robert wished that Marisee hadn't found her mother either. Marisee had been longing for her mother all her life, only to find out that her mother lived in the same city – and was the Goldsmith's accomplice. Marisee and Robert had passed the Tower of London so many times. Had Mistress Bee ever glanced out of a window and seen her daughter? Or had she been too busy doing the Goldsmith's bidding?

"Everything is finally prepared," the Goldsmith said, looking up from Mr Pipes' ledger. "London's seams are bursting with wealth from around the globe, but year after year we have foolish Lord Mayors who rely upon the Master Goldsmiths for advice. This city needs strong leadership. It needs me."

Miss Amelia was nodding so hard Robert thought her head might fall off.

"And you *need* all the wealth and riches too," Mistress Bee said with disgust.

"No," the Goldsmith said. "I don't need it, but I want

it." He stroked the cauldron. "And nothing nor no one will stop me."

But Robert was supposed to stop him! He and Marisee! Had they failed London this time? He looked around the laboratory for a way out. His eyes met Marisee's. She seemed confused and sad.

"A rogue Chad spirit raised an army of Sleepers that set fire to our streets," the Goldsmith declaimed, as if he was addressing the Lord Mayor and Aldermen of the City of London. "A foreign Fumi air spirit stole our city's music and woke a monster. Every day, we are at the mercy of lawless Elemental spirits that we permit to exist, untamed, in our human world." He glanced at Mistress Bee. "We have been generous in allowing many of the ancient practices to remain. London would not be London without the Elementals. Do you agree, Mistress Bee?"

She nodded, but didn't look at him.

"I have permitted Madam Blackwell, the Well Keeper, to continue her tasks," the Goldsmith said. "And her descendants to remain…" A smile played about his lips. "To remain unharmed. And of course they *will* remain unharmed if they obey my rules."

He beckoned to a guard holding a small trunk. It was bound with a heavy chain secured by a padlock, and it shook as if something inside was trying to free itself. The reek of scorched rotten meat seeped from beneath the lid. Robert knew that smell from the Lord Mayor's cellar. It was Dragon stink.

"Lord Gullinn wished to use the cauldron to create ratling spies and other Variegates," the Goldsmith said. "As, of course, will I. But that is the lesser of its powers. The Guild of Goldsmiths knew of this cauldron centuries ago. They understood that the Elementals must be controlled. Their secrets lie within this ledger."

The guard dropped the trunk on to a bench, pleased to be rid of it. A different guard handed the Goldsmith heavy leather gloves, which he pulled on. He clapped. Two Dragons flew down through the hatch. They stretched their wings over the trunk, jaws gaping wide, bodies smouldering black and orange. Only the Goldsmith didn't jump away from their heat. The first guard gave the Goldsmith a key. The Goldsmith fitted it into the trunk's padlock. It clicked.

"Dragons, be ready," the Goldsmith ordered as he started to unwind the chain.

The trunk shook harder, casting off the last coil of chain. The lid was flung back so hard it hung on one hinge.

"Ugghh," Miss Amelia said, waving her hand in front of her nose.

The tiny beasts that formed this Dragon surged out

of the trunk and clustered together on the bench. Robert recognized the hint of a jaw, a claw, a wing.

"Now!" the Goldsmith commanded.

The two Dragons he'd summoned blasted a short, searing burst of flame across the bench. The tiny beasts scattered then reformed in an orange-and-black ribbon. The Goldsmith moved the cauldron to the edge of the bench. More fire erupted from the Dragons and the tiny creatures changed direction, darting into the cauldron. The mouth of the vessel seemed to swell, pulsing like a throat.

The Goldsmith clapped three times, slowly. Suddenly, one of the two summoned Dragons turned on the other, its jaws gnashing, claws tearing. It buried its teeth into the other's neck, a relentless grip as its victim writhed and screamed. The weaker Dragon fell apart, thousands of creatures skittering across the benches and floor.

"Guards, collect them," the Goldsmith instructed.

The guards wore leather gloves too. They scooped up the scuttling Dragon-creatures and dropped them into the hungry cauldron.

The Goldsmith checked the ledger.

"Two Dragons for fire should be sufficient," he said. "Of course, the necro-alchemists couldn't test their theories. If more Dragons are needed, more shall be added. But let us move on. Water next. Mistress Bee?"

Mistress Bee didn't move.

"Mistress Bee," the Goldsmith repeated. His voice was threaded with menace. "Follow my orders."

"I have followed your orders, Goldsmith," she said, voice shaking. "I tainted the water in the Tower's wells so it was healthy for humans but not for the spirits. They were weakened. They forgot who they were and that there is a world beyond the Tower of London. I made this easy for you."

"That was just the beginning," the Goldsmith said. "Now the real work must be done."

He snapped his fingers and a raven flew, shrieking, through the hatch into the laboratory. It swooped towards Marisee, landing on her shoulder, its wing batting her cheek. She cried out as it steadied itself. Mistress Bee ran towards her. The raven snapped its beak, its claws tightening on Marisee's shoulder. She gasped in pain.

Robert had to help her! But what could he do? He couldn't fight the Goldsmith and his guards, as well as the raven *and* the Dragon that was now crouching on a bench by the tunnel door. He needed to think of another way to stop the Goldsmith, but the inside of his head felt as murky as Fleet Ditch.

The Goldsmith tapped the cauldron. The ringing sound was duller this time. "I'm waiting."

Mistress Bee glared at him. "You promised not to hurt Marisee," she said.

"I've kept my promise so far," he replied, "but you are testing me."

Mistress Bee thumped her hamper down into the middle of a bench. The bottles clattered as it hit the wood.

"Careful…" the Goldsmith warned.

Mistress Bee ignored him. She pulled out a painted porcelain flask, her hands trembling as if it was a heavy weight. She carried it towards the cauldron. She sniffed – she was crying.

"Mama?" Marisee whispered. "What are you doing?"

Mistress Bee twisted out the cork and began to pour. The water fell in three misshapen bubbles, writhing, streaked with a fine silver web of lines. Each bubble hovered for a moment above the mouth of the cauldron, then dropped. The cauldron seemed to widen, as if eager to catch everything. Mistress Bee stepped away. Her hands still shook as she held the empty flask in front of her.

"Next—" the Goldsmith started.

"Wait!" Miss Amelia held up her hand. She was hunched over the ledger. "That's not enough. It says we need five river Elementals."

Mistress Bee upended her flask. "There are no more," she said.

"There are always more," the Goldsmith said. "You subdued the Tower's Chads. There must be a well in this room. Bend these Chads to my will."

Mistress Bee wiped her eyes. Her voice wobbled. "I won't."

"Yes, you will," the Goldsmith said.

"Please!" Mistress Bee sobbed. "My daughter doesn't need to know every wicked deed you make me perform."

"Find the well, Mistress Bee." The Goldsmith's words were heavy with menace.

Fury rose in Robert. His mother had taught him to hide his anger to remain safe. He slowed his breathing and tried to clear his head. It was hard, but he imagined the furious thoughts turning to smoke, then mist, then air.

"Move that bench aside," Mistress Bee said.

She spoke the words like a lady ordering a servant. The Goldsmith frowned at her tone but told the guards to do as she had instructed. When the guards had heaved the bench to one side, Mistress Bee bent down and touched the flagstones. She paused by one, her eyes closed.

"The well's under here," she said.

A guard brought over a metal bar and levered up the flagstone. Beneath it, Robert saw the gleam of water.

Mistress Bee gave the Goldsmith an imploring look. "I can't do this," she said. "I mustn't do this!"

The Goldsmith nodded at the raven on Marisee's shoulder. She cried out as the bird's claws dug deeper. Robert moved to help her as a second raven flew into the laboratory. Guards grabbed Robert and held him still as the raven landed. He flinched as the claws grasped for a grip on his shoulder. The ravens called to each other, heads back, cawing as if laughing.

Mistress Bee turned to Marisee. "I don't want you to see this. Please look away."

Marisee stared back at her mother. Robert knew that expression. It meant she was going to stand her ground.

"Marisee," he said gently. "I think you *should* look away."

She gave him a searching look, then turned her back on everybody.

Mistress Bee mouthed "Thank you" to him, then faced the well. "Sorry, Mama," she said, out loud this time. "Sorry, Marisee."

She took a pouch from her hamper, loosened the drawstring and emptied some grains of ashy powder into her palm. She dropped them into the well. A cloud of steam rose from it.

For a moment, Robert felt calm, as if nothing would ever trouble him again. The moment passed. Mistress Bee had taken a hook, a bobbin and a bowl-shaped net from her hamper. The bobbin was wound with a thick silver thread that sparked with magic. She used the hook to tease out threads from the bobbin and wrapped them round the spindle, twisting and twisting until she held a thick silver coil.

He was glad Marisee wasn't watching. *He* didn't want to watch, but every time he moved, even when he took a breath, the raven strengthened its grip on him. The sharp beak was so close to his face.

"I need someone to help me," Mistress Bee said.

"I will!" Miss Amelia said, too quickly and too happily.

"No, dear," the Goldsmith said. "We don't want any *accidents*, do we? Robert will do it. He must be curious to know our plan."

Robert didn't want to help Mistress Bee with her cruelty, but the Goldsmith was right. He had become curious. The raven hopped into the air, but hovered close to Robert's shoulder as he moved towards the well.

"Bring the cauldron closer," Mistress Bee said.

Miss Amelia glared at her. "Never forget that we're your superiors. Speak with respect."

She banged the cauldron down next to Mistress Bee and stepped away. Wisps of smoke rose from it, bringing that faint stink of scorched, rotten meat.

"Take this," Mistress Bee said, handing Robert the net.

"Why do you need the thread?" he asked. He was almost certain that he'd seen thread like that before.

"It came from Lady Walbrook a long time ago," Mistress Bee said. "Don't touch it. It can't kill you, but it *can* hurt you badly."

I know, Robert wanted to say. *Because Lady Walbrook wrapped threads round your daughter's wrists. There's so much that you don't know about her, and perhaps never will.*

"Be ready with the net," Mistress Bee ordered him.

Was he supposed to catch … a Chad?

Robert crouched down next to her. As he peered into the well, a face stared back at him, wide-eyed, mouth open as if it was shouting at him. He blinked and it was gone.

Robert's breath was coming too quickly, his heart beating hard. The net was shaking in his hand. Mistress Bee twisted her hook into the thread on her spindle, creating a loop. She used her thumb and finger to tighten the loop. The thread left two dark scars on her hand.

"Hurry, Mistress Bee," the Goldsmith called.

"There's little left of the moss," Mistress Bee said. "It will take longer to work."

"You know that I'm a man of limited patience," the Goldsmith replied.

Mistress Bee touched Robert's quivering arm, moving her mouth close to his ear.

"We must do this to keep Marisee safe," she said quietly. Then louder, "Remove a Chad, Robert."

Panic coursed through Robert. He looked from the well to the net to Mistress Bee.

"Robert?" Mistress Bee's eyes bored into his.

He nodded and dipped the net into the water. He drew it back out. It contained a Chad, sleepy and ghostlike. Mistress Bee wrapped Lady Walbrook's thread round it twice, three times. She lifted the limp Chad from the net and held it over the cauldron until Lady Walbrook's thread had dissolved it, the dull grey sand joining the defeated Dragon's. Again, the cauldron seemed to stretch its rim and pulse like a throat. Robert had to clench his fists to stop himself from snatching the bobbin out of Mistress Bee's hands.

Soon all that was left was slack, damp thread.

"Once more," the Goldsmith demanded.

Tears ran down Mistress Bee's face as she made another loop, wincing as she tightened it with her fingers. On her command, Robert scooped out another Chad. This water spirit was shaped like a stag – a weary, limp beast. The cauldron swallowed it.

"And next…" Miss Amelia read.

"Please let my child go, Lord Goldsmith," Mistress Bee pleaded. "I've done as requested."

The Goldsmith beckoned to the guards holding the caged Fumi.

"We have no guarantee of success, Mistress Bee," he said. "The necro-alchemists could not agree on an absolute formula. Perhaps we must try many times."

"No!" Mistress Bee cried. "This is pure cruelty!"

"Is it crueller than poisoning your Chads, Mistress Bee?" the Goldsmith asked.

They stared at each other. Suddenly, Mistress Bee kicked out at the cauldron, trying to tip it over. The guards were quick, seizing her and pulling her away. Far above them, a Dragon roared and its heat poured down the wall, making Robert's skin prickle.

"Take her to the Tower!" the Goldsmith commanded. "Lock her in the Menagerie!"

The guards dragged Mistress Bee from the chamber, Marisee's eyes following her all the way.

"I'm so sorry, Marisee," Mistress Bee called to her. "Tell my mother how sorry I am for everything."

And then she was gone. Marisee stared after her, swiping away tears.

"Next," the Goldsmith said, as if nothing had happened, "we have the air Elemental."

The guards brought the cage with the Fumi, holding it above the cauldron. Its face flitted from side to side, the petals of colour bursting and exploding. Was it shouting for help? Yes, because then it called out in London English.

"No! No! No! A favour for a favour! A favour for a favour! Help me! A favour for a favour!"

Robert had saved a Fumi before – could he do it again now? As if reading his mind, the raven swooped back to his shoulder. A panel slid open at the bottom of the cage. The Fumi's face pressed against the glass walls, its pole-like body twisting in despair. Then the cauldron swelled like cheeks about to whistle and narrowed again. The Fumi was pulled out of the cage and dropped deep into the cauldron.

"Just one more element," Miss Amelia said.

"Just one more indeed," the Goldsmith said.

Robert felt a sick churning deep in his stomach. "What are you creating?"

"You're a clever boy," the Goldsmith replied. "You must understand by now. Fire, water" – he counted off each element on his fingers – "air."

"Now earth," Miss Amelia said excitedly.

Robert looked around the laboratory. Was there a statue in one of those trunks? They were the Magogs' spies, so drew some magic from the earth. Or a shard beast – the fierce glass-quilled creatures that protected the sleeping giants?

Robert's gaze flicked from the cauldron to the empty Fumi cage, then to the well and to the small trunk that had once held a Dragon. So many Elementals destroyed because of the Goldsmith's greed.

"You find it so easy to murder these spirits," he said. "What can be worth this?"

"This is a cauldron of *coalescence*," the Goldsmith replied. "It melds the ingredients together and makes something new, something better. Nothing dies."

Something better? Like the feathered animal with a beak like a rooster and the face of a rat? Robert shuddered.

"The Chads were turned to dust," Robert said. "How can that make them better?"

"Because they will meld with other Elementals as I create the Variegate of all Variegates." The Goldsmith stroked the cauldron. "It will have the strength of a hundred earth giants and the fierceness of a weyr of Dragons. Every air spirit will obey its commands." He looked directly at Marisee. "And every Chad will succumb to my creation, or face fire, earth and air. It will be an Elemental warrior, hundreds of times more powerful than Lady Walbrook and her filthy rivers, or any Council of Fumi Elders or giant that rises from the river." His eyes shone. A smile flickered across his mouth. "It will lead an army of Variegates, Robert. Across London, across England, across the world."

Marisee leaped towards him. The raven flapped its wings, pushing her backwards. She drew herself up to stand taller so she could look the Goldsmith fully in the eye.

"We won't let you succeed," she said.

The Goldsmith peered into the cauldron. "Forgive me, Marisee. These discussions are wasting time. I must continue before my ingredients are degraded."

"The earth, Papa," Miss Amelia said, her eyes glistening. "You must add that now."

"The earth," the Goldsmith murmured. "A creature that has a connection to the stones of this very city."

Perhaps they have captured a shard beast, Robert thought.

"Something that contains earth magic deep inside," the Goldsmith continued. "What does it say in Pipes' ledger, Amelia?"

Miss Amelia ran her finger across the page. "We must have all four elements, Papa."

"The Elements are the simple part, Amelia," he replied. "But for me to command the Variegate, it must be bound to a human."

Her mouth moved, then she looked up. *"For humans to be bound to the Elementals, we must offer the cauldron a man as his soul departs. It will anchor him, body and heart, to the Elementals."*

"And how convenient if that person contains earth magic too," the Goldsmith said.

Robert saw Marisee's eyes widen in shock, her lips form a scream, the raven tangling itself around her to stop her running to him. He felt the sharp sudden pain in his side and saw the flash of the silver blade in the Goldsmith's hand. Then he was shoved hard. The cauldron's mouth widened, widened, widened – and he fell.

ROBERT, GONE

Marisee didn't care about the ravens shrieking and flapping or the Dragons writhing and burning or the guards that had grabbed her arms, pulling her backwards. She didn't care that her shoulders were screaming in pain. All she cared about was Robert. *Robert!* She had seen the sweep of the knife in the Goldsmith's hand, the splash of blood, and then her friend, her best friend, had been swallowed into the belly of the cauldron.

"Robert!" she wailed, but she was being dragged out of the chamber and through a tunnel. Her feet bumped against the uneven stone, her eyes stung with tears. This was her fault! It would never have happened if she hadn't given up Mr Pipes' ledger! But she'd wanted to see her mother so badly.

The Goldsmith *had* stayed true to his word. She had met her mother – a mother who helped him to imprison Chads, and then… Those poor water spirits, tossed into the cauldron. She blinked away her tears. More came. Mama had tried to resist the Goldsmith's demands. Marisee had seen the pain in her mother's eyes, but still – the Mama in her head and the Mama in real life were so different.

Marisee stopped struggling. It was like all the earth and brick above the basement was weighing down on her. She sank to the floor, and when a guard picked her up and flung her over his shoulder, she let it happen. She closed her eyes until she heard a door unlock and she was dumped on to a cold cell floor.

She lay there, crumpled. There was no point in opening her eyes. It didn't matter where she was. Robert was dead. She had made the wrong choice and lost everything.

THE ELEMENTAL WARRIOR

Robert fell – or was he floating? He opened his eyes. He could see nothing but sensed the darkness curving around him, holding him inside it. He felt as though he'd been stung by a giant hornet, the venom burning its way through him. Was this dying? What would he see next? He hoped … *please* … that it would be Zeke – that wherever he landed, his brother would be waiting for him.

As he passed through the emptiness, he tried to bring back any memory of Zeke: the slightest image of him, a scent of him, a few words of a story whispered into the humid night air. Nothing came. The tithe-master had truly taken everything.

Robert landed on his back. Beneath him was warm metal. Of course! He was in the cauldron! The Goldsmith had… He clutched his side. There'd been a dagger and intense pain, but now it just tingled and itched and even that was fading away.

How could this cauldron be big enough to hold him? Ah – he had seen how its mouth had widened to swallow the Elements. Water, fire, air and … him. He felt a tickle of air on his face. A wisp of silver light flared and faded in the distance. He frowned. Could it be in the distance, though, if he was inside a cauldron? As he sat up, glowing orange sparks skittered around his feet. He felt their heat.

And he was growing stronger. He sensed the earth magic coming alive. His very bones seemed to shake with it – and rather than shaking him apart, it was binding him together. He breathed in and his head filled with the smell of damp clay and rotting leaves. The trickle of air was now a breeze whipping around his head.

Was that the Fumi? *It must be.* Tiny petals of colour scattered in the breeze – Fumi words that Robert could never understand. It had seemed to be dead, but now it wasn't. Robert felt his body grow air-like, as if he too could fly. The wisps of silver light curled into each other, then tangled around Robert. His hands were glowing, his skin damp. The curls lengthened into ribbons that tightened, pulsing with life.

The orange sparks at his feet rose into a column, moulding themselves into a long neck, a head with a wide brow, then loosening into a gaping jaw. Robert should have been afraid. This was a Dragon. It moved closer and closer, until he was staring into the darkness of its throat.

But why should he be frightened, when earth magic was teeming through him? He could wave his hands and scatter the Dragon across the cauldron. He could arch his back and break the watery bonds. And he was still growing stronger.

The Elements engulfed him, lifting him, binding him in water, coating him with fire. Every breath he took prickled with Fumi magic. Robert stretched. His fingertips touched the sides of the cauldron. And the magic was strengthening.

Was this how it felt to be powerful? How would it feel to be the most powerful of all?

What if he'd possessed power like this when he was imprisoned on the plantation? He would have freed everyone! He wouldn't have needed to search for memories of his brother, because Zeke would still be alive. Zeke, their sisters, Mama, Robert – they would all be together.

The Elements swirled around him, inside him too – the spark beneath his skin, water magic like a current surging through him, and that lightness, as if his body held no weight. And all the languages were inside his head – the Fumis' own language and the languages of birds and even weathervanes. He knew every language that the Dragons had learned in the millennia they had crept through the cracks to listen and absorb. He knew the languages of brooks and secret underground rivers.

Robert's shoulders pressed against the inside of the cauldron. His neck bent upwards. His heel thumped against the metal as if trying to find a way out.

There had to be a way out. Robert's earth magic had found the final shard of the cauldron. What if his magic gave him the power to shatter it too?

He was in complete darkness again – the other Elementals were part of him now. He kicked against the cauldron. The chime echoed and hummed. He kicked harder. The Elements seemed to shift within him, as if trying to pull against him and each other.

Of course, they'd been separate for thousands of years. They had squabbled with one another, even battled in the past. But imagine if they had shared their power? *They* could have controlled London! Robert stayed perfectly still, trying to understand this new feeling.

"Quiet now," he said to himself. "This is the time for the Elementals to work together."

Because Robert hated the Goldsmith! It was people like him who owned the plantations and bought and sold people to work them. Now Robert was Elemental, he was much more powerful than the Goldsmith. He could destroy him and all the people like him. He tensed, then kicked and punched out at the same time. The cauldron rang.

Kick! Punch! Kick! Punch!

Lines of golden light spread across the cauldron.

Kick! Kick! Punch!

Robert balled his fist and, in the tiny, cramped space that the cauldron had become, drew back his arm … and thrust it forward with all the human and Elemental strength in his body. His knuckles struck the metal – and went right through. He kicked and punched and elbowed as the cauldron broke back into shards around him.

His anger was rising – and so was the anger of the Elementals within him. The Dragon's fire burned inside his stomach. Could he roar flames? He knew that he had a Dragon's strength. It was humming through his body. He could smell the water surrounding the Tower and the spirits still imprisoned. The Chads inside him were calling to those on the outside. He could leap into the air and soar! No one could hold him against his will ever again.

How could the Goldsmith give him all this power and think that Robert would ever obey him?

He stepped from the shattered cauldron. The first person he saw was the Goldsmith, smirking and satisfied.

"Welcome back, Robert," he said. He beckoned to a guard. "Place the shards in that trunk with the book."

Robert bent his knees, ready to fight. He would summon magic from the depths of the clay beneath the Monument's foundations to crack this laboratory in two. The Goldsmith would never contain him.

"You wish to test your strength," the Goldsmith said calmly. "But in case you were considering disobedience, I have brought a guest for you to meet."

The Goldsmith stepped aside – and there behind him, with his hands in cuffs, was a man. His face was creased with exhaustion and fury.

"I would like to introduce you to Elijah *Hibbert*," the Goldsmith said.

Elijah! The man who he and Marisee had set out to meet on a night that seemed so long ago now. Elijah, who'd survived the cruelty of Lord Hibbert's plantation and walked from Liverpool to London to spread the word about the terrors of enslavement. Elijah, who had now been captured by the Goldsmith.

Elijah lifted his head and looked at the Goldsmith. "My name is not Hibbert!" he said loudly. His eyes met Robert's. "You mustn't save me. Don't do his work."

Robert looked from the Goldsmith to Elijah. What should he do?

THE TOWER PRISON

"Marisee!"

Mama was shaking Marisee hard.

"Marisee!" Hands rocked her to and fro, but she wasn't going to move. She would lie here with her eyes closed, curled up until the earth opened and swallowed her the same way that the cauldron had swallowed Robert.

"He's dead." Marisee couldn't hold back a sob. "He was pushed into the cauldron and it's all my fault."

"Robert isn't dead," Mama said. "Did you see him die?"

Of course he must be dead! Marisee had watched

that blade plunge into Robert's side. She'd watched Robert fall. But, no, she hadn't seen him die. Marisee slowly uncurled herself and wiped her eyes on her sleeves. No, she definitely had not seen Robert die.

"Remember! It's a cauldron of coalescence," Mama insisted. "What exactly happened, my darling?"

That nasty Amelia had read from Mr Pipes' ledger.

Offer the cauldron a man as his soul departs... Anchor him, body and heart, to the Elementals...

As his soul departs, not afterwards. So Robert really might still be alive. And, yes, it was a cauldron of coalescence. She'd seen the terrible rat-rooster creature. Robert had been used as an *ingredient* for a spell, like the animals, except this time it was with Elemental spirits.

Marisee opened her eyes and stared into her mother's face. "Even if he isn't dead," she said, "what is he?"

"He..." Mama started, then fell silent. "Whatever he has become, he will be the Goldsmith's weapon."

"No, he won't," Marisee said, sitting up. "I know Robert. He'll refuse. And I'll help him."

But how? She didn't even know where she was. She'd been carried down a long corridor and up stairs into the Tower's grounds. Then she'd been thrown into this round room. Small windows set high in the wall let in enough light for her to see cages, all with their doors open. They were filled with blankets. Marisee frowned. Were there shapes beneath the blankets? Animals? Or was that a child's foot? And a hand?

Suddenly, Mama threw herself in front of Marisee.

"Don't hurt her!" she shouted.

A pair of red eyes flashed from the shadows across the room. And then another pair.

"We won't hurt her, but we will hurt *you*," a voice squealed. "You could have helped us! You refused!"

"What could I have done?" Mama cried. "I would have tried anything to help you if I had known how. You ... you were created so long ago."

"You could have told someone," a soft girl's voice said. "You could have rescued us!"

"I was a prisoner here too," Mama replied. She was crying now and Marisee's heart twisted. "I was locked in the basement every evening with the cannons and saltpetre! Who could I tell?"

There was the sound of feet scuffling on the stones, and the children – a boy and a girl – crept towards Mama. Both had narrow faces, noses widened into snouts, round dark eyes that flashed red. Whiskers sprouted from the girl's cheeks and a long tail peeped from the hem of her skirt. The boy held his hands clenched in front of him; Marisee flinched at his long, sharp nails. Marisee knew them straight away. They were the rat-children from Mr Pipes' office, still alive over a hundred years later. Still the same. Marisee was filled with anger and pity for them.

"You could have rescued us!" the boy hissed.

"You could have told someone!" the girl repeated.

Their lips drew back, revealing long teeth.

"You could have rescued us!" they said together.

Their rat smell hung heavy in the air.

"We have been here for so very long," the girl said. "We pleaded to be released."

"Pleaded," the boy echoed.

"Used for the Goldsmith's ill will," the girl continued. "After he found us living in the cellars."

"How did you become like this?" Marisee asked.

"It was Mr Pipes' cauldron," the rat-children said together again.

Marisee was now so full of anger and pity that she thought it might burst out of her. The Dragon's memories had shown Mr Pipes as a good man! Had he been cruel as well?

"I thought that he'd refused Lord Gullinn's demands!" she said. "But Mr Pipes created you?"

The rat-children looked at each other. The boy's snout twitched. He turned his back on Marisee, his thin tail curling down around his leg.

"In a way," the girl said. "But he didn't mean to." She turned to the boy. "Please, Tommy. Help me tell the story."

Tommy didn't move. The girl sighed.

"My name's Helen," she said. "Or it was. No one but Tommy calls me by my name any more. When I was first brought to the Tower, this place was the Menagerie, but the Goldsmith's moved the animals to some sheds in Marylebone Park now. Me and Tommy and the other children were locked in the cellars, near where they kept the gunpowder. One day, when the guards opened the door to bring in more children, me and Tommy bolted. The guards couldn't chase us straight away because they had to keep the other children in, so we ran down some stairs and along a passage. There was only one door, right at the end. Tommy!" she begged. "I don't want to tell this story by myself."

Tommy turned his back to them. He spoke quickly, tail twitching.

"The door wasn't locked," Tommy said. "We thought we were lucky. The room was dark, but then we realized there were lanterns that didn't have no candles in them. And there was a head… A giant's head." He spun round. "I don't care if you believe me," he hissed. "A giant's head. That's what I saw!"

"I've seen it too," Mama said quietly. "I believe you."

Tommy's eyes flashed red at her.

"There was a pot in the middle of the room," Helen said. "It didn't seem special, but I could hear something inside it. I looked but couldn't see nothing. The pot wasn't that big from the outside, but I couldn't see the bottom. It was like a deep, dark hole. Tommy said that it was the devil's work. Then the door rattled. Someone was coming in."

"The cauldron opened up," Tommy said, "like it wanted us inside it. So we jumped in. Even though I didn't think that my head would fit in there, let alone the rest of my body."

"And it was…" Helen bit her lip with her long, pointed teeth. "Inside, it was bigger than this room."

"And there was something else in there," Tommy said. "I've always slept in places alongside the rats. I know what they sound like. All scuttling and scratching."

"It started to get warm," Helen said. "I thought me and Tommy were going to get cooked! Then I was shaking like my bones were being shaken right out of my body."

"It was the pot shaking," Tommy said. "Then all of me was hurting, like I'd caught the plague sickness. I was hot and my skin was scratching on the inside."

"Then the tail came," Helen said. "I felt it pushing out of my back like I had a creature inside of me. Me and Tommy were trying to climb out of the pot, but we couldn't."

"How did you get out?" Marisee asked.

"The pot got tipped over," Tommy replied. "We thought we'd been found by the guards."

"But it was Mr Pipes?" Marisee asked.

Helen nodded. "He just stared at us. Then he started crying. Me and Tommy looked at each other…"

"And we saw that we'd been cursed," Tommy said bitterly.

"Did Mr Pipes try to help you?" Marisee asked.

"We climbed in and out of the pot again, but nothing happened," Tommy said. "He told us that there'd been others made before us – a bit human and a bit animal – but not in the cauldron like us. He said he was going to read everything he could about the others, to see if there was a way of changing us back. There was a cellar under one of the towers full of old books and scrolls. He said the old alchemists left them. He read everything and wrote it down in his ledger. The problem was that none of the alchemists had ever seen the cauldron, so they were just guessing too. He told us it was like a puzzle and he was going to find the answer for us."

"But he didn't," Marisee offered.

"Lord Gullinn found us," Helen said. "But it was lucky Gullinn didn't know about the cauldron, not at first. It looked like any old pot. Mr Pipes kept a baby octopus in it that he'd found near Billingsgate. But then, after he found us, Gullinn knew Mr Pipes really could make Variegates."

"If none of the other alchemists had seen the cauldron, how did Mr Pipes find it?" Marisee asked. "And fix it?"

Tommy answered. "It was in the room with the giant's head," he said. "He found the pieces in a trunk. When he touched the pieces, he said that he knew straight away what to do with them. He fixed the cauldron easy, but there was a piece missing."

"But…" Marisee said. "A giant's head! Didn't anyone know that there was a giant's head in a room beneath the Tower of London?"

"There's lots of rooms under the Tower that no one knows about," Helen said. "Me and Tommy used to explore them before we got caught by Gullinn's spies. Someone in the old times had built a screen across the room hiding the head, so no one saw it if they looked through the door. Mr Pipes said he always felt that he was being watched when he was in there and couldn't understand why until he broke down the screen."

"And he wasn't frightened?" Marisee asked.

"No," Helen said. "He was sure it meant him no harm. He'd talk to it like he'd talk to his baby octopus. One day, the giant wanted to talk back. It opened its mouth and the missing piece of the cauldron fell out. It had been hidden in there all the time."

"It had happened that very same day," Tommy said. "A few hours before me and Helen escaped."

Mr Pipes *had* created the rat-children by accident. Marisee was pleased that she hadn't been wrong about him. "Then he gave the Guild of Goldsmiths the pieces of the cauldron in exchange for his life," she said.

"No one could put it together," Helen said. "Mr Pipes had a kind of magic that made it easy for him. One year, the Guild had a competition. They promised a bar of gold for anyone that could fix it. There was a woman who'd just came out of Coldbath Gaol. She put it together but there was a piece missing. They didn't give her the prize neither."

"So they were just waiting for the last piece," Marisee said. "Mr Pipes must have hidden it."

"I don't know why you're asking us," Tommy said. He stabbed a thin finger at Mama. "*She* knows everything. She saw how the Goldsmith made us trap more children and she didn't do nothing at all."

"Have you ever tried to escape from here?" Marisee asked quickly.

Tommy crouched down on his haunches, his red eyes boring into Mama.

"Sorceress!" Tommy's sharp face screwed up in fury. "You enchanted them water spirits to keep them tame! You could have made them carry a message outside. You could have done something!"

Tears poured down Mama's face. "The guards watched me every single moment," she said. "The Goldsmith threatened to hurt Marisee and my mother if I didn't obey him."

"There was no one to stop him hurting children like us," Helen said quietly.

There was movement in the cages, blankets being thrown aside, heads and bodies emerging. Marisee stared into the gloom. Were any of these children Garnet? Was she here?

The children were muttering.

"Who's going to stop them hurting us too?"

"I don't want to be a rat!"

Two small girls were huddled together in the back of a cage, clutching each other.

"If you'd have helped us, Sorceress," Tommy said, "these little ones wouldn't be here! It's your fault!"

Tommy sprang, thudding into Mama's chest.

"No, Tommy!" Helen yelled, but she wasn't quick enough to stop him.

"Mama!" Marisee screamed, running over to her.

Mama was sprawled on the floor. Tommy was crouched by her, teeth bared, eyes flashing. He lowered his head towards Mama's neck.

"One bite from me could end your life," he snarled. "Why shouldn't I do that?"

Mama was looking straight into Tommy's eyes.

"You're right," she said. "I deserve punishment for everything I've done at the Goldsmith's bidding. But I've already been punished by the years I've spent apart from my daughter. I left London when she was too young to remember me. And now ... now we are strangers." Her gaze shifted to Marisee. "But my child has a stronger heart than me. She *will* help you escape from here. And if you spare me, I will do everything I can to help her."

Me? Marisee thought. *Can I help them to escape?* It seemed so hopeless! They were locked in a room in the strongest fortress in London!

But she had helped to save London twice before. Could she and Mama save the children *and* London again? Yes! They could try! They *would* try!

As Marisee opened her mouth to speak, Tommy

squealed and lunged forward again. Mama rolled to the side just as Helen grabbed Tommy around the waist. Marisee threw herself between the rat-boy and Mama.

Marisee crossed her arms. "If you want to reach Mama, you'll have to pass me first!"

"No, my darling," Mama said from behind her. "It isn't your duty to protect me."

Mama might have done wrong things, but Marisee had given the ledger to the Goldsmith. That had proved the true power of the cauldron. She and Mama had to make things right together.

"It's our duty to protect each other," Marisee said. "And we must protect the children who have no one else," she finished.

"*Can* you help us?" The two girls had emerged from the back of the cage. The older one wiped her face with a dirty sleeve. "Can you stop us being turned into rats?"

"Yes," Marisee said. "We will."

Tommy was scowling in the shadows by the door. "Just the two of you? How?"

Marisee drew herself up to her full height. "I am the daughter and granddaughter of Well Keepers. My grandmother will come for us and she will not be alone."

She pushed back her doubt. How would Grandma know where she was?

Tommy slowly turned around, staring at the walls, the floor, the ceiling.

"Can you see any wells in here?" he sneered. "How will they get in? Unless your grandmother can squeeze through the window like a—"

"Like a rat," Helen said. "Like us."

"And no one's dropped your grandma in the cauldron, have they?" Tommy added.

Marisee glared at him. But … rats. An idea was sparking.

"You could waste your time mocking me," Marisee said, "or you can help us save London."

THE SUMMONING

The Goldsmith circled Robert and stopped close to him, his mouth by Robert's ear.

"So, we understand each other, don't we?" he murmured. "Do what I tell you and I will instruct Lord Hibbert to free Elijah. Perhaps Elijah has word of your mother and sisters. Don't you wish to hear it?"

Robert's sisters. What did they look like now? It had been more than three years since he'd seen them. They would have grown, would look so different. His memories of them used to shine brightly. His mother... He longed to take her hand in both of his, let their foreheads touch together like they had when he was a small child.

Elijah staggered.

"He's tired," Robert said. "Let him rest."

"Your will is my command," the Goldsmith answered. "Take him to the Bloody Tower."

"No!" Robert shouted. Elemental magic flared inside him, pressing beneath his skin. The room blurred and sweat slicked his forehead.

"The Bloody Tower was deemed suitable for Queen Elizabeth," the Goldsmith said. "I'm sure it will serve Elijah Hibbert until you have fulfilled my commands."

"Refuse him!" Elijah yelled as the guards dragged him away. "Don't fear for me. Follow your conscience, Robert. Do what you must do to save everyone else."

As Elijah's footsteps faded, Robert turned to the Goldsmith. "What do you want?"

No "sir", or "Master Goldsmith". He would have been punished severely for such blatant disrespect in the past, but now he didn't care. The Goldsmith's eyes flashed in anger, but he needed Robert. It was like they were playing some terrible game.

"I want you to summon a Fumi," the Goldsmith ordered.

Summon a Fumi?

"Prove your strength, Robert."

Robert laughed. How was he supposed to do that? He had never in his life been allowed to summon anyone, not even a scullery maid at Lord Hibbert's! Except ... he wasn't that Robert any more! He was Robert engulfed in Elemental magic. He was the heat of a raging fire. He was as light as the breeze, but held the power of a storm-laden wind. The streams bubbled within him, but the heaviness of the earth magic kept him tethered to the ground.

Robert squeezed his eyes shut, trying to nudge the thoughts of his mother and sisters into a different part of his head. *Could* he do it? Could he summon Fumis? Would that be so bad? The Fumi Elders had treated his friend, the Squall, very badly – and hadn't the Fumis forced him to find London's lost music last year? He could have been killed and the Fumis wouldn't have cared. The Fumis liked to lure you into owing them favours – they'd threatened to give Robert to the capture-creature if he didn't help them.

But what if he, Robert, could control *them* now? He stood perfectly still, feeling for the Elements inside him. He imagined hands sweeping aside the water and quelling the fire. The air magic was spinning, faster and faster. He stumbled, but the earth magic kept him rooted.

The air whirled, a typhoon of magic, but it wasn't enough. He needed more magic.

The magic swept through him. And the Fumi came. Dark, pungent smoke streaking down from the top of the Monument, scattering word-petals. The hatch above went hazy, as if the Fumi was bracing itself to halt its journey through. The air magic whirled so hard that Robert was sure his heart and everything else inside him was spinning too. At last, the Fumi was sucked down into the laboratory.

"Fire!" the Goldsmith shrieked.

The Dragon magic roared out from Robert before he could think. There were no flames – or Robert couldn't see them – but the heat came from within him and beyond. It enclosed the Fumi like a shroud. The Fumi thinned and disappeared, a few pale words fluttering around it.

Robert sagged. All the magic spluttered out, though he still felt it tingling through him. He had … he had killed a Fumi. He had to take big breaths to calm the sickness in his stomach.

The Goldsmith was clapping his hands.

"Excellent," he said. "Excellent. Those interfering airheads will think twice about whispering rumours into the wind again." His grin was so wide it reminded Robert of the bottom of the cauldron. "They'll think twice about disobeying me in any way at all. So, now I want you to—"

His words were interrupted as a cloud of ash dropped from above, as if it had been tipped from a bucket.

"What is this?" the Goldsmith said angrily, wiping his clothes.

Robert studied the pile of ash. It was moving across the floor – flecks of it scuttling in circles, glowing for a moment, then fading.

"One of your Dragons," Robert said. "When the fire came to me, I felt it drawing from a power outside me and it ... it killed a Dragon."

Is this what Robert had become? The Goldsmith's own Variegate assassin? How could he have ever thought that this power could be a good thing?

The Goldsmith nudged the ash with his foot. "You killed a Dragon?" he said. "Even more excellent!" He rubbed his hands together. "You can summon a Fumi and you can kill a Dragon. I want you to summon another Dragon *and* kill it."

Robert stared at the Goldsmith. "The Dragons are yours. Why deliberately kill one?"

"Not all are mine," the Goldsmith said. "Summon the Dragon from Mary-le-Bow Church!"

No! Not that Dragon! He didn't want to kill any Dragon, but this was worse. It would be like hurting Henry or the Squall – the biggest betrayal.

"Oh, Robert," the Goldsmith said. "You're not thinking of disobeying me, are you? Is there a choice to make? A mere Dragon or Elijah Hibbert – a human like you? A man with tales to tell of people you love."

The Mary-le-Bow Dragon wasn't a mere Dragon! She was the one who'd noticed that children were being taken. She was a lookout for London. She was his friend.

But *his mother and sisters...* With no memory of his brother, how could he let his mother and sisters fade too? Elijah would tell Robert everything he needed to hear. Was this really a choice?

He closed his eyes again, trying to steady his thoughts. Elijah or the Dragon? Elijah or the Dragon?

The fire magic scuttled and glowed beneath his skin. His head filled with a muddle of the Dragon's memories. The Thames – wide, bright and rushing through marshes scattered with a few houses. Men in tunics digging foundations and unloading blocks of stones from carts. A Fumi – rising, its smokiness almost transparent, before factories' stinking fumes filled the sky and tainted the air.

The fire magic throbbed its way through him, fiery flecks reaching for each other, trying to take a shape. It wasn't enough. Elemental magic was hungry magic. It fed from the magic within him but needed the Elemental power in the world outside too. The fire magic was calling, calling... And an answer came.

"No..." Robert moaned. He'd tried not to think about the Mary-le-Bow Dragon. Maybe another Dragon would come instead, but a ribbon of gold and black was already curling down from the top of the Monument, thinning and thickening as if it was trying to pull against itself.

It was too late. She was coming.

"Continue, Robert!" the Goldsmith urged. "Continue!"

Robert couldn't stop even though he wanted to. His fire drew the Dragon closer and closer, until the ribbon knotted into clusters that spread into one another, finally taking the shape that Robert knew. Her body filled the room, tilting upwards, tail poking out through the hatch.

"Is that all of it?" the Goldsmith asked.

The fire inside Robert had quelled. He nodded miserably.

"Now kill it!" the Goldsmith ordered.

Robert stepped back, shaking his head.

"Yes, you will," the Goldsmith said quietly. "Or Elijah dies. And perhaps not only Elijah. Madam Blackwell, her daughter, her granddaughter... I decide who lives and who dies, Robert. You cannot and you *will not* refuse me."

AMBUSH

Marisee and Mama stood on one side of the old Menagerie, Helen and Tommy on the other. The captured children were watching closely.

"How small can you become?" Marisee asked the rat-children.

"We don't want to be rats," Tommy said. "I'm not going to do it."

"It's the only way we can stop the Goldsmith," Marisee said patiently.

Tommy folded his arms. "I won't."

"Then you're condemning all these children to become rats too," Mama said.

"*You* can't tell us what to do!" Tommy countered.

Mama bristled. "I'm not telling you what to do. I'm telling you what will happen if you don't help Marisee."

Mama and Tommy glared at each other.

"I'll do it," Helen said.

Her voice came from higher up. The meagre daylight fell through three narrow slits in the stonework. She had already climbed on to a narrow ledge below the window. Marisee felt a quiver of excitement. The children were whispering too, clutching one another as they craned their necks up to watch her.

"Please come down," Tommy said. "You'll hurt yourself."

"Rats climb buildings," Helen explained. "It's … it's part of us now. We can do a good thing, Tommy. Help me. We can rescue these children. They don't have to be like us."

Tommy hunched down into himself. "And who will rescue us?" he asked.

"But you'll be free too!" Marisee said. "You won't have to do anyone's bidding ever again."

Mama lay her arm on Marisee's shoulder. "They will be free from this place, but the world outside isn't always a kind one."

"But they could find somewhere and—"

"And hide all our lives?" Tommy interrupted. "How's that different from here?"

"If you could be free of this place, what would you want?" Mama asked gently.

"I want to be me again," Tommy said. "Somewhere no one can hurt me."

Marisee thought she saw the glint of a tear, but he turned away from her quickly. Mama felt for Marisee's hand and held it tight. Mama's love warmed her in this cold, gloomy room. Tommy and Helen had never had that love. Who knew if the cauldron could turn them back into children? And if it could, they were so old… Would they be the age they were when they were taken, or their age now? If they were children, perhaps they could live with Marisee, Mama and Grandma.

"Where did you used to live?" Mama asked.

Tommy shrugged. "I was born in a house of correction and I got passed around my aunties until there was no one who wanted me. I lived down by Deptford for a while, searching the foreshore for coins. I liked it there."

"You were a mudlark?" Mama said.

"The guards are changing watch!" Helen called down. "If we're going to escape, we'd better do it now. Are you coming, Tommy?"

Tommy looked up at her and away. The child in the cage next to Marisee started crying.

Mama kneeled down beside Tommy. "If we fight the Goldsmith and win, I know that there's one place where you can be safe," she said.

She whispered in his ear. He looked at her, nodded, then sprang towards the wall. Marisee longed to ask what Mama had said. She shouldn't – mustn't – feel jealous that Mama had shared a secret with Tommy but not with her.

Tommy tapped the wall with a long nail, then rested his head against it, nose and tail twitching. Then suddenly he was climbing. He was barefoot and his toenails were as long and pointed as his fingernails. Soon, he was on the ledge next to Helen, tail arcing out to his shoulders.

Some of the children cheered, but could Helen and Tommy really squeeze through the window slits? The early necro-alchemists had wanted the unique abilities of the animals to be part of the Variegates – the things the animals could do that humans could not. And she'd seen it herself in Mr Pipes' ledger.

Rats have great flexibility of body. Squeeze through small spaces. Will make excellent spies.

They could fit an arm through the window and possibly a leg, but a torso? A head?

"I don't think they can do it," Marisee said.

"They will," Mama said with certainty. "Find the wells!" she called up to them. "Pull the magic binding away from the surface. Use your claws. Do it quickly. Swim through the tunnel and remove the binding from the other side. And try not to swallow too much water in case the sphagnum makes you sleepy."

And then the way will be free for Grandma to come, Marisee thought. *Because she will definitely come, with Turnmill and the Fleet Ditch Boar by her side.*

"We have to dive into a well?" Helen shouted back. "Won't we drown?"

"Rats can swim underwater," Mama said. "And the Chads should move the water aside when they know you're there to help them. Tell them…" She closed her eyes for a moment and took a deep breath. "Tell them that they'll be free from the sorceress's power. Tell them that you're seeking revenge for the Chads who were ill-treated by the Goldsmith."

Marisee squeezed Mama's hand.

It was approaching twilight. Helen and Tommy touched heads. First, they threaded an arm through the window slits, then a leg. Slowly and carefully, they folded their bodies like a blanket, and squeezed through the gaps, out into the evening beyond.

"They did it!" the children whispered. "We're going to be rescued! We're going to be rescued!"

Mama slumped back against a wall. "Now we wait," she said.

The shadows darkened. Church bells rang out another hour. The children whispered and cried. Mama moved among them, comforting them. Marisee knew she should help, but her mind wouldn't be still. She sat, leaning against the door, clutching her knees. How could she stay here doing nothing? What if Tommy and Helen had been caught? What if she and Mama and all the children were locked in here forever? Or, worse, used in terrible experiments in the cauldron?

And Robert! She had to find Robert!

The door was thumped hard on the other side, jolting Marisee's back. A hatch above her opened a tiny crack.

"Move if you want your food!" the guard shouted.

Marisee shuffled away from the door. It opened wide enough for the guard to throw in a bag of bread and bruised apples, before banging shut again.

Mama reached into the bag and held out an apple.

Marisee shook her head. "I'm not hungry."

"You'll need strength for when we escape," Mama said.

Marisee lowered her voice so the children wouldn't hear. "What if we don't escape?"

Mama sat down next to her. Marisee shuffled closer so their shoulders touched.

"We must have hope," said Mama. "I hoped every day that I would see you again, and at last here you are!" She squeezed Marisee's shoulders.

Marisee pulled away. "Why did you leave me? *I'd* almost given up hope. What was more important than me?"

Mama sighed. "London's rivers were becoming dirtier and dirtier. The Chads were getting sick too. I'd heard a sailor from Berbera talk about a plant that could keep water pure. I was so sure that it could help us. I persuaded Mama to let me sail with that ship, back to Berbera."

Marisee knew how hard it would have been for Grandma to agree to Mama sailing away. She must have regretted it every day afterwards. Sea journeys were always dangerous – there were storms and pirates, and some sailors swore that they'd seen sea monsters.

"Your grandma was furious at my plan," Mama said, reaching for Marisee again. Marisee let herself be reached for. "It was even worse, because I wanted you with me."

Marisee's eyes widened. "You were going to take me with you?"

Mama smiled. "Your grandma strictly forbade it. She would have locked me in a well for all time rather than let me take you with me. So I left alone. It was so difficult to leave you. But I believed it was better I went while you were so young and could barely remember me than when you were older."

Marisee thought hard. Could she remember the day of their last goodbye? No, but Grandma must. How would she have felt, waving her only child farewell on the dock? Perhaps taking care of Marisee eased the pain. Marisee wished Grandma was here now, so she, Mama and Marisee could be together again.

"What happened next?" she asked. *Because you never came back to me.*

"The luck of the Blackwells must have been with us," Mama said. "We sailed for almost ten months. We weathered the storms and saw no monsters at all. I had carried well water with me to tend the sailors' eye sickness, so they treated me well. We safely landed in Berbera, where we were due to remain for a week. The sailors were trading with local people. I went into the hills to search for the sphagnum weed. And goodness, Marisee!" Mama's smile made Marisee smile too. "I thought it would be hard to find, but it was everywhere! I gathered it and dried it, even though local people warned against it. The captain promised me free passage back to London if I gave him some for the ship's water."

"What happened when you returned to London?" Marisee asked. *London.* Mama had been so close all this time.

"When we docked in Deptford," Mama said, "the Goldsmith's guards seized me and brought me to the Tower. He threatened to harm you and my mother if I didn't do his bidding." Mama pulled Marisee closer. "So I did as I was told, hoping that you were both safe."

We weren't, Marisee wanted to shout. *He broke his word!* But that wouldn't help them now.

"The Goldsmith has the cauldron," she said instead. "No one is safe. I can't just sit here waiting. I have to go and help Robert."

"No," Mama said straight away.

Marisee folded her arms. "Yes," she said.

"No!"

Some of the children were looking at them, alarmed. Marisee and Mama stared at each other. Marisee's heart was bouncing like she was being chased.

At last, Mama said, "You'll go no matter what I say, won't you?"

Marisee nodded.

"Then I'll come with you," Mama said.

Marisee imagined it. She and Mama sweeping through the Tower of London together, rescuing Robert and saving London from the Goldsmith's cruel rule! But ... an idea was unfurling in Marisee's head. Her best chance of getting out of here was if she was alone.

She jumped up, took a deep breath and shrieked as loud as she could.

"The ratlings have bitten the children!" she screamed. "And now they're trying to escape!"

Would it work? Would it work?

"Marisee, what are you...?" Mama was shocked and confused. Marisee's heart hurt to do this, but time was running out. The children were staring at her, as confused as Mama.

"I need you to scream," she whispered to them. "Please! Make as much noise as you can. I want the guards to open the door again."

Mama grabbed Marisee's arm. "You cannot do this alone," she insisted.

"And the children can't be left alone," Marisee said. "They're frightened." She lowered her voice. "Imagine what will happen if Tommy and Helen are caught. The Goldsmith's punishment will be harsh. Stay and protect them."

Mama gripped Marisee's arm tighter, then let it go. She gave Marisee a nod, then threw back her head and shrieked.

"The ratlings have gone wild! Stop! Let go!" The last word ended in a scream.

The children looked at one another, then joined in, shouting and screaming. The door was flung open. Two guards ran in – one waving a club, the other with a flintlock.

"Stand back!" the second guard yelled, pointing his gun around the room. "Where are the ratlings?"

"They're in that cage!" Mama said, pointing to a high shelf. "I think there's a wounded child in there too!"

Mama gave Marisee a tiny nod.

Marisee slipped out of the door. She took a breath, glanced behind her and made herself walk steadily away, when she just wanted to run. She kept her head down, trying not to look like she was lost, though all she could see was a maze of walkways and towers. No one was following her – yet. She was free, but wouldn't be free for long if she acted like a fugitive.

"You!" a man's voice called out.

He strode out from a path that led to a square of dark grass. He was tall and barrel-shaped, wearing a red tunic and flat dark hat. His hand rested on the sword by his side.

"What are you doing here?" he demanded. "Lord Goldsmith ordered everyone to stay in their quarters!"

"I…" She should have had her excuses ready! "I…"

Could she outrun him? No, he had somehow moved so that she was between him and the wall behind. If she tried to dodge past, his sword would also be quick to move. He bent down to study her face closely. She turned to hide it from him, but he grabbed her shoulder and spun her round.

"You're that girl the Goldsmith locked up!" he said. A nasty grin crossed his face. "He said you were to stay locked up." He grasped her shoulder so tightly that it hurt. "Return to your prison or else!" He drew his sword.

No! She wouldn't return to the Menagerie, but she couldn't die here! The Goldsmith mustn't win! Something flickered beyond the guard's shoulder.

"Return to the prison or say your last words," the guard demanded.

Marisee placed her hands on her hips. "I am not returning to that prison!" she said.

His grin widened. His teeth reminded Marisee of the Fleet Ditch Boar's. "As you wish."

The sword swung back and Marisee threw herself sideways, just as the Fleet Ditch Boar himself leaped through the air, smacking the guard into the wall.

ROBERT STRONG, DRAGON-SLAYER

Robert's head throbbed. The Dragon magic had scorched through him. It felt as if his blood was on fire. He was going to betray the Mary-le-Bow Dragon in the worst way.

"I don't want to hurt you," he said to her. "But Elijah…"

"Look at me, Robert," the Dragon said.

The floor, the wall, even the Goldsmith's feet – Robert would rather look anywhere else than at the Dragon. But if he was going to end this Dragon's – this friend's – life, then the least he could do was meet her last request. He lifted his head and stared at her. Her shining eyes were flecked with gold. As Robert stared, the gold flecks stirred and the Dragon magic inside him swirled too, as if in answer.

Between the swirls he felt the Dragon's dream-like memories – the rage of the Great Fire, the stone masons and artisans bringing London back to life, the Monument slowly rising in the sky. The memories swirled, faded and, just for a moment, he saw someone he knew. He was watching her from high up, as if perched on a steeple. She was standing in an open doorway on a dark street of derelict houses.

Wait! He knew that house! It was the one near Fleet Street. The steps led down from its cellar, through to the Chads' tunnels. Why was Emma there? And she wasn't alone! On one side of her was the Fleet Ditch Boar, and on the other, Sally Fleet. Were they … were they coming for him?

"Having second thoughts, Robert?" The Goldsmith's voice oozed like ditch mud. "That would be unwise."

"No," Robert said as the Dragon's memory faded in his head. Had he really seen Emma with the two water spirits? Could he delay until they arrived? "It will take all my strength to … to kill a Dragon of that size. She'll do her best to fight back. I have to prepare properly because I'll only have one chance."

The Goldsmith clapped in impatience. "Stop making excuses, Robert! We have much to do today."

"Do what you must, Robert," the Dragon said, closing her eyes. "I'm old and tired. The Goldsmith has won. I could never bow to him. I won't resist you."

"Robert…" the Goldsmith urged, his voice edged with menace. "Kill it now."

Robert took a deep breath. The Dragon had shown him Emma with the Ditch Boar and Sally Fleet. Had she gone to them for help? If they didn't arrive in the next few minutes, it would be too late. He'd have to make a choice between the Dragon's death or Elijah's. Robert didn't even know how to kill a Dragon! The first time had been an accident.

What did he actually know about his new powers? He knew that his fire magic had summoned this Dragon to him, but it hadn't killed her. It had been the combination of air magic and fire magic that had turned the other Dragon to ash.

"You have another Dragon above us," Robert said to the Goldsmith. "Perhaps they should leave, in case…" He glanced down at the pile of ash.

"Agreed," the Goldsmith said. "Go!" he called to the Dragon above. "But stay close."

Robert imagined the departing Dragon splitting into streams of black and smouldering orange, scurrying over the top of the Monument, streaming into the cracks between the bricks.

"Now, kill this beast," the Goldsmith said. "My patience has worn thin. Guards!" he shouted. "Go to the Bloody Tower! Take the prisoner Elijah to the place of execution!"

"Wait!" Robert cried.

He couldn't delay any further. He had to do it. Tears streamed down his face and he felt for the air magic inside him. He remembered when he was a young child and strong winds had raged across the Hibberts' plantation. His mother had said that a hurricane was passing close to the island, making Lord Hibbert anxious about his crops. *Not about any of us people*, his mother had muttered. She'd prayed for the hurricane to blow every single cocoa tree away. The wind and rain had lashed the land, hurling the cocoa pods from the trees, knocking over carts and sending buckets tumbling across the yard. Two of the cabins had lost their roofs and the families that lived in them had crowded in with others, huddled together until the storm had ceased. Robert tried to recall every moment of that storm, using that memory to shape the magic.

His air magic was soon spinning within him,

gathering speed. Robert braced himself – he had to stoke the fire magic soon. It burned hard, swollen by the air. Sweat poured down his face. His skin prickled – the heat was pouring out of him. Suddenly, there was nothing he could do to control the rush of it.

"I'm sorry, Dragon!" he shouted. "So sorry!"

His eyes stung with sweat, but he could still see his friend, the Dragon, wavering as she no longer had the strength to hold her form.

"Good boy! Don't stop!" The Goldsmith was applauding. "I will scatter your treacherous Dragon ashes in the Houndsditch midden with the animal dung and cat carcasses. You will be a lesson! No Dragon will ever spy for anyone else but me!" He raised his hands in the air. "Robert! Make her burn!"

Robert didn't have a choice – he was ablaze with uncontrollable magic. He watched helplessly as the tip of the Dragon's golden tail collapsed into a mess of ashes and embers. Her flank was cracking, her wide brow starting to crumble. He felt his magic weaving together, spreading and smothering the Dragon's body. Her knees buckled and ash and embers pooled on the floor.

She turned to look at him. Her gold-flecked eyes were filled with sadness. His own eyes snapped shut as the fire magic exploded out of him. Someone screamed – perhaps it was Robert himself. When he opened his eyes again, all he could see was smoke.

And water. So much water.

"Move aside, Robert," Turnmill said gently.

She was standing, hands on her hips, with a river of Chads behind her and Madam Blackwell by her side. He tried to move, but the magic had taken over his whole body. It was fighting its way out of him. If he let it free, everyone in this room would die. His limbs quivered, his eyelids sank down.

Inside he burned, but the outside world was dark.

THE MONUMENT

Marisee quickly bent down to check the guard. He was unconscious but still alive. The Fleet Ditch Boar snorted, then raced across the green and leaped into a well. Marisee hesitated. What if the Tower of London Chads knew that she was the sorceress's daughter? Her mother had helped the Goldsmith keep them docile, and then… She tried to push away the memory of Mama forcing the Chads into the cauldron.

"What's happening?"

A guard had rounded the corner and noticed his comrade slumped on the ground. He was cocking his gun as he shouted. Marisee hurled herself across the green and into the well.

Two water spirits caught her. They were pale, wearing robes and crowns. They placed her on her feet without saying anything and quickly flowed away. She called, "Thank you," but they were already gone. Ditch was waiting further along the tunnel. She'd become used to the Boar's friendliness – she'd forgotten that he was a fighter too. But she sensed the urgency in the way he stood and the fury rolling off his scarred flanks. Those huge tusks were sharper than swords.

"Let's go and rescue Robert!" she said.

Ditch nodded and thundered ahead. The tunnel ran in a straight line, other small tunnels branching off it. Helen was waiting for her.

"You did it!" Marisee grinned.

"We did!" Helen grinned back. "This tunnel leads to the laboratory in the Monument. There's a well in there. Some of the others have gone ahead."

"Others?"

"The watery one in the breeches," Helen said. "The old woman. Other watery ones."

Old woman? Could that be Grandma?

"Are you coming?" she asked Helen. "You and Tommy have already risked so much to help us. You're free now."

Helen shrugged. "Free to do what? Go where? The watery one said there's a horse and cart waiting. Me and Tommy are going to make sure the other children have got out."

"And Mama," Marisee reminded Helen.

"And your mother," Helen said. "Then we're going to come to the Monument. The Goldsmith needs to be stopped. I want to be there when it happens."

Marisee nodded, picked up her skirts and ran. The tunnel felt endless, but at last she saw a small circle of light falling from above. A well mouth. Pale Chads, arms linked together, held back a wall of water. Ditch struck his hooves against the tunnel floor and leaped up through the well.

What was up there? Was the Goldsmith waiting to catch Ditch and throw him in the cauldron? A silver rope dropped down. Sally Fleet's face peered at Marisee from above.

"Are you coming?" said Sally.

Marisee gripped the rope. It coiled around her, lifting her up into the laboratory. The guards were slumped in a corner, unconscious. The Goldsmith was backed into another corner, guarded by Turnmill. His face was clenched in rage. Miss Amelia was staring, wide-eyed, at Ditch. The floor itself moved, black and gold specks clustering together.

Robert! He was alive! He was standing perfectly still. His eyes were closed. Sweat poured down his face. His skin was ash grey, rippling as if the tide flowed beneath it. She called his name softly. He didn't move.

Grandma rushed towards Marisee, pulling her into a hug.

"You're safe, my darling," she murmured. "You're safe."

When Grandma released her, Marisee noticed how old Grandma looked – as if every worry had etched itself into her face.

"I'm so sorry," Marisee said. "I shouldn't have run off without telling you."

"No," Grandma agreed. "You shouldn't have. Either of you." She took Marisee's hand and led her over to Robert. "He's very sick," said Grandma, "but I don't know what to do."

"Mama might know," Marisee said simply.

Grandma's grip tightened. "Is she … is she with you?"

Marisee shook her head. "Mama's taking care of the children that were locked up in the Tower. Did you … did you know she was here in London?"

"No," Grandma said. "Not for certain, but there were rumours. Every time a new Lord Mayor was elected, I'd ask, but the Goldsmith has always held so much power.

The Lord Mayors do what they are told – and they are told to stay silent."

"Why didn't you tell me?" Marisee sounded more plaintive than she'd intended.

"Because I didn't want to fill your heart with hope if it wasn't true," Grandma replied.

But perhaps a little hope would have helped, Marisee thought. She had to put that thought aside, however. There were much more important things to take care of. They needed to undo what the Goldsmith had started before it was too late.

"He mixed the elements in the cauldron of coalescence," Marisee said, throwing a furious look at the Goldsmith. "He made Mama… He made her…"

"I've heard what happened to the Chads here," Grandma said. She took a deep breath. "We'll talk about it later." She turned to the Goldsmith. "What's wrong with Robert? How can we help him?"

The Goldsmith stared back coolly. "I'll never help you."

"Papa," Amelia whimpered. "Perhaps we should—"

"No!" the Goldsmith replied sharply. "Tell them nothing, Amelia!"

"Look," Marisee said, pointing to the black and gold specks swirling into clusters across the floor.

The shape became solid – a shape that Marisee knew well. It was a Dragon's head, its body a glimmering band of gold and black snaking up through the hatch.

"It's the Mary-le-Bow Dragon," Marisee said. "Did the Goldsmith use you as *an ingredient* too?"

"Robert was ordered to destroy me," the Dragon replied. "He resisted for as long as he could, but the Elemental magic is too strong for him to bear."

"He must be trying to control it," Grandma said. "What happens if he lets it free?"

"He will destroy everything around him," the Dragon replied.

"And if he doesn't let it free?" Marisee asked, though she was sure she knew the answer.

Grandma's eyes were full of sadness. No words were needed.

"Then we must take the magic out of him!" Marisee cried. "Right now!"

The air rippled. For a moment Marisee's head was filled with the rush and grind of watermills. It faded quickly. Turnmill was trying to hold her own magic in check.

"We need to put this one under lock and key," Turnmill said, pointing to the Goldsmith. "His miserable daughter too."

Marisee met the Goldsmith's eyes. He looked pleased with himself. How could he? After all this destruction?

Thump!

Marisee spun round to see Robert falling to the floor. As Turnmill and Grandma rushed to him, the Goldsmith grabbed the ledger and a small trunk, before speeding towards the steps that led to the hatch.

"Papa!" Amelia called, eyes swivelling between her father and Ditch. "What about me?"

The Goldsmith didn't answer. Within seconds, he'd leaped up the stairs and slammed the hatch door shut.

Marisee ran towards the hatch and tried to push it open. It was locked from the outside.

"We must remove the magic from Robert," Turnmill said urgently. "Or he'll die! But I don't know how."

"Is the answer in Mr Pipes' ledger?" Marisee asked with hope.

"Perhaps," Grandma answered. "But the Goldsmith has the ledger, as well as the cauldron shards in the trunk. Did anyone here have a chance to read it?"

Marisee felt a pang of guilt. *She* could have read it, but instead she'd just handed it over to the Goldsmith.

"Lady Walbrook read it," Sally Fleet said. "It was in her library."

"Then we must take Robert to her!" Grandma said. "But someone must also stop the Goldsmith. If he has the cauldron and the ledger, he'll start all over again."

Marisee couldn't heal Robert, but surely she could stop the Goldsmith! She hammered on the closed hatch. Someone hammered back.

"Marisee!" a voice called. "Is that you?"

Emma? Marisee heard the scrape of metal and the hatch opened. A face looked down at her. It *was* Emma!

"How did you get here?" Marisee asked. She felt her cheeks flushing with embarrassment as she remembered how she'd abandoned Emma in the tunnels with Lady Walbrook. "And I'm really sorry... I shouldn't have given the Goldsmith the ledger. I was wrong."

"You *were* wrong." Emma gave her a gentle smile. "But all of us do things that are wrong sometimes." Marisee blinked back tears as Emma continued. "After you left, the Boar creature charged off and Walbrook disappeared. But the ... the Sally girl led me through more tunnels. At the end of one of them were the rat-children." Emma took a deep breath. "I knew they were the ones who'd taken Garnet and all the others. I really wanted to be angry, but when I saw them ... saw what had been done to them ... I felt sad for them."

"They just want to be back to how they were before," Marisee said.

Emma stood aside as first Grandma then Marisee climbed the steps out of the laboratory.

"I came up through a well inside the Tower of London," Emma said. "That was very strange."

"You were inside the Tower?" Marisee frowned. "I didn't see you."

"It was a well near the old Menagerie," she replied. "So I could help Helen and Tommy with the children. Some of them still thought they were going to be taken and turned into rats. When the children were out, we saw a horse and cart waiting outside. I couldn't find Garnet anywhere, but your mama said she knew where to look and went back in. She's promised she'll bring Garnet with her. I climbed up into the driver's seat with Tommy and Helen." Emma gave a little laugh. "None of us had driven a cart before, but the horse didn't need a driver. It brought us here without me doing anything."

Good old Red Rum, Marisee thought. "Thank you for rescuing me," she said out loud, her face still burning a little. "The Goldsmith locked us in. Do you know where he is now?"

"He tried to escape," Emma said, "but we wouldn't let him leave the Monument. He ran upstairs, instead. I think there's Dragons up there who'll protect him. Helen and Tommy have gone after him, though. They said they want to see it through until the end."

The entrance to the Monument was guarded by children, many of them clutching pikes or cudgels. Marisee recognized some of the faces. There was John, the mudlark she'd met on the foreshore. He held a small sword and looked furious enough to run the Goldsmith through with it straight away. They'd been freed. But the Goldsmith was also still free.

Marisee glanced up at the spiral steps leading to the top of the Monument. The rage flared inside her, as hot as Robert's fire magic. How dare the Goldsmith hurt her friend! How dare he refuse to help save Robert! But she didn't need the Goldsmith. She would find a way.

Marisee took a deep breath, placed her foot on the first step, then raced up, up, up the stone staircase that wound through the narrow building. Her sides ached and her chest heaved. The Monument rose so tall! She could see neither the bottom nor the top, only stairs below and above. She passed the recesses where visitors rested as they were climbing up to enjoy the view. Marisee wanted to flop down on the seat but she had to keep going. Narrow windows let in air that she gulped down to soothe her raw throat.

Up, up, and—

Marisee smelled it first – the rotten meat stink of one of the Goldsmith's Dragons. She turned a bend and found herself staring into its cruel eyes. It was fully formed. Its jaw gaped open and wisps of smoke curled around its snout. Its heavy body tapered into a long tail that coiled upwards through the Monument.

"Let me through!" she demanded.

"I haven't tasted human flesh for so long now," the Dragon hissed. "My master has ordered me to destroy you."

"Your master would destroy you too," Marisee said. "Didn't he use Dragons as ingredients for his experiment? Dragons you knew?"

The Dragon shifted its coils. "*The boy* destroyed my friend. He summoned my friend and killed him. When I have finished with you, I will kill the boy too."

The Dragon sprang towards Marisee, mouth hanging open, its throat endless darkness. Marisee flung herself back from it, towards the hundreds of stone steps spiralling downwards to the ground. She clutched for the rail – her fingertips touched it, but that was all. She tumbled, crying out as her elbow hit the wall.

The Dragon surrounded her, smouldering flecks of orange and black coiling around her, squeezing her.

"How do you want to die?" The words crackled

in Marisee's ears. "Will you fall to your death or be consumed by me?"

"She won't die today, Dragon!"

It was the creaky weathervane voice of a Fumi – and not just any Fumi… It was the Squall! The Squall hit the Dragon with its full force, blasting its body apart. The gold and black flecks hung in the air for a moment, before starting to recluster. But Marisee was falling. She tried to scream, but her voice stuck in her throat.

Arms caught her.

"I've got you," Henry said, holding her tight.

Marisee was shaking. Henry gently stood her up. She staggered and he held her until her legs had enough strength for her to stand by herself.

"The Goldsmith!" Marisee's voice was shaking too. "He's taken the cauldron and Mr Pipes' ledger! We have to stop him from using them again!"

The Goldsmith's Dragon was almost formed again, blocking their way once more.

"Well," Henry said, "if we can't go up the inside of the Monument, we must go up the outside."

"How?" Marisee asked. The only steps were inside the building.

Henry gave her a tired smile. "I may not wish to be in this body, but sometimes it has its uses." He unbuttoned his jacket and scooped up Marisee. "And my good friend does too," he said. "Squall? You ready?"

Marisee grasped Henry's waistcoat as he buttoned his coat back up around her. She was in darkness, cocooned in warmth.

"Hold tight!" Henry called.

Suddenly, he moved.

He must be on all fours, Marisee thought, because she was gripping as hard as she could, head first, cradled by his coat. They were going back downstairs, then a rush of cool air. They were outside – and bounding upwards, propelled by a strong wind. Helped by the Squall, Henry was climbing the outside of the Monument – and so was she! She squeezed her eyes shut, even though she couldn't see anything, and clung on to Henry so hard her fingers hurt.

At last, Henry slowed his pace. Marisee felt him tense as he pulled himself over the top of the Monument and into the viewing area. When he unbuttoned his coat, she was even more wobbly than before. Henry staggered back against the wall and slumped down. A small cloud of the Squall's flour rose from his coat.

"I'm much too old for tricks like that," he said.

"But what a rich life you've led." The Goldsmith was standing at the top of the stairwell, Mr Pipes' ledger under his arm. The trunk holding the shards of cauldron lay by his feet. "You should be grateful for those extra years."

"Grateful?" Henry gasped. "For being made part beast?"

"Yes!" the Goldsmith said. "Grateful! As a man, you were a common criminal! As a beast, you were dying! You became so much more! You were powerful!"

"Powerful!" Henry laughed weakly. "I was an assassin, at the beck and call of the Guild of Goldsmiths for more than a hundred years. But you and Lord Gullinn, your cruelty is the worst, because you hurt children. This must never happen again."

"Never again," Tommy and Helen echoed.

Side by side, they were at the top of the narrow staircase, blocking the Goldsmith's way out. They stood upright, trembling, as if it took effort not to drop back on to their haunches. Their teeth were bared and their eyes flashed red.

The Goldsmith held the ledger in the air. "Do you want to destroy the cure?" he taunted. "The cauldron of coalescence creates new from old, but with the right incantation it separates new *back into* the old. Human *from* beast..." He turned his sly gaze on Marisee. "The Elements from the human."

"Mr Pipes never found it!" Tommy said. "Or he would have cured us!"

"Oh, it wasn't Mr Pipes," the Goldsmith said. "The ledger made its way to a water spirit's library. Lady Walbrook read it most thoroughly. Her notes are scrawled beneath Mr Pipes' own. She found what Mr Pipes could not."

Marisee didn't want to believe him. The Goldsmith would easily lie to keep power. But ... she imagined Lady Walbrook turning the pages, studying Mr Pipes' words, contemptuous because she knew so much more than a mere Solid.

"Can the cauldron change Tommy and Helen back into children?" she asked. "Can it save Robert?"

The Goldsmith looked her in the eye.

"We could make a deal, Marisee," he said. "Give me my freedom and I will give you the ledger."

Marisee took a step towards him, her eyes on the book. Dare she believe him?

"Or perhaps we could not." The Goldsmith tucked the ledger back under his arm and clapped his hands. "Perhaps it's time for you to understand that I will always be more powerful than you."

Marisee smelled the Dragon stink oozing up the steps. It poured through the door, a mass of writhing flecks, batting Tommy and Helen away as if they were wasps. The Dragon perched on the gold flames of the urn that topped the Monument.

"Destroy her!" the Goldsmith yelled.

"No!" Marisee's rage was hotter than Dragon fire. "How can you serve this human? How can Dragons serve any human? You are older and wiser. Remember when the rivers were clear and the air was fresh, before humans built the cities and factories? Your memories are long. There was a time when you never did a human's bidding, because Dragons are guardians and warriors, not servants."

The Goldsmith laughed. "Haven't I always treated you kindly, Dragon?"

"He turned you against each other," Marisee said. "He made you fight your own kind to feed the cauldron."

"Dragons must never be weak," the Goldsmith said. "They were not worthy of being Dragons. You – you showed your strength."

"You locked me in a cellar," the Dragon growled. "How could I be worthy if I was locked in a cellar, away from all my kind?"

"That was for your safety," the Goldsmith said. "You were too wild to be free."

"I am *supposed* to be wild and free!" the Dragon

roared. "But you imprisoned me!" A tiny arrow of fire shot from the Dragon's mouth. It pierced the leather cover of Mr Pipes' ledger.

"No!" Marisee jumped forward. "Please! Don't harm the ledger!"

"I should have been free, but I was always your prisoner! Were you waiting for the day when you could kill me for your cauldron? You stole my friend's magic, Goldsmith! You killed her!" The Dragon's tail uncoiled, swinging back and forth. "You destroyed two of us today."

"But you are alive!" There was an edge of fear in the Goldsmith's voice. "I *will* free you, if that is what you wish!"

"I will never trust your promises!"

Another shot of fire, aimed at the Goldsmith's heart. The Goldsmith quickly held up the ledger to protect himself. The pages started to smoulder and curl.

"No," Marisee pleaded. "Don't destroy it!"

Small flames flickered across the book. The Goldsmith grimaced and dropped it. As he lifted his foot to stamp out the flames, the Dragon attacked, surging towards him, fiery mouth gaping wide.

"You will be free!" the Goldsmith shrieked.

Flecks of orange and black engulfed him like summer flies over stagnant water.

"Free!"

A final shriek and the Dragon's coiled tail wrapped around the Goldsmith. His arms waved and his legs kicked. His mouth opened and there was a whispered plea for help. Then the Dragon rose up from the Monument, bearing the flailing Goldsmith away into the night.

Marisee ran over to the ledger, but it was consumed by fire. Henry was still slumped, exhausted. Tommy and Helen were tending each other's wounds. And, somewhere below, Robert was burning up with Elemental magic.

TOO MUCH MAGIC

Robert heard voices but not words. The magic roared and raged and surged. His body was so heavy; his eyelids were weighed shut. But one word slipped through the clamour.

Dead.

Who was dead? Perhaps it was him, Robert. He was sure that he could never move again.

A voice whispered in his ear, a voice he knew well.

"Robert! I hope you can hear me!"

He *could* hear Marisee. He must still be alive!

"The ledger's been destroyed, Robert!" She sounded

distraught. "We don't know how to heal you. Our only chance now is Lady Walbrook."

Lady Walbrook? Didn't she hate Solids? She'd never help. The Mary-le-Bow Dragon's memories flitted through his head. Jars … diagrams … bones… Then the magic roared, shattering the memories. He willed his mouth to open, his lips and tongue to move, enough breath to move through his body for words to say goodbye.

But the magic was too strong.

"CAN YOU SAVE HIM?"

Marisee's chest hurt from racing back down the steps to the secret laboratory in the basement of the Monument. Would Robert still be alive?

She'd found Miss Amelia slumped in a corner, surrounded by open trunks. Her face was in her hands. She was sobbing. Marisee almost felt sorry for her.

Grandma was dabbing the sweat from Robert's brow with her sleeve. Marisee tried not to blink her tears on to his face as she leaned over him. He was dying and there was nothing that she or Grandma could do. Where *was* Lady Walbrook? She should be here, healing Robert!

Grandma had devoted all her life to helping the Chads, fighting Lord Mayor after Lord Mayor, trying to keep the rivers clean and flowing above ground. If it wasn't for Grandma, the rivers would be even filthier or covered up, so rich people could build houses over them.

Suddenly, Marisee heard marching feet, but not in her real world – in her head. Her skin tingled as if flecked by the cold spray of a surging river. The sound and the feeling stopped as Lady Walbrook swept into the room, followed by Turnmill and Sally Fleet. She glanced disdainfully at Marisee and Grandma. But Marisee didn't care. She was here!

"Can you save him?" Marisee asked desperately.

Lady Walbrook bent down to examine Robert's face. His face twitched as if he could sense her there.

"The magic must be taken out of him," she said.

"So you *can* save him?" Grandma said.

"I did not keep Pipes' ledger simply to adorn my shelf," Lady Walbrook said. "I read every word. I remember every word. I cannot remove all the magic, but I will take back what was stolen from us."

"You can only take the water magic?" Turnmill said. "What about air, fire and earth?"

"That is not our business," Lady Walbrook said.

"Not yours," Turnmill said. "But Robert is my friend,

so it's certainly mine." She called into the air. "Mary-le-Bow Dragon! Squall!"

"And what of the earth magic?" Grandma said quietly.

Before Turnmill could reply, a shriek filled the air.

"It's Robert! Is he dead? Please don't be dead!" Garnet raced across the room towards him. "What's wrong with him? Wake him up!"

"Shh, Garnet," Emma said, gently pulling the girl away.

"Take her home," Grandma said. "She needs to recover."

"No!" Emma said. "We won't leave him."

Garnet threw herself down on to her knees next to Robert.

"I'm going to sing to him," she said. "That will make him better."

FIRE, AIR, WATER

The magical fog thickened inside Robert. But, at its edges, a song trickled through. *Do you know the muffin man?* Garnet's favourite song. Was it really her or just his imagination? He wished he could open his eyes to see, but he felt as if he was sinking into the earth. Little jabs of heat prickled beneath his skin. The fire magic was shifting. And shifting. And reaching out for more fire magic from beyond him.

Was he being called upon to destroy again? No! He wouldn't do it! He twisted and thrashed as the magic scorched him. Firm hands held him down.

"It's hurting him!"

It was a girl's voice, a friend's voice, but he heard it through the roar of a fire. The heat was gathering inside him – it was unbearable.

"Open your eyes, Robert," a different voice coaxed. "You'll see that we're not trying to hurt you."

Was that Madam Blackwell? He forced his heavy eyelids to open. The world wavered around him.

"Well done, Robert," Madam Blackwell said. "We're all your friends here. We're going to remove the Elements from you, one at a time, by…"

Robert couldn't hear her words now – he must have fallen into a wasps' nest. Thousands and thousands of stings, a black and orange and gold haze, a flare of memories from so long ago, then… He breathed out smoke and heat. The fire magic was gone.

All the faces in front of him were sparkling clear – Madam Blackwell's, still worried, and Marisee, worried but smiling, and the flickering gold and black face of the Mary-le-Bow Dragon. She closed her eyes and her smouldering flank twisted and spun, mottled with orange too. Two black and orange ribbons separated from the Dragon's body and formed their own shapes – two small Dragons that collapsed again into tiny scurrying creatures that streamed up the walls and through the hatch.

"Are those the Dragons that ... that I killed?" Robert stuttered.

"We are harder to destroy than the Goldsmith could ever imagine," the Mary-le-Bow Dragon said.

Then she too scattered into spots of gold, floating on her own breeze back to her church.

"Air next," Madam Blackwell said in a determined voice. "Are you ready, Robert?"

Ready? What was going to happen this time?

A Fumi's pale floury head appeared above him. Was that the Squall? The air inside Robert pulsed and bulged until he thought he would burst. At last, the air magic flew out through his nose in a mighty gust.

Two Fumis hovered in front of him – the one that had been imprisoned in a cage and dropped into the cauldron, the other that had been summoned by Robert to be destroyed. Both were alive! They spoke their own language, word-petals of every shade dropping around them. The Squall grew wider and darker as Robert's air magic filled it.

"Go, now!" Madam Blackwell said.

The air spun and the Fumis disappeared, leaving a cloud of flour and the tang of factories and coal smoke. Robert tried to rub his sore nose, but his arms were too weak. It wasn't only his nose that hurt – his whole body was sore, inside and out.

A glint of silver caught his eyes, a knotted web of silver threads. *Lady Walbrook.*

"You mustn't hurt him," Madam Blackwell said sternly.

The riverhead didn't reply. As Robert looked up, her cold eyes stared down at him. Her skin shifted from pale brown to slate grey to silver. Her web floated over his body, not touching his skin. The water magic rippled inside him. Without the fire, he felt as if he was lying in a freezing puddle. His skin stung with cold. The magic surged out of him and into Lady Walbrook. Still without speaking, she glided away.

Madam Blackwell stroked Robert's cheek. Her mouth moved — she was talking but his ears seemed full of mud. No, his whole body was made of mud. If he moved, he would crack like dry clay, because there was only cold, heavy earth magic left. It was part of him. If that was taken, what would remain? He tried to lift his head to talk, but his neck was too heavy. The weight was pushing him into the ground. Soon, the earth would reach up and claim him. He was sinking, like Gog and Magog, the giants who lay sleeping at the bottom of the Thames.

He must have said their names out loud because suddenly he was scooped up.

"I'm taking him to the river!" Turnmill said.

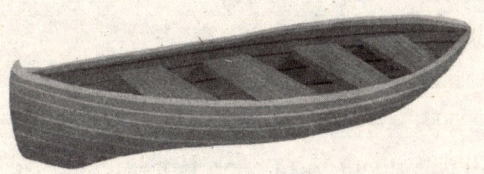

MAMA AND GRANDMA

Marisee was confused. "What river?" she shouted as she followed Turnmill, who was rushing from the laboratory with Robert in her arms. "It's earth magic, not water magic, that's left inside him!"

Grandma touched her shoulder. She was puffing from running after Marisee. "She's taking Robert to the giants," she said. "To Gog and Magog. They must claim back their magic."

"But they're sleeping on the Thames riverbed!" Marisee said.

Grandma nodded.

Marisee stared at Grandma. "Is Turnmill going to throw Robert into the river?"

Outside, Turnmill was lifting Robert into the back of a cart. Marisee recognized the horse. It was Red Rum! Turnmill was fluent in London Horse – she had only to whisper directions into Red Rum's ear and he would drive to the destination.

Mama was standing by the cart, her dress sparkling like water.

"Mary-Bee!" Grandma was gazing at Mama. "My darling! Oh, my darling!"

It was as if Grandma could say no other words. Marisee understood. All her own feelings felt too big to explain.

"My darling, Mary-Bee!" Grandma half-hobbled, half-ran towards her daughter. "You're home!" she gasped, reaching out to Mama. "I've ached for this day for so long!"

"So have I!" Mama clasped Grandma's hands.

For a moment, they studied each other, but then Grandma was clutching Mama as if she'd never let her go.

At last, they pulled apart. Grandma ran her finger down Mama's cheek, wiping away a tear.

"I thought I'd never see you again," Grandma whispered.

Mama smiled over at Marisee. "I thought I'd never see either of you again." She freed one arm and beckoned to Marisee. "Come, my beautiful one."

Marisee threw herself towards them. Mama scooped them all together – Marisee, Mama, Grandma. Marisee sank into the warmth and the love, laughing and crying at the same time.

"You came back," Grandma muttered. "You really came back."

"And I'll never leave again," Mama said.

When Mama pulled away, the air around Marisee felt cold and lonely.

"The children are free and safe," Mama said. "But Turnmill said that Robert's very sick."

"They're going to throw him into the Thames," Marisee said bitterly.

She was pleased that Mama looked as shocked as Marisee felt.

"Throw him into the Thames?" Mama repeated. "Why?"

While Grandma explained, Marisee climbed into

the cart next to Robert. She covered him with a blanket and held his hand tight – it was cold and clammy. Mama was nodding.

"Oh," she said, looking at Turnmill. "I see. Is there no other way?"

Turnmill shook her head.

Mama met Marisee's eyes. "If Robert is to live, then that's what we must do," she said. "But he won't make that journey alone."

Turnmill and Mama exchanged a glance, then Mama climbed up and settled next to Marisee and Robert. Mama's fingertips touched Grandma's. They stared into each other's eyes as if they were speaking a silent language. Marisee wished she knew what they were saying. Grandma turned away, crying.

"We must go now if we're to save him," Mama said firmly.

Grandma moved quickly, hobble-running to the front of the cart. She climbed up into the driver's seat.

"And I'm coming too," she said.

Turnmill travelled through the underground tunnels. It was quicker and safer for her.

First, though, she whispered into Red Rum's ear and he set off. He drew the cart carefully, with no sudden starts and stops, which wasn't easy in London's traffic. Would they get to the Thames in time? Marisee had to press her ear hard against Robert's chest to hear a heartbeat.

The cart headed east, passing Billingsgate fish market and Custom House on the road towards Wapping. Finally, Red Rum pulled into an abandoned woodyard. Marisee heard the splash and tumble of water. Turnmill waited by a crumbling well, with the Ditch Boar and Sally Fleet at her side.

"There are steps down to the Thames behind the sheds," Turnmill said, unhooking the back of the cart. "And a boat is waiting for you."

"How will I know when I'm in the right place?" Mama asked.

"He will tell you," Turnmill replied, looking down at Robert's limp body. "The magic will know."

"Why Robert?" Marisee sobbed. "Why did the Goldsmith choose him?"

Grandma joined them. Her fingers entwined with Marisee's, and her other hand clasped Mama's.

"The Goldsmith heard that Robert could talk with the statues," Grandma said. "He understood that Robert had earth magic in him."

"But the Goldsmith could have used a shard beast,

or" – Marisee felt guilty even suggesting this – "or a Variegate like Haakon. Why Robert?"

Grandma gave a sad laugh. "The Goldsmith thought that he could control Robert easily. But he was very wrong, wasn't he?"

"Yes," Marisee said. "He was very wrong."

A rowing boat was bobbing on the tide by the water steps. Robert was laid in the hull. Mama, Marisee and Grandma crowded in after him. The boat swayed even more. In the past, Marisee would have worried about falling out, but now all she cared about was Robert.

"You can row?" Grandma asked Mama.

"The bays around Berbera were shallow," Mama said. "I would often row myself from the merchant ship to shore."

The boat headed east, weaving between the sloops and the schooners and the wherries carrying passengers between the north and south banks of the Thames. No one spoke.

Suddenly, Robert started shivering. His skin was as cold and damp as the foreshore at low tide. Marisee tried to lift his hand to hold it, but she couldn't. It was like something magical was trying to pull him through the bottom of the boat, into the water.

"This must be the place," Mama said.

"It must be," Grandma said, so quietly that Marisee could barely hear her.

Another look passed between the two women.

Mama took Marisee's hands and kissed her fingertips. Then, before anyone else could move, Mama grabbed Robert around his middle and tumbled off the boat. The two of them immediately disappeared beneath the filthy water.

"Mama!" Marisee screamed. "Robert!"

THE HAND

Something – someone – pinched Robert's nose tight. He had so little strength left that he wasn't sure he could breathe anyway. He was in the river now. The tide shoved his body, but a stronger power dragged him down.

He wasn't alone. He was being held firmly around the waist. He opened his eyes. Mistress Bee stared back at him. He shook his head and tried to wriggle free. She mouthed words back at him.

"Not alone."

Down, down, down through the water, as seaweed tangled through their hair and shells and fragments of wood clipped their skin. The river hummed in Robert's ears as if it had captured London's lullabies and was trying to soothe him.

Down, down, down, with the weight of the river and boats and jetties over him. Mistress Bee's eyes were closed, her grip still tight.

Suddenly, he was hurtling towards the riverbed as if a rope had looped around his ankle and yanked him. Mistress Bee's eyes flew open, her face creased in distress.

Stop, Robert wanted to yell. *She can't breathe!*

But *he* could breathe!

He thought that the dark shape heading towards him was driftwood, but as he blinked the water from his eyes, he realized that it was a hand – an enormous hand. The fingers were curled, and Robert and Mistress Bee were drawn into them. The fingers closed around them.

Robert was in darkness, but it was a living darkness. The giant's skin throbbed with earth magic that flowed into Robert and through him to Mistress Bee. She gasped and went limp.

No! he tried to shout, but not with his mouth. His words came from his whole body. *Don't let her die!*

The reply was felt by his whole body too, as if the giant's words flowed through his blood.

Touch her face!

Robert touched her brow – it was warmer than the water around him. Her eyelids fluttered. Two bubbles of air swelled and shrank beneath her nostrils. She was alive.

It's time for us to take back what's ours, the giant said. *Are you prepared?*

Robert wasn't sure if he *was* prepared. *Can't I keep some of it?*

The hand shook as if the giant was laughing. *Everyone has some Elemental magic buried deep inside them. Yours was close to the surface. We saw your magnificence when others did not.*

Images flashed through Robert's mind. The statues stepping from the steeple of St George's Church in Bloomsbury – a lion, a unicorn and a king.

"I see you," the king had said.

The golden cherub on the Fortune of War tavern had called down the same words to Robert: "I see you."

The Panyer Boy and his basket of knowledge, who others could hear, but who would only answer Robert.

They had all seen Robert as a real person, when so many other real-life human people had not. But there were other humans who had shown him kindness and love – Lizzie the Hibberts' scullery maid, Madam Blackwell, Marisee, Emma, Garnet.

As the last of the magic was drained from him,

warmth spread through his body. No matter what happened next, he knew that he was loved.

The giant must have opened his hand, because Robert and Mistress Bee were sinking again, further and further into the murk. Robert's nose filled with water; his chest heaved painfully. He held his breath and tried to kick his legs, but he was too tired. Someone grabbed his arms and tried to pull him upwards. It was Mistress Bee. Her skirts flowed out around her, dull grey in the dark water.

"Kick!" she mouthed. "Help me!"

He tried, but he might as well have been a statue. His legs were as heavy as stone. Mistress Bee tugged his arms. Her face was screwed up with the effort of pulling him and holding her breath.

"Please, Robert!"

He tried to pull free. "Save yourself."

Mistress Bee shook her head.

She closed her eyes and shuddered. His eyes closed too.

Zeke, I'm ready to be with you now.

And then he was rising. The water fell away from him like rotting rags. His ears popped. He opened his eyes, blinking away the river grit. Mistress Bee was looking at him, eyes wide, lips pressed together as if to keep hold of every tiny breath. There was a small puff of air left inside Robert's lungs. His chest burned as he held it in, but he would hold on to it because he could see light above him. They would break the surface soon. Robert looked down. He and Mistress Bee were standing in the centre of the palm of a hand. Dirt was etched into the lines. The nails were long and jagged.

"Thank you," came a rolling voice from below. "I am back with my kin."

There was a glimpse of a face. Was that a thick beard swaying in the tide or a river weed? Was that a smile or stones? But that was definitely a strip of red, just like the velvet across the platform that had been wrapped around Myrr's head.

"Here!" came Marisee's voice from above them. "Grab on to this!"

As Robert reached up for the oar shaft, the giant's hand fell away beneath him.

Robert's fingertips grazed the wood. Mistress Bee grabbed the back of his shirt and heaved him up with her. He clutched one side of the oar; Mistress Bee clung to the other.

His head broke the surface of the river as he gasped for breath. He stared up into Marisee's tear-stained face. It was only when Mistress Bee appeared beside him that

Marisee smiled – a wide, brilliant smile that seemed to warm his whole body.

Then her smile was so wide that he couldn't help smiling too, even though he was shivering and his hands were so weak that, if Madam Blackwell hadn't held on to him, he would have slithered back into the Thames.

As they rowed to shore, the tide was high. Dark river water lapped the top of the water steps. Madam Blackwell and Marisee struggled to control the boat in the tumbling tide. Mistress Bee was shivering, despite Madam Blackwell wrapping a blanket around her.

Marisee had tried to rub warmth into her mother's hands, and Robert had felt a jab of jealousy. They looked like a complete family, while he had no idea if his family were still alive. He guiltily pushed the thought away. He should be happy for his friend and he knew in his heart that Madam Blackwell thought of him as her grandson. But... He sighed to himself. What if *he* could find *his* family?

Tommy and Helen were crouched beneath the wharf, waiting. The rattiness of their bodies was hidden by heavy loose jackets and hats.

"Where are Tommy and Helen going?" Marisee asked.

"Where they want to be," Mistress Bee said. "Where they should have been for such a long time now."

Marisee shook her head. "I don't understand."

Robert did. He already knew how it felt to be weary to the bone, and Tommy and Helen had lived much beyond their years. The rat-children crouched low on their haunches, then threw off their coats and waded into the water.

Marisee tried to jump to her feet, but the boat wobbled. "What's ... what's happening?"

Robert took Marisee's hand. It was so much warmer than his.

"Wait," he said.

Marisee stared out at the dark water. "I can't see them."

"Look towards the foreshore," Grandma said.

"The tide's high," Marisee said. "There isn't a foreshore. Oh."

There wasn't a foreshore, but there *was* a foreshore. The river was still lapping at the quay, but Marisee could also see the stones and sand. It wavered a little, as if underwater, but for a moment it was clear.

A boy and a girl walked out of the water on to the shore. A woman stepped out from under the quay, her arms outstretched. She was dark-skinned with short hair, her ears heavy with gold trinkets. She wore a dark grey shimmering dress, its bodice embroidered with intricate rippling silver.

Robert breathed in the scent of spice and oranges.

"Mama Tems," Marisee whispered.

"And Tommy and Helen as they once were," Mistress Bee said.

Mama Tems folded her cloak around the two ghost children. The three of them looked up at the boat and smiled. Then the foreshore wavered again and all Robert could see was the deep, rippling river.

Madam Blackwell glanced towards the road. "Is that a horse I can hear?"

Red Rum appeared, pulling a cart behind him. He neighed once and stopped on the wharf.

"Time to go home," Madam Blackwell said.

TWO WEEKS LATER

Marisee and Mama finished painting the new sign. Standing back, Marisee held up her lantern to admire it, the light flickering over the words.

> Blackwells' Medicinal Waters.
> Proprietors: Madam Mary-Ay Blackwell
> Mistress Mary-Bee Blackwell
> Miss Marisee Blackwell

Grandma sighed. "I never thought this day would come," she said.

Marisee reached for her hand. "Me neither."

Mama grasped Marisee's hand. "Nor me."

In the distance, an owl hooted, as if cheering their happiness. Reluctantly, Marisee let Grandma's and Mama's hand go.

"We have to leave or we'll be late," she said. "Don't forget the hampers."

Red Rum drove them down the hill towards London. They stopped in Cattle Court first. The Red Guard Gang's den was now … well, maybe not as cosy as Grandma's cottage, but no longer a tumbledown ruin. The walls, windows and roof had been fixed. There were rugs and curtains. A shelf was cluttered with pots and pans above a fireplace for cooking. One of the cattle stalls in the yard had been made into a chicken coop that already housed five hens. Garnet loved collecting the eggs.

The little girl ran out as soon as she heard the cart. Her sickness had passed quickly, thanks to Robert's medicine and Emma's care. She was hand in hand with Maud, the mudlark, who lived here too but couldn't resist going to the foreshore to meet her old friends and hunt for treasures. Turpin and Duval hung back in the shadows, always wary. They still made their trips to Covent Garden. They'd been doing it for so long they couldn't stop, but

Emma had made them swear an oath that they would not steal anything from anyone. Marisee hoped that they kept their promise.

Spindrift strode out from one of the stalls. He was carrying a hammer and a pail of nails. His wide-brimmed hat was pushed back so that his face was no longer in shadow. He seemed older, no longer a child. Almost a man. He'd promised to care for runaway children that needed a place to stay, just as Robert had done when he'd escaped from the Hibberts. Spindrift, Emma, Robert and Marisee had cleaned the rest of the stalls and built sleeping bunks. They'd made sure that there were shelves and trunks for the children's precious things.

"Are there muffins?" Garnet asked, lifting the lid from the hamper.

"The finest," Mama replied. "And butter and apples and pies and…" She gave Turpin and Duval a little wink. "Sugar plums."

"The Guild of Goldsmiths has deep coffers," Spindrift said.

"They do," Grandma said seriously. "And I really wish we could refuse their money, but…" She waved towards the restored house. "I'm prepared to tell no one about the Goldsmith's terrible experiments if they continue to give money to support poor children. Aren't you?"

Spindrift nodded, though he didn't look happy. He paused.

"Madam Blackwell," he said. "I'm deeply sorry for suggesting that you were the sorceress."

"Yes, me too," chorused Turpin and Duval.

"Think no more of it," Grandma said. And Marisee knew that she meant it.

The cart moved on to Fleet Street, stopping in a narrow, dark alley. Mama and Grandma followed Marisee down the steps to the furrier's cellar. It was lit by lanterns so that the way was easier, but the stink hadn't changed.

"Whooo," Grandma said, fanning her nose.

"This is nothing compared to months on a ship with unwashed sailors," Mama said.

The door to the tunnel was open. They walked on for a little while before the tunnel widened. They entered the chamber arm in arm.

The room with the stone benches was filled with people. Nearly every single person was an African. The one person who obviously was not African was Emma, who sat by Robert's side.

All the humans had come through the furrier's cellar, walking along the tunnels, excited, curious, suspicious. They'd been told that a secret benefactor was allowing them to use his hidden chamber, safe from prying eyes, but no more questions must be asked. Turnmill had been strict – no Chad should go anywhere near the Solids. The audience was still whispering uncertainly, perhaps sensing the magic.

A man clapped loudly and stood up.

"My name was Elijah Hibbert," he said. "I was Lord Hibbert's 'property'. But no human being is another's property. Tonight we shall plan how this abominable trade will be destroyed, because it *must* end." He pointed to Robert. All eyes were on him. "We suffered on the same plantation," Elijah continued. "Before I escaped the cruelty, I promised Robert's mother that I would find him. When she knows what you've achieved, Robert, she'll be so proud of you."

Proud? *Yes*, Marisee thought. *And so am I. Proud of my kind, loyal, brave friend.*

Robert stood up, shoulder to shoulder with Elijah.

"My name *was* Robert Hibbert." He looked every person in the eye. "I, too, was Lord Hibbert's 'property'." His gaze fixed on Marisee, Grandma and Mama. He smiled – the biggest, warmest smile he'd ever given before. "With my friend Marisee, I have saved London from evil three times," he said. "And now I have vowed to accompany Elijah to tell of the evils of the plantation. I have found my strength and courage – because I am Robert Strong."

Acknowledgements

It takes a whole team to make a book! Thank you to everyone at Scholastic and beyond: Lauren Fortune, Aimee Stewart, Wendy Shakespeare, Camilla Chetty, Tina Mories, Kiran Khanom, Ellen Thomson, Hannah Griffiths. Thank you, also, to my illustrators Paul Kellam, Amanda Quartey and Luke Ashforth, and proofreader Philip Ridgers.

As always, special thanks to Emma Roberts, who has had my back for so long now, and Claire Wilson and Safae at RCW. And a big-up to Sophie, Darren, Nenna and Adam – the Writers Hour posse, who let me rant and make me focus!

And, finally, my enduring gratitude to the scholars who burrow beneath established history and tease out a myriad of hidden stories, including Catherine Johnson, doyenne, and Gretchen Gerzina, whose impressive book, *Black England: A Forgotten Georgian History* was invaluable for my research.

Read how Robert and Marisee's story began and step into a London lit up by the Elemental spirits: the fiery Dragons, the airy Fumis, the watery Chads and the earthbound Magogs.

When a sleeping sickness descends upon on the city, Marisee and Robert are the Elemental Detectives chasing the clues to prevent London from slumbering for all eternity...

"Bristling with magic... I loved it!" Cressida Cowell

Elemental Detectives Marisee and Robert are back to solve another mystery on the streets of multicultural eighteenth-century London.

An orchestra explodes in Vauxhall Pleasure Gardens and suddenly the music of London disappears ... and a terrifying monster stirs off the Greenwich peninsular, threatening to trample London underfoot.

A page-turning mystery and exploration of fractured families, long-buried secrets and the power of friendship…

Nervous Ayrton was stolen away from his mum as a baby. He was returned safely, but now Mum won't let him out of her sight. Curious Stanley has a Forbidden Grandmother. His mum won't even talk about her. Homeless Sen has finally found a place to live, but she'll be out on the street if she upsets her secretive landlady. What happens when their paths cross…?

"Masterful storytelling weaves together the lives of the three protagonists in a page-turning mystery with a fierce heart"
The Scotsman